ALWAYS YOU

RUGBY BROTHERS BOOK 2

TIARA INSERTO

DIGITAL ISBN: 978-1-949823-04-2

PRINT ISBN: 978-1-949823-05-9

Cover design by LLewellen Designs

CHAPTER 1

Neela sank against the front door, her breathing still hard and erratic after taking the steps two at a time. She darted her eyes back and forth, scoping the familiar surroundings. Was there another way to escape the place she had started to regard as a refuge from the past?

She pressed her fingers to her forehead, wanting to calm the relentless pounding in her head. She knew its source all too well.

It was a feeling so strong, it threatened to drown her in a sea of darkness.

Until five minutes ago, she'd thought she would never need to fight from being afraid again. She realized now that she was just used to living with fear all the time.

She closed her eyes and tried to even her breathing.

Not working.

Eyes now opened, she focused on the window that kept the small unit full of light. They lived on the second floor. Could she survive a jump?

She shook her head, scrambling to reach the rational part of her mind. *Be smart! Think through this! Just stay quiet!*

The door was double-locked. He wouldn't know which unit she lived in. He couldn't have seen which door she had entered; she would have heard him if he were closer. There was no way he'd know where she lived.

"Neela!"

Her gasp sounded loud even to her own ears. *Breathe… breathe… He doesn't know you're here. He can't - know…*

"Neela Smyth! I saw you!"

She breathed in and out rapidly through her mouth, this time switching to techniques she had learned in the field to control the adrenaline pumping through her. Frowning, she willed herself to concentrate, to listen. She pushed slightly against the front door, her ear pressed against the dark wood panel. Heavy footsteps made their way up the stairwell; her name repeatedly being called by a voice she'd never wanted to hear again.

Then it was silent.

Neela shut her eyes as she released her breath. Her heart continued to pound loud and fast.

Warily, she crept across the room to the dining area. Without thinking twice, she grabbed a chair and wedged it against the door. She stared at it, tempted to test how well it would stand against a forceful push.

The loud, brash knock on the door made her take a sudden step backward as if the sound had shoved her.

"Neela!"

She bit back the cry that was close to escaping. She started to shake and wrapped her body with her arms. *There's no way he can see in. He doesn't know you're here. You're safe… You're safe…*

"Neela!"

Her body jerked in response.

She kept her eye on the door handle as she inched toward her bedroom. *Don't try it, Kyle. Leave me alone!* She had long since given up reciting prayers, but she was praying now. The ringing in her ears became louder with each step she took, and the floor seemed to be moving again. She should call the police… but say what?

There was another loud knock—an impatient one. Neela's heart raced. She rushed into her bedroom but was careful to shut her door quietly. The click that confirmed it was now locked did little to ease her anxiety.

"Go away, Kyle," she whispered.

She let her arm fall and felt for the phone she'd thrown into the pocket of her jacket earlier that day. She should call Mano. He'd know what to do.

Her hand rested on the cold screen, but she didn't pull the phone out.

She didn't want to be a burden again. Not to Mano. Once was more than enough. He couldn't know she was still afraid. Her beloved cousin had done so much to help her get out of the situation in the first place. She wanted him to get on with his life, especially now that he'd found someone. He should only be focusing on Margot right now. He deserved that.

It was quiet now. Her body began trembling uncontrollably. Was it from relief? Fear? Both?

She shut her eyes and covered her ears with shaking hands, wanting the incessant ringing inside her head to stop. Kyle would have left by now, surely. He was not a patient man.

But she didn't want to leave the room.

It was safer here. Locked behind two doors, it was safer. She was safe.

* * *

Neela woke to the sound of a low buzz. She groaned as she felt the stiffness in her lower back inch up her torso. She had fallen asleep at an awkward angle, still hunched against her bedroom door. She stared at her bed, only a few steps away, her doona still tossed haphazardly at its foot.

Buzzing pulled her attention back to her phone. She caught the time before she pressed the green button. It'd been two hours since she'd come back from her run, two hours since she and Kyle had locked eyes over a crowded crosswalk, two hours since she'd tried to outrun her past.

"Hello?" she asked hesitantly.

"Are you home? I can't get the door open. I think something's stuck against it."

Corrine!

Neela scrambled off the floor and ran out of the bedroom to the front door. She pulled the dining chair from the door, reminding herself to smile as she greeted her flatmate.

"Hiya! Sorry about that. I was... uh... trying a new workout."

"What kind of workout has you putting the chair against the door?" Corrine asked, frowning at the piece of furniture that was still in Neela's hand. She shook her head and picked up the grocery bags at her feet. "Never mind. I don't want to know. Do whatever you need to do to get to Rio, my friend. I want bragging rights when this is all over."

Neela smiled cautiously, then peeked into the hallway quickly before shutting the door. She made sure the deadbolt was turned and pulled on the door handle again. She ran her hands through her hair and willed herself to keep her smile on. She walked towards the kitchen to help with the unpacking.

Keep it normal. He's gone.

"I have my dates for Papua New Guinea. Looks like it's finally happening," Corrine said as she passed a box of pasta to Neela to put away. "Are you sure you don't want to hang on to the unit? You'll like the girl who'll take over this place. I don't think she's found a flatmate yet."

"No, the contract with Christchurch is a good one. I might not even need a full-time job to pay the bills. It's a good team, and one of the girls from the team has a room available for me to rent."

Corrine paused. "You seemed so settled here. I'm just surprised. I thought you liked being in Auckland."

"I do. But with Rieann being sick…"

"How is she doing?"

"As far as I can tell, she's as good as she can be. They still don't know what's wrong with her. She's going through a lot of testing. She and Trey are coming up next week to meet with some specialists. Mano's been great at giving her some advice about who to see and what questions to ask."

Corrine sighed. "Unfortunately, he would be one of the few people who could have that discussion with her."

"Yeah." She glanced at Corrine, whose back was still to her. They had an unspoken agreement to not discuss her cousin's girlfriend. Neela reached into the bags for more cans but decided to ignore the whispers of caution in her head. "Have you heard more about how Margot is doing with her treatment?"

Corrine stopped what she was doing, her chest rising and falling as she took a deep breath. She turned and leaned against the counter, her blue eyes troubled. "No. Now that I see how secretive everyone is about it, I guess I'm lucky to even know she's sick."

"He didn't say it outright," Neela said. "But I think Mano believes it's because of who he is that she's not talking to anyone about her cancer. She wants to fight this privately."

Corrine removed the last few cans from the grocery bag and began handing them over to Neela. "We all deal with things differently. I guess I wanted Margot to need me, but she has Mano and her parents now."

Neela didn't miss Corrine's quivering lips, bitten down quickly as the latter glanced away. Neela returned the cans to the counter and reached for Corrine. She hoped her attempt at some physical comfort made up for her inability to find the right words. Were there any that could adequately address the sadness in her friend's quiet voice?

She knew of the silver frame on Corrine's desk that held a

photo of two beautiful young women with arms tightly wound around each other. Windblown hair, broad smiles, and animated eyes were caught for eternity in a moment that spoke of a deep bond. It was a photo Neela caught Corrine staring at often.

Corrine squeezed Neela's hand one last time before stepping out of their embrace. With another deep breath, Corrine returned her attention to putting away the last of the shopping. "Anyway, while I'm surprised, I'm glad you've decided it's time to go home. It can't be an easy decision. But I think it's the right one. Your sister will need you close."

Neela recognized the unspoken request in Corrine's eyes to change the subject. "Time will tell. Rieann hasn't asked and won't. But Mano reminded me that Mum would have wanted me at home, to be there for my niece and nephew, so Trey can concentrate on being there for Rieann. He's right as usual. As much as I love living here, there are now more reasons for me to go than to stay," she admitted. *And after today, getting as far away as possible from Kyle would be one of the major ones.* But Corrine didn't need to know that.

Neela shut the cupboard door. "What about you? Ready to leave Auckland? It's been your home for five years." Corrine smiled excitedly as she launched into a list of things she was looking forward to doing.

Corrine had the gift of joy, Neela thought as she listened to her flatmate's plans for Papua New Guinea. But behind the soft-spoken woman was someone with a will of steel. In their year of living together, Neela had watched Corrine systematically overcome challenge after challenge to fulfill her lifelong ambition of doing missionary work overseas. Corrine might have the face of an angel, but she attacked her dreams like a predator.

Mano had known Corrine for years through a youth program they were both involved in. When he learned she was looking for someone to share her flat, he'd called Neela immediately. He'd merely stated that there was a room in a nice area in her current budget. When Neela expressed her hesitancy at moving, he'd asked bluntly, "How many times does a man have to hit you before you leave?"

She had hung up on him then.

But the question had stayed with her all day, forcing her to confront what her heart needed. If she had listened to her heart, she would have stayed, wanting her love to be enough to change Kyle, to inspire him to control his temper and anger.

Except the hits were getting harder, and his promises to do better, to be better, were becoming less frequent.

The next morning, after Kyle left for work, she'd phoned Corrine and asked if she could move in that afternoon.

In hindsight, it should have been an easy decision. But in the first month after she had moved out, she'd found herself dialing Kyle's number half a dozen times. When sleep didn't come quickly, she would reach across the bed, finding only cold sheets, and would wonder if he was thinking of her, or if he still loved her.

After today's encounter, she had her answer.

Seeing the anger in his eyes, even from a distance, was all the validation she needed that she had — indeed — made the right decision.

"Oh, I almost forgot," Corrine said, pushing a folded piece of paper toward Neela. "This was taped to the security door when I came in. It has your name on it. Probably from one of your fans."

The pounding in Neela's head returned with a vengeance. She recognized Kyle's handwriting immediately.

She hoped Corrine didn't see her shaking hand when she picked up the note. "Thanks. It's my turn to cook, isn't it? Would a simple soup and salad do? In an hour?"

"Sounds good. Want any help?"

"No worries. You did the shopping. How much is my share?"

Corrine smiled. "My shout. I know you need to get a new exhaust pipe for your bike."

"So you were listening while I had my mini-tantrum?"

"A little hard to miss. Our walls aren't that thick."

"Thank you."

"Happy to do it and glad I can. I know how tight things are, especially now, with all the training for the Games. But I'm really proud of you. Imagine that—a year ago, you weren't even playing at the provincial level. And now you've got a real chance of representing our country at the Summer Games!"

"Yeah," Neela said quietly, her fingers tightening on the note. Nothing good was going to come from it.

Instead, she smiled. "I'll start on dinner after a quick shower." She walked towards her bedroom, resisting the urge to crunch up the note and toss it straight into the bin.

It wasn't until later, after Corrine had gone to bed, that she opened the folded piece of paper with trembling hands.

We need to talk. You owe me. Call me, or I will come back and wait outside until we do.— K

She didn't imagine the chill that went through her body. She bit down hard on her bottom lip, wanting to focus on the physical pain instead of the one that was gnawing from within. She reached for her phone instinctively. Mano would want to know that Kyle had contacted her.

For the second time that day, she stilled her fingers. She returned the phone to where it had lain.

She wasn't going to depend on her cousin.

She wasn't going to depend on anyone.

She'd figure a way to deal with this herself. She had to, or Kyle would always be a part of her life.

CHAPTER 2

He had turned his head randomly just as she entered the pub. A split second later, he would have completely missed seeing her.

Neela Smyth?

After all these years?

He watched her walk tentatively past a group of people before she reached the bar with her head down. She was dressed casually: a leather jacket covered a simple white shirt and jeans.

Her gaze moved over the other patrons at the bar. A look at the door suggested she was searching for someone. She raised a hand to massage the back of her neck before returning it to find its partner, nervously wringing them as she continued to scan the busy room.

Blake frowned. He had difficulty associating telltale signs of nervousness with the rugby player who was expected to be part of the team heading to Rio next year.

The pub door opened again and drew Neela's attention. Her shoulders sagged. In relief?

Blake's frown deepened.

Was this the girl from his childhood he credited as the reason he had made it out of primary school in one piece? This couldn't be her, could it? That Neela Smyth had been fearless.

"Hey, are you all right, mate?"

Blake reluctantly drew his gaze away from the bar and automatically smiled at his teammate. "Yeah, fine."

"For a minute, you looked like you'd seen a ghost." Jason Williams looked past Blake, then smiled knowingly. "Looks like you picked up some interest from over there."

Blake turned around quickly, returning his attention to the bar. He frowned and tried to find Neela among the group of bodies that now crowded the area.

"No, near the window, mate. The redhead."

Blake reluctantly followed Jason's gaze to the table near the pub's entrance. He shook his head. "No, mate. More your type."

Jason winked as he stood up. "Maybe you're right. I'll go say 'hello' real quick."

"Hey, we agreed we're sticking together for the birthday boy."

Jason slapped Blake's back. "You National Team boys don't have to work as hard as we do to get some attention. I'll be right back. Promise."

Blake grinned as he watched his club's vice-captain saunter with uncharacteristic swagger toward the redhead in question. He lost the smile a few seconds later when he spotted a thick-set man walking in. The stranger's face suggested an unkind history. A well-worn leather jacket didn't hide the broad build or the tattoos that wrapped around a thick neck. The stranger spat out a toothpick as he scanned the room, his gaze finally settling on the bar — straight at Neela.

"Not him. Don't let it be him," Blake murmured.

He looked back at his table. The rest of the fellas were preoccupied with whatever tale the birthday boy was telling. Laughter burst out, merging with the sound of voices and the soft strains of a guitar being played on the small stage deep inside the room.

Neela was now standing with her back to the bar, her hands shoved into the front pockets of her jacket, her head down. But her eyes were trained on the stranger. Whatever relationship there was between Neela and the man walking towards her, Blake knew one thing for certain: there was no joy in this reunion.

Blake scanned his table quickly. "I'm going back for another round. Anyone?"

Two of the lads nodded. He moved swiftly through the crowd, thankful that people were giving him and the team some breathing space. It was one of the reasons that this was a favorite place for professional athletes such as himself: there was an unspoken rule among the patrons to keep to themselves.

Still, there were always gawkers, and it wasn't unusual for him to spot a phone here and there being raised for a quick photo. The never-ending attention was just part of being a member of the country's most famous sports team. He was used to it by now and had arrived wearing a cap that effectively shielded part of his face. The distinctive tattoo on his arm, always on display at matches, was hidden under a light cotton Henley.

He nodded at a young woman who was trying to catch his eye. On a different night, he might have smiled and stopped to make conversation, but tonight, his focus was on the scene at the bar.

When he reached the bar, he hesitated. He didn't actually know what he should do. Neela wasn't asking for help. Maybe she wasn't scared. And was it even really her? It had been more than a decade. Still, his instincts were screaming that this wasn't a good situation.

A space at the bar suddenly opened up behind Neela. Blake squeezed in before he could think twice.

Her back was still to him. He didn't think she knew he was there. He was just another body angling for attention from the bartender on a busy Saturday night.

He could just hear her voice.

"Please leave me alone, Kyle. We both need to move on from the past, from each other."

"I've been trying to get in touch with you for months."

"We've said all we have to say to each other. I've told you I don't want to see you again."

"I deserve to know where you are. You owe me that, at least."

"I don't owe you anything!"

"You owe me five grand, Neela Smyth," Kyle threatened.

"You stalking me is about money?"

"I'm not stalking. I'm just coming for what's mine. After you left, there was never going to be anything between us again. I don't live with quitters. I just want what's owed to me."

"I never asked you to help pay for my training! You said it was a gift! That you believed in me!" Neela hissed.

"A gift? What kind of people are you hanging out with these days, Miss National Team Player? No one I know would put that kind of money into me," Kyle growled. "You were an investment. You're famous now. You should be rolling in it. I want my money back…with interest."

"I don't have money like that! I'm not on *the* National Team! It's women's rugby, Kyle!"

"With all the publicity you're getting, I don't believe you! I read the papers. You're up for a contract, aren't you? You've got money coming in!"

"Kyle, let go of my arm."

"Not until we talk."

"Please let go. You're hurting me!"

It was nothing more than a whisper, but Blake recognized the fear in it. That was all he needed to hear. A rush of anger blocked out everything else in the room.

He didn't realize he had moved until he felt the stranger's muscled arm in his own firm grip.

"She asked you to let go," he said quietly.

Years of learning to move at a moment's notice helped him

escape the full impact of a clenched fist, but he couldn't wholly avoid contact. Fierce pain moved instantly from his jaw through his body. He continued to hold on to the arm that was still keeping a tight grip on Neela's arm as he met the eyes of the person who had hit him. He expected to see fury but only saw cold indifference.

The sounds of multiple chairs scraping against the wooden floor brought all conversation in the pub to a stop. Blake didn't need to turn to know that his teammates were probably all standing in anticipation of a word or a sign from him. He had help if he needed it.

Kyle took a quick look past Blake. He must have noticed Blake's teammates behind him, but he didn't seem intimidated by the sight of six professional rugby players ready to move. Instead, he returned his attention to Blake, his eyes now assessing. "Who the hell are you?"

Blake felt Kyle's arm move under his grasp, and Neela's gasp suggested Kyle was tightening his hold on her. Blake responded similarly, adding pressure to his grip on Kyle's forearm. He kept his gaze firmly on Kyle's face, unintimidated. "I'm a friend of the family. Let go of her."

"Make me," Kyle dared.

"You don't want me to do that. Let go of her, mate."

Kyle sneered, his eyes now lighting up in recognition. "I know you. You're that rugby player. You get into a fight, and won't you be done with the National Team? Only the perfect play for our country, don't they?"

His free hand was now clenched. Kyle was looking for a fight and apparently didn't care if the odds were against him. He glanced at Blake's teammates again and his lips curled, almost in amusement. "Your pretty boyfriends over there don't scare me, either. You blokes just look tough on the pitch."

Before Blake could respond, a calm voice coming from behind the bar said, "The police will be here in two minutes. Break this up, now."

Neither man moved. Blake prepared himself for another strike. He was a quick learner and never forgot a mistake, especially a painful one. His sixth sense also told him that his teammates would make sure he didn't get hurt again, that they would handle Kyle. At the very least, they would give Blake the time to get Neela away from this madman.

But as soon as he felt Kyle's muscles relax a fraction, Blake let go of Kyle's arm. His priority was to keep Neela safe, and he couldn't do that if he were fighting. From the corner of his eye, he saw her pull her arm close to her body, using her other hand to massage the tender spot. Blake moved in front of Neela, his arms now crossed.

Kyle ignored Blake and stared at her. "We still have some unfinished business, Neela." He didn't wait for a response and purposefully pushed past Blake as he walked out of the pub.

Blake released the breath he hadn't realized he'd been holding. He didn't want a fight. The bastard was right: a public brawl would mean an automatic fine and possible suspension from both the club and the National teams. He would take whatever reprimand came from keeping Neela out of harm's way. But he didn't want his rugby brothers to suffer. He knew at least one of the fellas counted on every paycheck.

He turned to look at his teammates and nodded. They returned his nod before they sat back down, signaling to the rest of the pub that all the excitement was over. Slowly, the noise generally associated with a busy night returned.

Blake returned his attention to Neela and inhaled sharply. Vacant eyes stared back but didn't see him. A pale pallor had spread through her bronzed skin, and her breathing was shallow. Trembling hands were clasping and unclasping.

"Neela? Hey? Remember me? Blake Stanton? It's been a few years, eh? We were in school together when we were kids." He pushed back the instinct to put his arms around her.

"Blake Stanton?" she repeated. She kept her face away from him, and her voice was small and distant.

"Yeah, that's right," he encouraged.

"You live with Mano." She was looking at him now.

He nodded. "I do. Maybe we should give him a call. Let him know…"

"No!"

He cursed silently as she stepped backward automatically. She frowned. Her eyes darted back and forth as if trying to understand the environment she was in, to process the noise, the lights, her feelings.

Dark brown eyes, wild with emotions he wasn't sure he understood, eventually settled back on him.

"No, no. Don't call Mano," she said faintly. "He'll be so disappointed if he knew I met him…"

Blake rushed his hand through his hair. "Let me take you home. Please? I think you've had a bit of a scare. Or I can drive you home if you show me where your car is. I can take a taxi back here."

Neela only shook her head and started for the exit.

Blake turned quickly to the bartender and pulled out his wallet. "Sorry about that, mate. Let me shout the drinks for the fellas over there. If I'm short, here's the number at my club. Leave a message with the amount I still owe you. I'll swing by tomorrow to settle up."

"No worries," the bartender replied. "This should be more than enough. Good luck with your lady friend, Blake. Never seen that bloke before, but he's bad business if you ask me."

Blake turned and bumped straight into Jason.

"You all right? What was going on?" Jason asked.

"It's all good. I've got to go. Will you let the others know?" Blake looked past his friend. The front door was just closing.

Jason nodded. "We got it. See you back in Christchurch?"

"Yeah." Blake clasped Jason's arm and quickly returned his hug. It was the same as it was on the pitch. Jason would be there to help when he was needed. No questions asked, no answers required.

A rush of cool air greeted Blake when he left the pub. Different from the high energy inside, the front gardens were filled with a more varied age group of patrons. The large number of heating lamps plus an unusually warm August evening no doubt contributed to more people being outdoors than usual. He noticed a phone pointed at him. A few more faces smiled in his direction. He started to move. The last thing he wanted tonight was more attention.

"Hey! Watch it!"

Blake followed the sharp voice and caught sight of Neela holding her hands up in silent apology to a large man shielding his still-full glass of a rich amber liquid.

She moved away briskly, head down.

He ran towards her and was by her side in a few seconds. Her hand was still massaging the spot Kyle had grabbed.

He kept up with her hurried pace. "Hey, are you all right?"

His hand was slapped away, and her face grew horrified at what must have been an unplanned reaction to his touch. She exhaled loudly, then met his gaze. She started to speak, then stopped herself. He recognized her attempts to regain control of the situation, but the pulsating vein in her neck suggested it wouldn't happen quickly.

Blake shoved his hands into his pockets. He wanted to draw her close, to comfort her physically, but this was Neela. Neela, who never needed anything or anyone. He suddenly felt as if he were in primary school again, unsure of how to behave in front of a girl he practically worshipped, worried that the wrong word, the wrong move, would send her away.

"I'm sorry," she said, her dark eyes studying him. "Blake Stanton."

He shrugged. "Yeah. Do you remember me from school?"

"Yeah. A bit. I know *of* you better now, of course."

Blake gave her half a smile. "Bet you didn't think the kid you protected on the field would end up winning a world championship, eh?"

"Well, my cousin saved your ass a couple of times at last week's game against Australia. Still lost, though."

Blake laughed. "He did, and we did. I owe him a few favors. How about I repay one by taking you home?"

She turned her head again, her eyes returning to the brightly lit garden now behind them. "I can pick up a taxi."

"You might have to wait a while. It's a busy night. My car's not too far from here. Do you want to go straight home, or can I take you somewhere?"

She whispered, but her words shook him. "I think he knows where I live."

Think, Blake, think. Keep her safe. "Uh…how about a friend's place?"

"I don't want him to know about anyone else in my life, Blake. He mustn't know more than he does already."

Unexpected anger welled up within him. Who was that bastard? He made an impulsive decision, knowing his best friend wouldn't mind. "I'm staying with Tim Molloy this weekend. You know him too, right? It wouldn't be like you're staying in some strange place or anything. There's an extra room there."

"No, I can't."

"Neela, that fella in there, the one who laid his hands on you? You're telling me he knows where you live. And it doesn't sound like it's something you want him to know," he said gently. "He left here angry."

He didn't expect her false bravado to crumble so instantly.

His eyes widened. *Oh, shit.* Neela was crying? Neela Smyth never cried. He remembered her falling out of a tree when they were ten. She had dusted herself off and strolled casually to her mother, telling her she thought she'd broken "a couple of bones." At the same school picnic, twenty minutes earlier, he'd had to stop himself from wailing out loud in front of his friends because he had a splinter in his finger.

Blake gave in to his instincts this time. He put his arm around her and drew her close.

Hiding her face in her hands, she didn't resist his attempts of comfort. Her body shook as she sobbed quietly.

He wasn't sure how long they stood in that position. He only knew he would hold her as long as she needed him to.

He moved them deeper into the shadows of the shrubs, away from any prying eyes and snap-happy fans. When he could no longer hear her soft cries, he said, "I'll take you back to the Meriton. It has one of the best views of the city, I promise you."

Neela nodded, but her shoulders slumped as she walked out of Blake's arms and wiped her tears. He hadn't expected the urge to pull her back into his arms, to keep her safe.

She now stood apart from him, eyes red and swollen. The pulse in her neck returning to the volatile pace he had witnessed earlier. "Where did you park?" she asked.

As they walked to the car, Blake sent a quick to message to Tim, asking him to get the room he was staying in ready for Neela. He offered to sleep on the sofa. He sighed with relief when Tim responded immediately.

Tim: **She can stay in the mstr. Call when U arrive. I'll be up.**

He didn't try to strike up a conversation with Neela, hoping instead that music would ease the awkwardness that naturally came when a vulnerable moment was shared between strangers.

And they were that. Despite their shared past and a number of mutual acquaintances, they didn't know each other.

Strains of an aria flooded the small confines of his older brother's car. He glanced over, expecting the usual reaction at his preferred choice of music, but Neela didn't move an inch. Her sad, vacant eyes stared straight ahead.

Just as he was getting used to the silence, she spoke unexpectedly. "Who's this?"

"Maria Callas."

"It's nice."

He drove into the garage of the exclusive condominium complex just under an hour later. When they arrived at the unit, Tim was standing at the doorway. He went straight to Neela to give her a hug. Blake met Tim's eyes and recognized the questions in them. He shrugged, then shook his head. He didn't know how she was doing, either.

"You poor little sausage," Tim said as he led them into the condo.

Neela gave a small laugh. "It's been a while since anyone's called me that." She looked around the condo before turning to face Tim and Blake. "Good to see you again, Tim. It's been quite a night of reunions for me."

"How long has it been, Neela?" Tim asked.

"A few years, at least. I still remember your choice words to the ref in the Test against England. Very colorful for a scientist."

Tim smiled. "We talked about getting together one day, but even moving in with your cousin hasn't increased my chances of seeing you."

"Life has been busy. And I haven't lived on the South Island for almost ten years now. But I do keep up with the news. Congratulations on the Shorland Medal."

"How did you learn about that?"

"Hey, when one of Canterbury's own makes it big in any field, we all know. Even the nerds."

"I was part of a team." Tim smiled, but his voice turned serious. "You all right?"

Neela's lower lip began to quiver, and she bit on it before nodding quickly. "I just need a good night's sleep. I hadn't expected Kyle to be so aggressive in public. He never was before. I thought it'd be safe to see him in a public place."

Tim glanced sharply at Blake. They both heard what she didn't say.

Blake asked cautiously. "Has he ever been ... rough ...with you in private?"

She turned her head slightly at the question, but she avoided looking at Blake directly. Her eyes were distant when she looked up again, acknowledging but not seeing the two men in the room. "I should go to bed. It's been a long night. I'm sorry to impose, but…thanks. I can sleep on the sofa."

Tim shook his head. "No chance and no apologies. We're glad you're here. Just head down the hall."

Blake watched Neela make her way to the master bedroom, her back straight, her head up.

When they heard the door shut, Tim turned to Blake. "What the hell happened at the pub? Your message of 'Neela. Need room 4 her. I sleep on sofa. Fight.' could have meant a million things. And your jaw looks like it's swelling up, mate. You'd better get some ice on it."

Blake automatically touched his face. He had forgotten about the punch until then. He went to the kitchen for an icepack. "Honestly, I don't really know what was going on between her and that fella. It's the first time I've seen her in years. For a minute, I wasn't even sure it was her. She just looked scared when she walked into the pub. "

"Don't you two have some sort of history?"

Blake shook his head, then opened the fridge and peered inside. He would love a strong drink. "Who? Me and Neela? Not really. I mean, we went to primary school together for a bit."

"And there is that video."

Blake rolled his eyes. "That was a million years ago."

"People still talk about it."

"I was twelve. I'm bigger and better now. You'd reckon with a championship and a few club titles under my belt, we could stop talking about that video."

Tim grinned as he joined Blake in the kitchen. He took the bottle of beer Blake offered. "Aren't you having one? I think you deserve it tonight. I won't tell."

"Can't risk it. It's a week until we leave for England. I had my one indulgence earlier."

Tim raised his beer. "You and Neela are part of rugby folklore with that video. I think my sister has included it in one of her syllabi."

Blake sat down at the kitchen table, ice pack in hand. "Your sister scares me."

"My sister scares most people, but I've learned a lot from her. She volunteers with Women Refuge. One in three women will be part of an abusive relationship at least once in their lifetime."

Blake shook his head. "That's a shocking statistic. But it's Neela Smyth we're talking about. You grew up on the South Island and follow rugby. She's expected to be on the team preparing for the Summer Games next year. Talk about folklore. Everyone who knows their rugby knows she doesn't take shit from anyone."

Tim shrugged. "Neela wouldn't be the first woman who's hidden having an abusive boyfriend. I'm glad you brought her back. Best let Mano know she's here."

"What should I say?"

"The truth. She's like a sister to him."

"Yeah, I know," Blake said. "But I don't think Neela wants him to know."

"Phone him, Blake. Let him know what you saw. He'd be angrier if he found out you knew and didn't tell him. And you know he'll find out. He always does."

Blake grimaced. "Feels like at least one of the cousins isn't going to be happy with me."

"You're about to leave for England with Mano. Not the best way to foster team unity. Remember when you made a pass at Liana at the last Championship?"

"I didn't make a pass! All I did was invite her to my nan's birthday! I didn't know anything was going on between Liana and your brother then. No one knew!"

Tim grinned. "Mitch hasn't forgiven you."

"He should. They're married now. Hey, would Mitch and

Liana want to know she's here? I don't want you to get into trouble with Mitch."

"They won't mind. Mano's like family to them, which means she's family," Tim said. He glanced at the clock on the wall and made a face. "I better turn in now. I'm driving to Piha with Professor Roberts, and he's a stickler about leaving on time. But wake me up if you need anything. Or if she does."

"Yeah, I will."

"I'm not sure what time I'll be back, but…"

"Go to bed, Tim. I'm sure I can handle it. Thanks for staying up, mate."

"No worries." Tim looked toward the master bedroom again. "She may be Neela Smyth, but she can get hurt like any one of us. Phone Mano, yeah?"

Blake sighed. He was tempted to wait until morning, but he couldn't chance someone putting something out there on social media about what had happened at the pub. They might not know Neela, but anything that involved a National Team player these days garnered attention. He knew it wouldn't be farfetched if tonight's incident were already making its mark somewhere in cyberspace.

"Blake?"

Blake nodded before taking the ice pack off his face. "I'll phone him right now." It was the right thing to do, even though he was silently praying that the call would go straight to voicemail.

No luck.

"Blake?" Mano's gruff voice greeted him suspiciously.

"Yeah, it's me."

"You've been arrested, haven't you?"

Blake grinned. "No. I'm good."

"Was Tim arrested? If he is, call his brother. I'm just the landlord."

"Tim's good."

"Then why are you calling me at one in the morning?"

Blake took a deep breath. *This is the right thing to do.* "She's fine, but Neela's with us at the Meriton. I was at the pub with some of the team. She was also there, and was in some sort of… well, it wasn't exactly a fight, but there was this fella…"

"Kyle? She met with Kyle?"

"Yeah, that's what she called him."

"Did he hit her?"

Blake's heart sank. "No."

Mano was quiet on the phone. "And she's at the Meriton with you? Right now?"

"Yeah."

"Is she hurt in any way?"

"I don't think so. He grabbed her pretty tight around the wrist, but he didn't touch her otherwise while I was there."

"Right. Listen, you have to keep this quiet. Neela doesn't want anyone to know about Kyle. I think it's a mistake, but that's her choice. Margot needs me tomorrow, but I'll get on the first flight I can. Will you keep an eye on her until I arrive?"

"Yeah." Blake hesitated, then realized there was more to this situation than he knew about. "Uh, she said this fella — Kyle? — knows where she lives."

In all the years Blake had known Mano, he had never heard the usually quiet and amiable man use a derogatory term even once. Either on the pitch or off, Mano kept it clean. So for Blake to hear his team captain use several expletives in a row only highlighted how dangerous things really were for Neela.

"If I know her, she'll want to leave as soon as she wakes up. She'll want to pretend it didn't happen. Don't leave her alone tomorrow," Mano instructed.

Blake shifted in his seat.

"Blake? Mate?"

"I'll do my best. But I don't know her well enough to insist that she stay," he said. "We haven't seen each other since we were kids, and, well, you know… She may not listen to me."

"Do what you have to do. Keep her there until I arrive."

Blake rubbed his forehead.

"Come up with me to Auckland," Tim had said.

"Enjoy some time with the boys before we leave for England," Mano had encouraged him.

That was the last time he'd listen to his flatmates.

Blake inhaled deeply. "I'll do my best."

"That's all I'm asking."

CHAPTER 3

Neela opened her eyes to a color that wasn't the soft cream walls of her bedroom. A whisper of lavender hung in the air, its comforting scent a contrast to the cool gray of the doona cover she lay under. She stretched her fingers, sliding them back and forth over dark linen she was reluctant to leave. Turning on her back, she pushed herself deeper into pillows that only encouraged her to stay where she was.

Definitely not her room, but her instincts told her she wasn't in any danger.

Then the events from last night came back swiftly, in images that promised to sear themselves into her memory: Kyle, the pub, Blake showing up out of nowhere. This wasn't a nightmare she could dismiss after she woke up.

Neela shut her eyes and pulled a pillow over her head, hoping to vanquish the onslaught of fear that threatened to manifest itself in a flood of tears. She swallowed the scream that wanted to come out.

Sitting up, she forced herself to relax her shoulders, then closed her eyes again. "Breathe. You can do this."

She fingered the area of her forearm where Kyle had held her so aggressively the night before. Without looking, she knew there'd be visible bruising.

Wherever she was this morning, she was there because Blake had insisted she go back with him. What would have happened last night if he hadn't shown up? Would she have allowed Kyle to drag her out of the pub? Would she have fought back?

Kyle.

She shivered.

He had kept his violence toward her private. Last night, for the first time in their history, he hadn't been afraid to show his true colors in public.

She could admit now that she had been in an abusive relationship and had chosen to stay in one for months. Now, almost a year later, she wondered how it had spiraled into a situation where, if it hadn't been for the intervention of her cousin, she might never have seen how much danger she really was in.

But it wasn't over. Kyle was back. For money. Money she didn't have.

Was that all she was to him in the end?

How was it possible to feel so much for someone who didn't care for her as deeply? She'd believed him when he said he loved her. But she'd also believed him when he apologized repeatedly with promises to never to hit her again, that the first slap had been an accident, that he just needed to learn to control his temper.

She could call the police, but she couldn't deny that she owed him money. Like it or not, he had paid for all the extra training that had brought her back to the level where she needed to be.

Neela sighed. Life had just started to become understandable again when her past had to rear its ugly head.

Still seated in the middle of a king-size bed, she followed the lines of the morning sun to the bureau against the wall. On it, a collection of framed photos of various sizes was on display. An ornately decorated frame caught the light, its blue and pink rhinestones sparkling.

She got out of bed to study the collection of photographs found in most families' homes: a wedding, several pictures of a much-loved baby, and a close-up of a beautiful girl with startling blue eyes. But among the everyday family snapshots were also photographs which depicted lives that were far from ordinary.

A discreet knock interrupted a rare insight into the Molloy family. "Neela? Are you up?"

"Yes, I'm up," she replied, taking one last look at the wedding photo of New Zealand's most famous sporting couple.

"Good. There's coffee if you're interested," Blake said through the door. "I can make tea if you prefer that."

She took a deep breath, knowing she was going to have to face Blake sooner or later. Leaving the house without saying 'thank you' wasn't an option, though it was tempting.

She hated that he had been part of last night. Being a woman who needed to be saved wasn't a role she coveted, but she was also honest enough to admit that if he hadn't been there, she could have been the recipient of Kyle's next punch.

Wincing at the memory of Blake's face when Kyle's fist had made impact, she recognized the mask of control that had immediately replaced the shock at being hit. The horror of that moment accompanied the instant recognition that with Blake next to her, Kyle couldn't hurt her.

"Neela, are you all right?"

"Uh, yes. Sorry. Coffee would be fine. Thanks. I'll be out in a minute."

"There are clean towels in the ensuite if you want to take a shower."

"Thanks. I might do that."

She stood under the rush of water longer than she should have. Even though she had to wear the same clothes she had slept in, at least she could face Blake Stanton feeling somewhat lucid. She needed all the emotional armor she could muster to meet another part of her life she had thought was long since over.

As she left the bedroom, Blake's rich baritone voice accompanied a soundtrack that filled the condo. She leaned against the entryway that led from the bedrooms to the kitchen and dining area. She couldn't quite decipher the words. Italian?

Blake's love for opera was a well-known fact, and he was often quoted as saying that the invitation to sing at the city's New Year's Eve celebration had been one of the highlights of his life. She wasn't a fan of opera, but even she could hear that he was good. Or at the very least, able to carry a tune.

She walked toward the kitchen counter, making a sound as she climbed onto one of its barstools. Blake turned with a ready smile on his face, but she frowned when she caught sight of the darkened area just below his jaw.

"I've been hit worse." He smiled wider and held up a mug. "Coffee, you said?"

"Coffee will be great. Thanks."

"I'm just about to have a protein shake. Tim made an extra serving if you'd like one."

He pulled out a plastic pitcher filled with an ominous green liquid from the refrigerator.

She raised her eyebrows. "Tim made that?"

"Yes. Scientifically proven to do...uh...something. I tune out when he starts bringing out reams of data. How about it, eh?"

"I'll give it a go. Tim still here, is he?"

Blake shook his head as he poured Neela a tall glass of the green shake. "He left before dawn. Collecting data by the coast. Something to do with slugs and water salinity." He pushed the glass towards Neela. "What do you reckon? Give it a go?"

She reached for the drink. Different textures and flavors teased her taste buds: lemon, apple, celery...mint? She took another look at the glass in her hand, swirling it gently. "This isn't as bad as I thought it would be."

Blake laughed. "Tim's quite the nutritionist. He eats far better than Mano or me. When we're in training mode, he has no problem dobbing us to the team nutritionist."

Neela smiled at the idea. "Mano dobbed in for bad eating habits? That's not like him."

"No." Blake grinned. "But you know he can't say 'no' to a bucket of fried chicken."

"No, he can't. It's a weakness that runs through the whole family. Our nan's fault. Her fried chicken is the centerpiece of our family reunions." She reached for the mug now in front of her, shaking her head at the offer of milk. She inhaled the aroma of the dark liquid. "I hope I didn't keep you from anything this morning."

Blake shook his head. "No, I take Sundays off. I was going for a swim, but I'm under strict instructions from your cousin to keep an eye on you until he arrives."

She spat out her coffee. "You're under what?"

Blake offered her a serviette. She took it, trying to temper the building anxiety at what her cousin could now know. "He's in Christchurch. I know he is. Margot has one more dose of chemo this week."

Blake leaned his large frame against the counter, his index finger idly following the curves of the tall glass that held his shake. "Yeah, well, he said he'd get the first flight from Christchurch to Auckland tomorrow. He just sent me his itinerary. He'll be here in the morning."

"You told him about last night, didn't you? Everything?" she asked. A tedious thumping began in the back of her head. She didn't want Mano involved again.

"Yeah."

Their eyes met. He was no longer the boy she remembered from primary school, but his face —and physique—were all too familiar. He was on half the billboards throughout the country. But now, separated from him by a wide, smooth granite countertop, she took in his keen brown eyes, the sharp nose that had miraculously escaped being broken over the years, and the practiced smile that had graced the covers of dozens of publications. His thick neck and broad shoulders were the expected results of years in the gym. Although not tall, he filled up space. The top of her head would just reach the tip of his nose.

She knew how his body worked because she studied him as diligently as she did some of the all-time greats of the sport. While he wasn't on the same lofty levels as legendary rugby players such as Mitch Molloy and Connor Dane, Blake Stanton continued to be an integral part of one of the world's elite sporting teams. He was known for being tenacious on the field. Despite all the attention he garnered with his colorful social life, there was no argument among the fans and critics that he deserved his place on the National Team.

Yes, she was fully aware of the very public image of Blake Stanton.

But off the field, she was less sure of the man. He had a friendly face, the kind of face a mother would like to see on her daughter's date. He smiled in all his marketing pictures and came off as easy-going and fun.

She was also now sure that the same focus that took him to the highest level of professional rugby could be equally potent in whatever else he felt he needed to do. She had seen that last night. She might not know the reason why he'd stepped in when he did, but there was no doubt in her mind that – at that moment – he was committed to being there for her.

Except she didn't want his help anymore. She especially didn't want another man in her life who thought he knew better than she.

"I wish you hadn't said anything to Mano," she continued. "He has a lot on his mind. I don't need to be one more thing."

He crossed his arms. "I had to. It didn't feel right not saying something to him about last night. We know how much you mean to him."

"Look, he's not my keeper. I know you mean well, but Mano flying over from the South Island is overreacting. This was his last break before the National Team leaves for the World Championship."

"I don't tell Mano what to do."

"You could have told him I was fine, that I wasn't hurt."

"That would have been a lie because I wasn't sure if you were 'fine.' I'm still not sure if you are. And you have bruises."

"So do you," she retorted, then instantly regretted her outburst.

Neela placed both of her hands, palms down, on the countertop. "I'm sorry. That was uncalled for. You did what you thought was right, and if I know Mano, there was nothing you could have said last night that would have changed his mind. But I'm going home after I finish my coffee."

"I promised him I'd keep an eye on you until he arrives."

"I don't need a babysitter."

"Hey, if there's one person in the world who doesn't need convincing about that, it's me. You were always the one in charge when we were kids."

Her eyes narrowed when she recognized the teasing quality in Blake's voice. It was the one he used in his interviews, especially when the reporter was a woman.

"No," she began slowly. "I don't remember that. Primary school was so long ago."

"Neela Smyth, you can't tell me you've forgotten how you were the one who always divided the players up into teams. And you must remember how no one would tell you any different, whether we agreed with you or not."

"Was I fair?"

He laughed, his eyes lighting up, and she suddenly understood why reporters—both women *and* men— would finish their segments smiling. Blake made people like him. He must have picked up that attribute when he was older because she didn't remember him being more than the smallest kid on the field, full of energy but lacking any real skill. And he definitely hadn't always been liked.

"You were, actually," he said. "Though, when I think back,

you taking me on your team was more of a testament to your strength as a player than to mine."

She couldn't stop the smile that rose up at that concession to their shared past. That part, she did remember. Blake had been such a puny little thing when he was a young boy. No one had wanted him on their teams, nor had any of them suspected he'd go on to be one of the youngest players on a world championship rugby team.

"You're not going to distract me from trying to leave, Blake." She finished her coffee and jumped off the barstool. "I'm sure you have more important things to do today than go over childhood memories. I need to go home."

"I'll come with you."

She paused and turned around slowly. Hands on her hips, she hoped he heard how serious she was. "No."

"Come on, help a fella out. Mano's still my landlord, and he's one of my captains. If I fail, he may kill me."

"He won't kill you."

"Come on, Neela, please?"

She couldn't help it, but the exaggerated look on Blake's face dampened the irritation she wanted to feel for him. But she also wasn't naïve. Rugby wasn't the only reason his name was in the public eye so often.

"This is new territory for me. Is the famous Blake Stanton trying to charm his way with me? Because you know that won't work with this girl. Save it for your adoring fans."

"I'm not trying to do anything. Come on. I made a promise I intend to keep. If you won't stay here, I'll have to go back with you."

"No."

"I'll wait outside your place all day if I have to. I'd rather not because it's not how I want to spend a beautiful Sunday. But a promise is a promise between brothers."

She groaned. "Oh, don't give me any of that 'rugby brothers' rubbish."

"You'd do anything for your rugby sisters. I know you would; I've seen your team play. There's real chemistry there. You're aiming for the gold in Rio. Whatever happens, whether or not you make the team, you lot support each other. That's just how it is. You understand that I'll do nearly anything Mano wants me to do because I know he'd do the same for me."

Neela hated being pushed into a corner, especially by the likes of Blake Stanton. They weren't exactly friends, but they shared a social circle that encompassed both the rugby world and the small town they had grown up in.

Then there was his relationship with Mano. Her cousin didn't let many people into his life, and Blake was one of the few. She had heard his name often during the last few years, and she was quite sure that if Blake Stanton said he was going to do something, he would. She didn't doubt he'd follow her or even wait outside her unit all day. That would go over well with the neighborhood once word got out that a famous rugby player was hanging around for no apparent reason.

She decided on a compromise. "I'm going home. You can come back with me if you like, but it isn't necessary. You can't stay over, though. My flatmate's very particular about guests, and our sofa is too narrow."

"I'm sure I would fit."

"I doubt it, but it's a moot point. You're not staying the night."

"We'll see."

"Blake!"

Blake grinned, holding up his hands in mock surrender. "If I have to sit in the car all night, I will. I don't break my promises."

An hour later, as Blake parked the car outside her building, Neela scanned the quiet street for anyone who looked remotely familiar. The Kyle she knew would never be up this early, especially on a Sunday. Or would his ego prompt the unexpected? She didn't know anymore.

Before she could dwell on the possibility, a sudden rap on the window startled her.

Twelve-year-old Leon Liu was staring unashamedly at the driver of the black sports car that screamed 'money.' Neela lowered her window for her upstairs neighbor. "What are you doing out here, Leon? It's a cool morning, and you're only wearing a jumper."

"Just went to the shops to pick up some bread. Mum has one of her headaches," Leon explained, his eyes still on her companion. "Is that who I think it is?"

Before she could answer, Blake leaned over, an easy smile on his face. "Hiya, mate. You all right?"

Leon raised his hand for a wave. "Hiya. Yeah, I'm fine. You a friend of Neela's?"

"Yeah. I live with her cousin."

Leon glanced at her before turning his attention back to Blake. "You live with Mano Palua? That's a cool house to live in."

He grinned. "It's not bad. But only if we win. When we lose, Mano's a terrible flatmate."

"Yeah, I bet. Well, I better get the bread back home. Mum gets all weird if she doesn't start her day with toast."

"Nice meeting you, mate."

"You too, Mr. Stanton."

She watched the boy make his way back to their building.

"You know him well?" Blake asked, his eyes also on Leon's retreating figure.

"I babysit on occasion. His mother works late at a local restaurant."

"His dad?"

"Never met him. I'm not sure if he's around. I don't ask, and neither Leon nor his mum talks about him. She's a good mum, and he's a good kid," she said as she got out of the car. Rolling her shoulders, she breathed in the fresh morning air.

"How long have you been living here?" Blake asked when they reached the security door.

"About a year," she replied as she entered the code.

They walked up two flights of stairs and Neela unlocked the door. After Blake had entered the unit, she instinctively looked up and down the stairwell before she locked the door behind her. She exhaled quietly and hoped her thundering heart would calm down quickly.

Blake had made his way to the console near the window. He picked up the picture that had been taken on the night of Mano's debut on the National Team.

"I remember this," he said. "He scored two tries that night. He was unstoppable."

"It was the first time I'd been to Eden Park. Mano flew my parents and me over. I was excited and so nervous. He introduced me to Mitch Molloy, Connor Dane, and Jay Morrison afterward. I couldn't believe it. Mum said I slept with a smile on my face."

He put the photo down and picked up the next one: a picture of Mano the night New Zealand had recaptured the world title. He smiled, possibly remembering the thrill of a long-awaited victory. Like the others on the team, Blake had become a national hero that night.

Neela came to stand next to him and looked at the photo in his hand. "That was quite a night. You played full-on for eighty minutes."

"You were there? You didn't come over to say hi or something?"

"No."

"Why not?"

"I had my own hero to fawn over. Besides, I didn't know whether you would have remembered me after all those years."

"You're one person I would never forget, Neela," Blake said softly.

Something in his voice made Neela look at him. She wished

she hadn't, as she found herself suddenly caught in an intense look. Whatever he was remembering, she was being swept up in it, and it held on to her. *Who was that girl you remember, Blake?*

She swallowed and dug deep to break the hold his gaze had on her. Refocusing her attention to the picture, she said, "Mano's embarrassed that I have this out, but I love that shot. He's never looked more happy or free if that makes sense. He took the Championship seriously."

She felt him still staring at her but didn't look up. Then she heard a quiet sigh before he spoke again.

"All the senior members did," he said. "The difference between how we prepared for the last tournament and the upcoming one is like night and day. There's always pressure, you know. But in getting ready for Twickenham, it's a different kind of expectation. This time, it's really for ourselves."

"Still like the pressure?"

"Still love the game. And that's what counts the most." Blake turned from the console and surveyed the room. "This is nice."

"Mano found the place for me," she said. "He introduced me to Corrine. The timing couldn't have been more perfect. She's sweet. Teaches music at the college."

Blake's gaze stopped on the very narrow blue sofa that faced the small TV.

"You are not staying over," Neela said firmly.

"It's not that narrow. I could fit."

She didn't bother hiding her grin as she shook her head. "Look, you asked to be here, but don't expect me to entertain you. I don't need you here, but I also believe you're hard-headed enough sit outside just to keep a promise."

"You don't need to entertain me. I'm a grown man. I can take care of myself. Mano, Tim, and I do our own thing most times."

"Suit yourself. You're welcomed to put on the telly if you like."

"If you have the all ingredients, fancy some choc chip cookies?"

Neela knew she looked surprised. She couldn't help it. Those were the last words she had expected to hear from Blake. "You bake?"

"Yeah. And I promise you, my choc chip cookies will bring you to the brink of ecstasy."

Neela blinked. "Do you say that to all the girls, Blake?"

"Yeah, I do, actually."

"Shameless."

"But it's true."

"Well, go ahead, then. Knock yourself out in the kitchen."

Blake started singing as Neela closed her bedroom door. Again, she shook her head, but this time with a smile on her lips.

* * *

Later, Neela tried very hard to stop from groaning as the first bite of chocolate chip cookie literally melted in her mouth. She couldn't prevent her eyes from shutting at the onslaught of texture and flavor—chocolate, vanilla, nuts, and was that a hint of cinnamon? —warmed her mouth.

"Not bad, eh?"

Blake was watching her, amusement danced in his eyes.

"These are deadly," she admitted before taking another bite. This time, she forced herself to keep her eyes open, but a sigh escaped.

"Told you," he said smugly. "It's my nan's recipe, and she said it came from her mother. The ingredients aren't a surprise. It's the technique in the mixing that makes the difference."

Blake's phone buzzed, and he glanced at it. The amusement in his face disappeared as he answered the phone. "Hello? Yes, I'm with her. She insisted on going home, so that's where we are." He held out his phone to her. "Mano."

She grimaced but took the phone. "Hey. Where are you?"

"Don't give Blake a hard time. You and I need to talk about what happened," Mano said.

"Nothing happened."

"Look at your arm and say that again."

Neela threw Blake a suspicious look. He offered her another cookie as if he had sensed the reason for her ire.

He was always such a dibber-dobber.

She took the cookie, bit into it, then returned her attention to Mano. "Okay, I'll admit that Kyle was a little rough. But I'm fine. Yes, I was lucky Blake was there. I won't make that mistake again."

"You promised you wouldn't see him again, especially without me."

"I met him because he promised he wouldn't come to my building again. I thought it'd be safe at a pub that's always full of people. I'm not stupid. I wouldn't have met him alone. And I don't like having a babysitter, so you can let Blake off the hook by telling him he can go home."

"No."

"He won't fit on my sofa!" she yelled. "I'm fine. I was in a little bit of a shock last night. It's been almost a year since I last saw Kyle. I've learned my lesson, Mano. I won't let him come near me again."

"Let Blake stay with you girls tonight. I can speak to Corrine if you like. She won't mind."

"I'm sure Blake has more important things to do than be here with me. Tell him to go home."

"I haven't forgotten what you went through that night. Kyle could have really hurt you."

She responded with silence.

Her automatic rejection of his statement didn't come as easily as it would have a year ago. She had since learned to face those demons, to accept the truth. She hadn't forgotten that night either. She could still feel Mano's gentle hands as he lifted her off the floor and wiped the blood from her face. The anger and sadness in his eyes that night would forever be seared in her memory.

Recognizing that she was the cause of his pain and fury woke her from the cloud of denial she had created for herself. She had never thought of herself as a victim. Victims were weak. She was strong. Her mother taught her that. She was raised to be strong.

"Neela? Are you still there?" Mano asked.

She felt Blake's eyes on her and blinked away the tears that were threatening to spill. She wasn't going to cry in front of Blake again. Far too many tears have already been shed because of Kyle.

"I've moved on, Mano."

"We'll talk tomorrow. Promise me you'll let Blake keep you company until I arrive."

"Flying to Auckland is overreacting."

"RugNZ needs me there by the end of the week anyway. This just pushes things up by a few days."

"Margot?"

"Her parents are with her. She's doing well and is comfortable. I want to make sure you're okay."

Neela looked at Blake. He raised his eyebrows and gave her a thumbs-up. She rolled her eyes, which only made his cheeky grin grow wider. "He can stay today, Mano. Only today. I have a say in how I want to live my life, okay?"

She tossed the phone back at Blake before she walked to the kitchen. She opened the fridge, found the milk, and reached for the large tin of Milo in the kitchen cupboard. Today called for chocolate. Lots of it. She could hear Blake talking but couldn't distinguish his words.

"So, we both agree that I'm here because of Mano?" he asked as he entered the kitchen.

Neela poured the milk into a mug then shut the microwave door. "We shouldn't let him bully us. I'm related to him, so I can't quite escape him. Why are you living with him? You've got money. Don't you want your own place, something really fancy, with a view of the water or something?"

"How often does one get a chance to live with a legend? He

took me under his wing and kept me straight about dealing with everything that comes with being on the National Team. I'm not perfect, but one thing I've always known is to stick close to those with experience."

"Are you going to move out when he retires?"

"Or if he and Margot get married first."

Neela smiled at the thought. "Do you think they're talking about it?"

"You know your cousin. He doesn't say much. But it's something he wants with her."

The microwave sounded. Neela reached for the mug and began scooping Milo into the warmed milk. "Would she agree, you think?"

Blake gave her a lopsided grin. "I don't see why not. He's not a bad catch. They're perfect for each other."

She sighed. "They are. Some couples are just that way, aren't they? Is that the way it is with you and your latest? What's her name?"

He looked surprised at the question. "Lindsay."

"She seems nice."

"Yeah, she's good."

"You don't think she'd be worried about you spending the night with another girl?"

"She's in Los Angeles visiting her mum."

"You didn't answer the question, Blake," Neela grinned.

"We're not doing anything that would make her upset."

"How long have you two been together now?"

"Almost two months, I think. Do you know her?"

"No, but she comes across well in the media. Not like that other girl you saw for a while. The redhead? She loved all the attention."

"Carla was all right."

"I understand that the exclusive she gave on your breakup was a good read. The magazine was sold out the day the story came out."

Blake crossed his arms as he shrugged. "She checked in with me before she agreed to talk to the reporter."

"You didn't mind?"

"I trusted her to tell the truth about our relationship, and for the most part, it was a fair account about why we broke up." Blake shrugged again. "She's a nice girl, hard worker. What they offered her for the story gave her a bit of a break with her finances. Everyone could use a hand once in a while, eh?"

Neela pushed over the mug of Milo. "Here. Unless you want something else?"

Blake grinned. "I was hoping you'd share."

"Why wouldn't I?"

"You didn't when we were twelve. At the end-of-school-year picnic, remember? You took the last Choc Cherry, and I asked if we could share."

Neela snorted. "No one in their right mind shares a Choc Cherry! And why do you remember such odd things?"

"Some things I don't forget. My first try at school, being invited to the National Team, winning the World Championship, and not getting a Choc Cherry when I was desperate for one."

She put another mug of milk in the microwave. "Your family left for England after that picnic."

"Yeah. Dad was stationed there for four years."

"What was that like?"

"It was all right. My boarding school was great. That's where I got serious about rugby. Had a good coach there who made me feel like I could really give it a go."

"Do you miss it?"

"England? Nah. Mum hated it. We were all glad when we moved back. This is home. Always will be."

"Is that why you didn't take up the offer to play in England? Must be nice to be able to turn down all that money."

Blake moved from the counter and sat at the small table in the breakfast nook. He looked out of place at the tiny dinette set, covered with a yellow tablecloth with lacey edges. He gingerly sipped at his mug, his shirt tightening at his controlled movements.

He was fit. All muscles. Solid all over, especially his thighs…

Neela pulled her eyes back from the shorts that clung tightly to Blake's body.

"Er, how many spoons of Milo do you usually put in your milk?" He was staring pointedly at her mug.

She looked down. Peaks of the malted-chocolate powder were threatening to spill over. She didn't turn around to look at Blake. Was the room getting warm?

"I like a lot of Milo. Don't change the subject. England?"

"The money was very tempting," he said. "I could have set myself up really well if I'd spent a few years in England. It was also a good club with a real chance of winning a few trophies. But it didn't feel right, you know. I like it here. I make good enough money. My family's here. I have my mates. What more do you need?"

"I would have gone in a heartbeat, but even getting to your pay scale at home would be a dream."

"It'll happen. The men's game didn't reach this level for a long time. Women's professional rugby is still new when you think about it."

Neela turned to lean back against the counter as she brought the Milo to her lips. She considered the history of their sport, one so deeply associated with their country. He had a point: the opportunity to become a professional rugby player had only started in the mid-nineties. Even now, the pioneers of their sport —the men who had brought the sporting world's attention to their country—continue to move in different directions after their playing days were over. Few were able to live off their successes from their time in rugby.

"So, what should we do now, Mr. Babysitter?"

"I see you have a couple of video games there."

"You're on."

* * *

Blake turned over and found himself face-down on the carpet.

He groaned, sat up carefully and rubbed his face. Then he moaned again. This time, his hand went to his forehead.

He'd known he was going to pay for drinking all that beer. Being a teetotaler most of the year had turned him into a light-weight when it came to alcohol, but he couldn't think of a better excuse to stay.

Fortunately, Corrine hadn't even hesitated to offer the sofa when he mentioned how much he had drunk. He also hadn't missed the look of suspicion in Neela's eyes. She'd known what he was trying to do. At least he'd be able to face Mano knowing he had tried his best. But, damnit, he'd forgotten about the headache that always came after a night of too much drinking.

Thank goodness the sofa wasn't particularly high, but Neela was right. It was too small for him. A faceplant on top of a bruised jaw was going to be hard to explain to Lindsay. Still, he had slept on worse. He'd recover.

He glanced at his watch. Almost six o'clock. He looked at the still-closed door of Neela's bedroom.

They had spent all of yesterday inside.

They had played video games, and she'd schooled in him Super Mario and Halo. He'd taken his revenge in Scrabble and would have claimed outright victory if she hadn't 'accidentally' tipped the board. He'd met Corrine, and the three of them had had a pleasant dinner of pasta, salad and more of his choc chip cookies. It was the most adult evening he had experienced in a long time.

After Corrine had turned in, he and Neela had stayed at the table and talked late into the night.

They led parallel lives, sharing the same profession, common acquaintances, and a part of their childhood. Yet Blake realized that until yesterday, he had barely known Neela Smyth beyond who she was on the rugby pitch. He hadn't realized they both had grown up idolizing the same sports heroes. They both despised politics but were up to date with world events. She ran religiously. She didn't know a thing about opera but would watch any movie musical.

Scary Neela Smyth, the most intimidating person from his childhood, was actually someone he had a lot in common with as an adult.

"Hey, are we running or not? Hurry up. I've to get to the gym by eight. Meeting a new trainer. Fell off, didn't you? Told you it was too small." She had suddenly appeared in the living room, already dressed in her running clothes.

Blake winced as he got up from the floor. He reached for the nylon bag he had dropped at the foot of the sofa last night, unzipped it and stared at his running gear. Maybe he should skip the morning run.

"You sure you're up for this? I can go alone."

And there it was: the unmistakable challenge in Neela Smyth's tone. It had haunted him as an adolescent when he wasn't clear whether he wanted to meet the challenge for her or himself. It shouldn't have bothered him as an adult. He knew he had nothing to prove to anyone anymore.

Damn headache…

"I'm fine," he mumbled as he walked to the bathroom door. "Just give me ten minutes."

They were on the road fifteen minutes later.

Neela led, keeping a brisk pace. She didn't even glance at him once, so lost in her own world. Headphones relegated him to the role of an anonymous running partner.

It must have been a route Neela used often. As they ran, there were occasional waves from storekeepers opening up their shops, and she even stopped briefly to say 'hi' to an elderly couple sitting on a bench outside the bakery. When they hit a local park, she increased the pace, and Blake concentrated on keeping his breathing and strides even.

A cross-back fitted tee showed off her toned body, but it was the combination of grace and strength in Neela's movements that Blake appreciated more. He made a mental note to pay more attention to how she moved at her next match. He had no doubt that she'd bring the same kind of speed to her game.

About half an hour into their run, they reached an intersection that temporarily stopped them. While they were waiting for the light to change, they jogged in place. Still no word exchanged between them. Blake's gaze lingered on the dark area above Neela's wrist. He ground his teeth. It wasn't his business. No, that was a lie.

It was now.

Suddenly, Neela stopped. Her eyes were focused across the street. Blake saw the sudden change in her body; she was now tensed and alert. He turned his head and tried to see what she was seeing. The morning rush was just beginning. People moved quickly and automatically.

"Neela?"

She looked at Blake with eyes that were wild and afraid as if she had forgotten he was there.

"What's going on?" Blake asked.

The light changed. "Let's go," she said. "Let's just go."

She was running faster, her strides uneven. Keeping up with her wasn't a problem, but the casualness of their morning run had become urgent. She wanted to get back home quickly.

When they reached her building, she went straight to her room in silence.

Blake shook his head and reached for the towel she had given him last night. Something—or someone— had spooked her. Could Kyle have followed them? He walked towards the bathroom but stopped in front of Neela's door. Leaning in, he strained to hear something, anything. But he heard nothing.

"Neela? All right?"

No answer.

"Neela? I'm going to take a shower now, okay? Neela?"

Silence.

When he came out of the shower, he saw Corrine in the kitchen.

"Good morning! How did you do on the sofa?" she asked, offering him a mug.

Blake took it and caught the aroma of freshly ground coffee. "Good enough. Has Neela left?"

"Yes. She always leaves early. On Mondays, she works out with a trainer. I've never met a more disciplined person. She left you a note," Corrine said, pushing a folded paper towards Blake.

Thanks. Neela

That's it?

Blake refolded the note and drank his coffee. He had technically fulfilled his promise to Mano, but he couldn't forget the look she'd had during their run. She was still scared, and his instincts said all that fear was because of Kyle.

He reached for his phone, then cursed silently. He didn't even have her phone number.

There were only a handful of gyms in the area that could cater to the needs of an athlete of Neela's experience and skill level. He could ask Corrine... No, what was he thinking? Her leaving before he came out of the shower was a clear message.

She didn't want his company.

CHAPTER 4

CHRISTCHURCH, NEW ZEALAND, OCTOBER 2016

The soft but persistent ring of the alarm woke Blake from a pleasant dream that involved sun, sand, and coconuts. Not a rugby ball in sight. The temptation for another couple of hours of sleep was there, but it was time to get back into a regular training schedule. After a long nine weeks away from the game, he finally received the green light from team doctors.

He stretched his arms over his head and followed the circular rhythm of the ceiling fan. He listened for a sound from next door.

Nothing.

Tim must have left already. Was it fish or frogs that his scientist flatmate needed to count today? But if he knew Tim, even with more important things on his genius mind, there'll be a jug of green protein shake in the fridge.

He glanced at the clock again. Would he see Neela this morning? It'd been six months since he'd first spotted her in a corner of Hagley Park. She and someone he assumed was a teammate had been practicing a series of sprints and bounding exercises. A week later, he took a gamble that, like him, she followed a disciplined training schedule and convinced himself that a good brisk morning walk was a perfect way to begin the day. She was alone that time but still practicing. He recognized the precision of movements that were meant to be automatic when it mattered. She was working. Hard. It wasn't the right time to say "hi."

Just as he was about to walk away, she looked in his direction. Their eyes met, and even though they were a good fifty meters apart, he could see both her surprise and indecision. But whatever misgivings she harbored, she ignored them, raising her hand to acknowledge his presence with a wave.

He waved back.

Then she turned around and walked away. And that was that.

She wasn't there the following week.

When he tried to bring up the idea to Mano about inviting her over— "Since she's family?"— Mano just glared. Unspoken message received.

Before he could think of another way to re-establish contact with Neela, he became injured, and life as he knew it was on hold.

A second glance at his clock caused him to frown. His phone should have gone off precisely ten minutes after the alarm. He reached for it on his side table: no charge. He sighed.

Well, he was up, and whatever messages that had come in overnight would just have to wait until he came back from his run.

Blake hit the pavement twenty minutes after he woke up. It was to be a slow, controlled jog to build up the endurance he had lost in the previous weeks. It was far from his favorite thing to do, but he nevertheless enjoyed the sensation of an ankle he could once again put some weight on. He couldn't remember having been away from rugby this long before. But if missing the last couple of months of the club season had been rough, the reason for his injury made it worse.

One day he wouldn't be embarrassed by how it had happened. The video of him tripping over the same ball he had scored a try with just a minute earlier was worth a chuckle, but when people would rather remember that instead of the good things he had accomplished on the pitch… Well, it was starting to feel tiresome.

"You're earlier than usual."

Her voice was so unexpected, Blake stopped immediately and stared.

Neela returned the stare with a frown on her face. "What?"

"We're talking to each other now, are we?"

She shrugged and re-started her run.

"Are we?" he repeated when he caught up with her. "Because you barely said anything the last time we met. It's like our day together in Auckland didn't happen."

This time, she was the one to stop. Hands on her hips, she looked away before facing him again. "It did happen."

"So why did we—Tim and I— have to learn that you've moved back to the South Island from the papers?"

"I was busy. You of all people should know what it's like. I was training for the Games and then dealing with everything that came with it afterward."

"I do know what it's like, and that's not a good enough reason. Try again."

She blinked at his words as if unused to being pushed. She folded her arms and shuffled her feet. "I was busy."

"It's a small city. Smaller still, since we're both ruggers." He began his run but stopped when she called.

"Blake! Look, it's not easy for me to say 'thank you.' I wasn't expecting to see you in the park last time. I'm still embarrassed about what happened last year."

"There's nothing to be embarrassed about."

"But I am." Her voice was so soft that he wasn't sure he'd heard correctly.

"Why haven't you come by? Tim really wants to see that

medal of yours." This time, he was confident of the flash of regret in her eyes, and something inside him softened.

"I'll bring it around one day." She sighed. "I'm not good with people from my past, okay?"

"We're friends. We were friends when we were ten, and we can be friends now."

"O-kay," she said cautiously. "Do you really want to be friends?"

"Maybe. If you had a Choc Cherry on you, would you share?"

"No."

Blake grinned. "You're honest. That's all I ask from my friends."

The sides of her lips almost formed a smile. Almost. "Want company this morning?" she asked. "I usually run alone. I don't want to interrupt your training."

"No, run with me," he said impulsively. "I've had enough time alone. But it's my first time out on hard ground."

She nodded and kept to the pace he was setting. "Why are *you* up so early?"

He smiled. He could hear the strain in her voice in her effort to be friendly. "Same as you. Staying in shape. Does your coach know you put in some extra work on those legs?"

She glanced at him suspiciously. "Running clears my mind. I'm not overdoing it."

He laughed, earning himself another unfriendly look.

They ran in silence, following a circular route around Hagley Park. They were far from alone. A cool, crisp morning attracted many early-risers. As he neared one of the entrances to the park, Blake slowed his pace. She matched it before they both completely stopped.

"Good news about Margot," Blake said as he began to stretch.

Neela nodded. "Yeah. A year in remission."

"Let's hope for two. Mano's so chuffed, he actually smiled," Blake said. "How's your sister?"

"Rieann? She's six months in remission. How did you know?"

"Mano."

"Thanks for asking."

"Saw the list in the papers yesterday. Congratulations on making the squad for Dubai. Are you training here or in Wellington?"

"Wellington, but I'll be staying down here until a couple of weeks before we leave. We don't have the budget for longer training sessions."

There was no resentment in her statement of fact. Nor did he want to sour the longest conversation he'd had with Neela in over a year with a discussion on sports funding. Tim's sister had given him an earful about the disparity in pay and support the last time she visited her brother.

He stood up. "It's most of your team from Rio. You'll all be in good form."

Neela took off her baseball cap and shook her shoulder-length black hair loose, framing a face that was still flushed from the run. Blake blinked at the transformation. She didn't smile in a lot of her marketing pictures. Now that she was, she actually looked pretty.

"That we will be," she said. "I haven't heard back from Mano, which is unusual, but will you let him know I'll phone if I need a lift to Rieann's next weekend? Otherwise, I'll just see him there."

"Okay."

Neela started to walk in the opposite direction from where he was headed.

He called out. "Hey! Thanks for the company. Another time, maybe?"

She paused before answering. "Maybe."

He grinned. *Honest to a fault...*

"By the way," she continued. "That latest video on YouTube? Best one of you yet."

An uneasy feeling slowly began to grow in his gut as he watched Neela walk away. He had expected she would have seen the video of him tripping on the ball by now, but the knowing grin that had come with her last statement planted a seed of suspicion that she was talking about something else.

When he reached the townhouse, he found a dozen missed calls on his now fully charged phone, half of them from his mum. The other half was from his agent. Neither was a good sign so early in the morning.

Blake went straight to his laptop. As he typed his name into the search engine, the heavy feeling in his gut grew wider and deeper.

And there it was. A new video of him uploaded to all the major social media platforms.

Trending.

It was clearly him: in the hot tub in Los Angeles with his ex-girlfriend, a month after the Finals at Twickenham. The amount of water splashing suggested that only one thing could be happening between him and Lindsay.

He glanced at the corner of the screen, then groaned. Half a million hits already. *Oh, shit.*

He didn't want to see anymore, but he knew he was going to face questions from the Club, the National Team…his mother. Blake hit his forehead with the palms of his hands. Who should he call first? His agent or his mother?

"Neither!" came the cowardly voice he hated hearing from.

He ran his hands through his hair, wanting to deny that it was him. He took a deep breath and replayed the video, wondering who and why anyone would have put this up.

He remembered that night. He'd been close to asking Lindsay to move in with him on that trip. While his face was clearly seen, she couldn't be distinguished as easily. He'd recognize those curves anywhere, but the shadows cast by the trees that surrounded the hot tub kept her miraculously anonymous. He was glad for that, at least.

Blake leaned back in his chair, trying to remember the details of their holiday rental. She had made the arrangements for them. Having lived in Los Angeles for a while, she knew the neighborhoods. She was excited about the small cottage in the Hollywood Hills, central to all the tourist-oriented activities they were going to indulge in but isolated enough for them to have their privacy. If he remembered correctly, there was nothing but wild bush behind them. That was probably why he'd felt comfortable doing what they did. They were alone, or so he'd thought.

The phone rang. Blake grimaced when he saw the name that flashed on the screen. He knew better than to ignore it this time.

"There you are!"

"Sorry, Mum. I was on a run."

"I suppose you've seen it by now."

"Yes."

"Well?"

"Mum…"

"Your father hasn't seen it yet. He had an early golf game. I'm not sure how's he going to react. It's quite a spectacle."

"I didn't plan on it being filmed."

"You don't plan on a lot of things being on YouTube, but they tend to be. You're such a high-profile figure, Blake. When are you going to learn that with the privilege of success comes certain expectations?"

"Mum…"

"I don't mind the underwear ads. Those are quite well done, actually, if I do say so myself. But the videos that are posted up aren't really flattering, darling. What does Scott say about this?"

He took a deep breath. He bet his agent would have a lot to say about it, but he hoped that Scott would dig in his magical bag of agent tricks and find a way to turn this into something positive. Scott always had in the past, but this was something completely different from breaking up with his latest girlfriend, him singing in public, or falling over his feet.

"I'll call him next."

"Oh, Blake, what are we going to do with you?"

"I thought you liked a good scandal, Mum."

"Only the ones that were created because of who you are, and not who you think you should be."

He sighed. He wasn't going to be able to brush off this one quickly.

A yell came from downstairs. Blake glanced at his closed door and checked his watch. Tim was back early. "Gotta go, Mum. Have to give Scott a call."

"How does Lindsay feel about all of this?"

"I don't know. I'll phone her sometime today. I've only just seen the video. Trust me, this isn't something I'm happy about, either."

"All right. I'll make sure Dad doesn't call you until he's had a glass of wine or two."

"Thanks, Mum."

"Though I expect your brothers might call soon."

"Fantastic."

But he did smile when he heard his mother laugh at his discomfort. She was disappointed but not angry. That was good, at least.

He tossed his phone casually onto the desk and rubbed his eyes. This wasn't really happening, was it?

"Blake!"

"In here, mate!"

The door opened after a single knock. The tall, bespectacled man who stood in his doorway smelled like fish. "I'm trying to count an endangered species while I'm knee-deep in river water that's going faster than I'd like, and I keep hearing my phone go off," Tim said.

"Why were you in the river with the phone?"

"I forgot to take it off, but that's not the point."

"I guess you heard."

Tim threw himself on the unmade bed. "I had twenty messages from the boys asking if that was really you in the video. Wasn't one viral video this year enough?"

Blake heard the teasing tone in Tim's voice. He blew out of his mouth and raised his hands to catch the back of his head. "Falling on a ball during a game is funny, even if I was the one who landed on his face. But I think I'm in serious trouble with this one, Tim. RugNZ isn't going to take this lightly."

Tim shrugged. "What could they do? You're not on the team for the next tour."

"I think that's what I'm most nervous about. What *could* they do?"

"And it's not like you were shagging some stranger. You and Lindsay were in a relationship. And didn't all that take place on private property?"

Blake turned his chair around to face his flatmate. Tim pushed his glasses up his nose, something Tim did when he was particularly confident.

Blake studied the figure now lying flat on his bed. "You've analyzed things fairly well."

"You're the one with the law degree. You should start thinking like one again, you know, just in case."

"Stanton!" A loud voice came from downstairs.

Blake and Tim looked at each other. "I didn't think he'd be back from Auckland until tomorrow," Blake said.

"Well, here's your chance to see how RugNZ will react," Tim said as he pushed Blake out of his chair.

Blake rolled his shoulders and took a deep breath, but his reluctance to face Mano increased with every step.

Mano waited for them at the base of the stairs, arms akimbo and his dreadlocks tied back as usual. Dark brown eyes greeted Blake with curiosity rather than anger. He had his first sign of hope that things weren't as dire as they seemed to be.

"I was barely off the plane before a reporter asked about this new video," Mano said as Blake reached him.

"Am I talking to my captain or my friend?"

Mano paused. "Your friend. But in fifteen minutes, when Barnsey calls, I may put on my captain's hat."

"Barnsey's going to call?"

"Given the current climate about how professional athletes conduct themselves in public, you should be expecting a call. Management will need to issue a public statement about this."

"Bloody hell."

"It could have been worse. We could have seen body parts," Mano pointed out. "It's suggestive but not indecent. Well, not completely indecent."

"And at least there wasn't any sound," Tim quipped as he joined his flatmates at the dining table. "Lindsay could be pretty loud when she was…uh…in the moment."

Blake glared. "You're not helping, Tim."

Tim turned one of the dining chairs around and straddled it, his cap turned backward. "Hey, I liked Lindsay. I'm just trying to look for all the positives in the situation."

"I wish I knew who filmed it. And why now? That trip was so long ago," Blake said.

"I think you'll have a hard time discovering who recorded it," Mano said. "This wasn't about someone being in the right place at the right time. They'd have known in advance you'd be at this particular rental. People follow you all over social media. If someone was determined to find out where you were staying in Los Angeles, I think they could do it. You know privacy is one of the first things we lose."

Blake looked at Mano. "What do you think I should do?"

"Let's see what Barnsey has to say first."

"Do you think I'll be suspended?"

"Mate, I don't know."

The rest of the day went by in a haze, with Blake spending

most of the day on the phone, talking about a topic he'd rather forget. His head was hurting by the evening.

"It could have been worse" was the refrain he kept hearing—and repeated—throughout the day. His agent was on damage control, and they agreed to meet at the townhouse the next day to discuss the fallout from the video.

"If I ever find out who did this…" Blake muttered to himself as he fixed dinner.

Tim was at his parents' farm for dinner, while Mano was spending time with his girlfriend. Typically, when Blake was alone, he'd head to a local restaurant or pub, but the thought of facing anyone today gave him an ill feeling.

This was his life, damnit! What gave people the right to blast a private experience to the rest of the world? He slammed the saucepan harder than he had intended, and the clash of metal made him wince. Half the water was now on the floor. It'd been a while since he'd last lost his temper. He had learned a long time ago that nothing ever went right when he did.

Blake reached for a washrag and threw it on the floor, then stepped on it gently before refilling the saucepan with water. When he lit the burner, the flames danced wildly, hissing as they made contact with the still-wet surface. He braced himself against the edge of the counter, wishing he could go to the gym, to the field, even on a bloody run just to burn off the frustration that was building inside him.

He had always known privacy was one of the sacrifices that came with being a public figure. But he had studied the players who had come before him and had learned from their examples and mistakes. He had also learned that he didn't mind the spotlight, that he was comfortable with the attention. But he wanted to think he wouldn't do just anything to grab attention. He certainly didn't appreciate having his sex life become the trending video of the day.

At least the phone call with the National Team's head coach hadn't gone as badly as it could have. Barnsey wasn't pleased, but neither did he suggest that this had been Blake's fault. Even so, Blake knew he wasn't entirely off the hook; he'd have to fly to the headquarters of RugNZ for a discussion with members of management and the senior players. The National Team players were expected to represent their country both on and off the pitch. Being on the disabled list for the next tour might mean he would escape any severe reprimand for the incident, but it didn't dismiss the distaste of his private life being so public.

When the water began to bubble, he tore open the packet of pasta, threw the contents into the pan, then reached for a wooden spoon.

He replayed the conversations he'd had all day. First with Mum, then Tim, Mano, Barnsey, his agent, his dad, his brothers—both of them. Their conversations fell into a similar pattern: *There you go again, Blake. When will you stop mucking about and grow up? Isn't it time you were more responsible?*

The irony about those questions was that he was just who he was. For all his successes on the pitch, too many people didn't take him seriously off it.

CHAPTER 5

Neela didn't see Blake the next morning on her run. After she had finished her workout, she stood at the entrance to Hagley Park, watching the path they had completed their run on yesterday.

His absence in itself wasn't unusual, but today, her conscience had nagged her from the time she woke up.

When she'd mentioned the video to him, she'd thought it would be just one more funny thing to associate with Blake Stanton. But the media storm that surrounded it was more significant than she'd predicted. Something she'd thought was suitable for the gossip magazines had evolved into a social commentary on the role of professional athletes in New Zealand, with opinions coming from all walks of life, including Parliament.

Poor Blake.

He didn't need her sympathy, Neela reminded herself. He was as successful as they came. By all indications, he had reached a rare level of financial security through sport, and despite currently being on the injured list, he was still considered a marquee player for the Club. Nor did anyone doubt he'd be invited to sign for another year with the National Team.

No, Blake Stanton didn't need Neela's concerns.

But she did have them. Plus, she owed him more than an apology for her lack of communication this past year.

He was right. It would have been easy enough to reach out. After all, she knew where he lived. But she hadn't lied either.

Once she'd made the team for Brazil, she'd thrown herself into everything the coaches demanded and more. It was simpler to convince herself that her note to Blake was a sufficient form of gratitude.

Then she'd seen his face across the field in Hagley Park a few months back, and her mother's voice had rung loud in her brain. "Us Smyths don't owe anyone anything."

She owed him.

Not the way she was in debt to Kyle. What she owed Blake was more than money. She might not have asked for his help, but he had protected her from the full wrath of Kyle's temper. Most people would have avoided getting into someone else's mess, but he hadn't. And he'd gotten punched in the face for it.

Half an hour later, after she'd taken a quick shower, her sister's number flashed on her phone. She was tempted to let it go to voicemail because her instincts were telling her there was only one thing her sister would be calling for. But a promise was a promise.

She took a deep breath. "Hello, Rieann."

"That wasn't so bad, was it?"

"What?"

"Answering the phone when you knew it was me."

Despite herself, Neela smiled. "You know me too well."

"Don't you forget it, little sister. And you know me just as well, so should I say why I'm calling?"

"You want me to answer the invitation to Dad and Laura's anniversary party."

"Yes! It's pre-stamped and addressed. All you have to do is check the box and put it in the postbox."

"Can't you say you've heard from me already and that you know I'm coming?" Neela asked, walking out of her bedroom.

"This makes it official."

"I'll save you the stamp."

"Neela Smyth, you're one of the toughest rugby players in the world, and you're scared to mail back a card to your stepmother."

"I still have a hard time seeing her like that."

"What? As our stepmother? Get with the times, Neela. She's not an evil witch. She really loves Dad."

Neela bit her bottom lip.

"It's because she's only a couple of years older than you, isn't it?"

"No."

"It's Dad's life. The rest of us are okay with it."

But I'm not like the rest of you.

She knew the party was important for Rieann. It was the first event her sister had insisted on organizing since she'd entered remission. Neela's attendance would be as much for Rieann as it would be for her father and stepmother.

Tension crept up her neck. She'd rather be tackled hard than spend time with her father. The last time she'd seen him—and Laura—was at her brother's for Sunday dinner a month ago. The whole family had been there, but even with the endless chatter and mindless chaos that came with such a large gathering, it was awkward and uncomfortable.

This party was something entirely different. She was to be a guest at an event that honored the reason she'd left home in the first place.

She sighed.

That wasn't exactly true. The engagement was just a catalyst. She would have left sooner or later. Without Mum serving as a buffer, things between her and her father weren't getting any better. It was either silence or shouting.

Rieann was right: it really had nothing to do with Laura. Neela barely knew the woman. When her father introduced Laura to the family, everyone had been shocked. She seemed nice. Quiet and soft-spoken. Her siblings said her father's new wife was as committed to the success of the family business as they were.

While there continued to be tension between her father and herself, Neela *not* going could very well be the final nail in the coffin of their relationship. There'd be no chance of building anything with Malcolm Smyth if she missed the celebration. Never mind the hell Rieann would raise.

Neela had made enough mistakes during the last few years to realize how much she still wanted to have her family in her life.

"Okay. I'll put it in the post today," Neela said.

"If I hear from Laura that she hasn't received it by the end of the week, I'm driving up to Christchurch to watch you actually post it!"

Neela laughed. "Don't be like that. A promise is a promise."

"You'd better. Or even worse, I'll call Mano. He feels so bad that he can't make it that he'll do whatever I ask to make sure his most beloved cousin hosts a great party."

"You're evil sometimes, you know." Rieann's laugh made Neela smile.

"You're not the only one in the family with a competitive spirit, little sister."

After ending their call, Neela walked towards the console that held all the mail. She flipped through the various envelopes before she found the invitation in question. She felt the heavy parchment paper, admiring how her name had been written so elegantly in calligraphy. She knew it wasn't Rieann's hand that had written it. None of the Smyths were particularly artistic. Rieann must have hired someone to address all the envelopes, an expense that was unusual for the ordinarily money-conscious family.

She reopened the envelope and pulled out the simple card printed on white stock with gold lettering. The weight of the card and the quality of the print screamed *expensive*. The Smyth siblings were making a big 'do' out of it, but Neela was sure it wasn't as much for Laura as it was for Rieann.

Whatever misgivings she had towards her father and step-mother, she had offered to help pay for the party. It was meant to be a celebration hosted by the children, all of them. But Rieann had brushed away the offer quickly, asking only for two things from Neela: to always answer when it was one of her siblings calling and to actually attend the party. The former still took some work, but she had yet to avoid a phone call. As for the latter…well, even her sister wasn't sure she'd make it.

She had chosen to come home and knew she couldn't pick and choose what the move back included. She remained uncomfortable with her father's remarriage, but Rieann really wanted this. For all the reasons Neela had for not going, breaking her sister's heart would trump them all.

Neela reached for a pen. She checked the WILL ATTEND box and inserted the response card quickly into the stamped envelope.

One day in purgatory won't kill me.

Family obligations now out of the way, she gasped when she saw the clock: ten minutes before she had to leave the flat to get to work on time. It was the usual midweek break from training, but Wednesdays were her longest days at the art store.

After signing with RugNZ, she'd had the option to quit working. The precious contract—still all too rare for those in her profession—would ensure she had a decent living wage. However, she was well aware of how fleeting financial stability could be for a professional athlete. Plus, she still had a couple thousand dollars more to go before her debt to Kyle was finally paid.

A shiver went through her body. At least he stayed away while the checks kept coming. Once a month, she sent a significant part of her salary to a P.O. box in Auckland. She was more than halfway to repaying the debt. Whatever it took to keep him away.

Or so she had hoped.

She thought she'd seen him at one of her games. After the final whistle blew, she'd searched the crowds, but she hadn't found him among the scattered groups of strangers.

Maybe it was never him, but she was looking over her shoulder more often these days. She'd caught herself scanning the stands before her last match, wondering with nervous antici-pation if her gaze would settle on a man whose face she had once memorized because she was in love.

The same face now haunted her, and she hated him for that.

She grabbed her backpack and helmet before running out of the building to her parked motorcycle. The traffic gods were good to her as she made it to the art shop in record time.

Before entering, she took a minute to admire the new window display. A collection of artworks in various media, sharing a similar color palette, was creatively curated and hung. Neela smiled when she spotted the small painting of a vase full of sunflowers in the corner. It was that same painting that had first drawn her into the "Karen's Art Shop" a year ago. Mum had something similar hanging in her kitchen.

Is it still there? Or did Laura replace it?

Dismissing the questions, she tapped on the glass door. A head popped up from behind a table, followed by a wave.

"Good morning!" Karen Liu said as she opened the door, dressed in her signature red smock covering her black top and pants. She locked the door again after Neela came in. "I've got six people booked this morning to try out some of the new colors for glazing. The pink is especially divine! Could I borrow you for a few minutes to help set up? Running late as always!"

Neela smiled, accustomed to last-minute setups on the first Wednesday of each month. She returned from the back room with the stools, then unwrapped the smocks from dry-cleaning bags and left one on each seat.

"Did you have a chance to look at the calendar for January? It's quite a long trip, I'm afraid."

Karen waved her hand dismissively. "No worries! My niece will be here right after Christmas, so I'll have extra help."

"If I haven't mentioned it before, thank you for being so flexible with my playing schedule."

Karen beamed. "You've mentioned it plenty, Neela. Of course! You're a good worker, and I'm delighted it's working out for the two of us. Besides, how many people get a chance to say they have a silver medalist working for them? I'm the only person I know, and you being here has given me some credibility with my sons."

As soon as the first artists had arrived for the morning's workshop, Neela excused herself to the back room.

Karen had already turned on the small desk fan, and its low hum kept the small, functional room from being completely silent. A radio had been brought in a week after she started, but Neela never needed it. She preferred the sound of solitude. It was a nice change from the physical exertion that took up so much of her week.

She could sink into the world of numbers quickly. They were logical and understandable. Everything fit into neat columns. Things had their own places.

When she next spoke to Karen, the day had already flown by, and it was close to five o'clock.

"Neela? Mano's here to pick you up. How are the numbers looking?" Karen asked as she stepped into the room.

Neela glanced up at the clock wall. He was early.

"Good," she said as she closed the spreadsheet she had been working on. "Last month's accounting is saved. I have your checks ready to go out. We're up to date on everything."

"Lovely! It's been a while since I've seen your cousin. Anything special I should know of?" Karen paused, then frowned. "Please tell me it's not your birthday."

Neela smiled. "It's not my birthday." She gathered her things and reached for her backpack. "No, just a quick catch-up. He leaves for a month's tour soon."

"My son said Mano may be leaving for good."

"Your son knows more than I do at the moment."

"Lawrence would be devastated. Mano's his favorite player."

"Yeah," Neela said softly. "He's mine too."

As she entered the central part of the store, she spotted the significant figure of her cousin. Hunched over slightly, he signed the back of a t-shirt, whispering unknown words to the young fan still wearing it. The young boy's face lighted up as they both followed a woman's direction for a photo. "Over here, please!"

Her cousin's smile softened the harsh planes of a face which belonged to a man known to be merciless on the field.

Mano spoke briefly to the woman before taking the young boy's hand and walked towards her. "And this, Tommy, is my cousin, Neela. She's one of the first rugby players in New Zealand to ever win a medal from the Summer Games."

"Wow," Tommy said, his eyes widening even further. He swallowed. "May I have your autograph? Next to Mano's?"

"Of course," Neela said, taking a pen. "There you go. Are you a rugger, too?"

"I'm trying, but I'm the smallest in my class."

"It's never only about size," Neela said. "It's about technique. And heart. Mano always told me that when I was growing up."

After a few more pictures and another wave to their new fan, Neela turned to Mano for a hug. "How was your trip?" she asked. It'd been a few weeks since they'd last seen each other.

"Good enough," Mano said. He touched the bruise on her cheek. "From training?"

Neela shrugged. "An elbow got in the way. No big deal."

"Watch out for elbows."

"I'll do my best."

Mano gently squeezed her shoulder. Soft-spoken and careful with his words, her cousin was always the odd man out at the family gatherings. The only time anyone would see Mano Palua yell was on the pitch.

When she was younger, her older brother Joe had once

commented that watching Mano play was like seeing Bruce Banner become the Incredible Hulk. "Like two different men," he said when their cousin made a particularly vicious tackle during a Test match.

But Mano was never uncomfortable among the din that their extended family would create. He just sat in the corner, usually with their grandmother, content to observe rather than participate. He'd speak when spoken to but never more. If he were asked to play some footy with the family, he'd join in, but a passer-by would be hard-pressed to identify who among the mess of bodies was the professional player.

"Shall we pick up some takeaway and go back to my place?" Mano asked.

"Your place?"

Mano narrowed his eyes. "Why the surprise?"

"You've never invited me before," she said.

"Sorry. I've not been there a lot with Margot being sick," Mano said. "I should have done so when you first moved back. Blake brought it up, but he would turn our place into a pub in five minutes if I let him. Fella has a thousand friends."

Neela smiled. She didn't think Mano was exaggerating. "I rode my bike over. Why can't we just eat out? Save you from cleaning up."

"I'll drive you back here after dinner. There's something we need to talk about, and I'd rather not have that conversation in a public place," Mano said.

"This sounds serious."

"After dinner."

She knew better than to push for more information. After she'd said her goodbyes to Karen, they walked a couple of streets down to a pita restaurant they both liked and had frequented before.

She asked Mano about his upcoming tour—his farewell tour.

"It'll be bittersweet," he said. "Being on the National Team has been the focus of my life for so long, but it's time. I'm ready for a change."

"I read that you had a few offers from abroad?"

He kept his hands in the pockets of his jeans. "Yeah."

Neela smiled at Mano's reluctance to share details. "Oh, come on. What does that mean?"

"Thinking about them. They're all good offers."

"But?"

Mano glanced at her. "Margot's here."

"You'd be set for life."

"Not quite, but yeah, the salary some of the teams are tossing about will give me some breathing room to help Margot's family. They're still recovering from all the treatment costs. I won't lie— a higher salary would be attractive. Being away from Margot isn't."

"What other things are you looking at if you're not playing overseas?"

Mano frowned. "Your father offered me a job at his company."

Her heart sank, as it always did when she heard of her father. "You spoke to him recently?"

He paused before responding. "I speak to him every week."

She knew she shouldn't feel betrayed by that knowledge. Of course, Malcolm Smyth would make an effort to be in touch with his favorite nephew. Mano had lived up to everyone's expectations.

"Neela, he's a good man."

She inhaled sharply. "I never said he wasn't."

She could hear the anger in her voice, but she couldn't help it. Almost ten years after leaving home, she still didn't give herself permission to understand when — or why — she'd stopped feeling like Malcolm Smyth's daughter.

"You'll like working for him. He's fair," Neela said, digging deep to be gracious. She meant what she said, although her voice sounded hollow.

Mano put his arm around Neela's shoulders and drew her close. "I know. He's family. He'll always be family. And family look out for one another."

She didn't want to hear it. She shook off Mano's arm, walking a step ahead. She'd heard that all her life: family first, family first.

But only if you fit in the family.

When they returned to the townhouse, Tim greeted them at the door.

"Took you long enough! Hello, Neela! Long time no see! How are you? I think it's your first time here, ever. Where's your medal? Are you joining us for dinner?" Tim bent to give her a quick kiss on the cheek before he grabbed the bags of food out of Mano's hands. "I'm starving. I hope you bought the one with the mint sauce." Then Tim turned around and yelled, "Scott? Blake? Are you two done yet? I want to get into the kitchen."

Neela followed Tim inside. She recognized Blake's physique immediately. He stood with his back to her, leaning against the kitchen counter. The man he was speaking to glanced up at her entrance and did a double-take. His action caused Blake to turn around, surprise showing on his face. He looked past her to Mano, then back at her. He raised his hand in greeting. "Hi."

Before she could say anything, Scott moved in front of her, eliminating Blake from her sight.

"Neela Smyth!" Scott exclaimed. "You being here has just made this day fantastic again. You're on my top five list of people I hope to meet this year. You were brilliant in Rio."

Neela returned his firm handshake. "Thank you. Top five? I guess I'm honored. But who are you?"

"Sorry. I'm Scott Warren, Blake's agent. You're not working with an agent now, are you?"

"Knock it off, Scott. Pay attention to me," Blake said as he walked out of the kitchen. He smiled at Neela. "I didn't know you were coming over. We would have had dinner ready if we knew Mano was bringing guests."

"Last-minute change of plans," Neela said.

Scott reasserted himself in front of Neela. "You know, I've had a few companies contact me, wanting some high-profile female athletes to represent their products."

"Watch out for him, Neela. He's a bit of a shark, this one." Blake's voice came from behind Scott.

Scott didn't turn at Blake's interruption, his study of her continuing. "That's why he has all those sponsorship deals," he said. "You're really far more beautiful in person. The camera is going to love you. If you're not working with an agent—and I'm surprised no one has snapped you up yet—we should talk."

His hand held on to hers. She smiled. It had been a while since anyone had flirted with her so blatantly.

"Scott? How about we talk more tomorrow?" Blake said.

"I have no plans for dinner. Why don't we finish our discussion tonight? There's enough food for one more, isn't there, Mano?" Scott said as he kept his eyes on Neela.

Mano suddenly appeared in front of her, his massive body now blocking Scott from her. He put his large hand on top of Scott's and broke the long handshake.

"Why don't you help set the table?" Mano said, his voice low and cold.

"Of course! Everyone dining together? I love a good family gathering!"

Mano rolled his eyes at Scott's enthusiasm.

Scott was apparently not a stranger in the townhouse. He found the plates and flatware without asking for help and set the table as he continued to talk with Blake about the fallout from the hot tub video. But he was clearly still interested in talking to her. He pointedly asked Tim to move over so he could sit next to Neela, which elicited another unfriendly stare from Mano.

"Anyway, most of your sponsors aren't worried," Scott continued as he helped himself to one of the stuffed pitas. "The underwear people, even if they didn't say it exactly, probably liked that this was a pretty sexy video."

"It's not sexy, it's embarrassing. Mum saw it," Blake said, then glanced at Neela. "We have a guest. How about we save this conversation for later?"

Neela waved a hand. "Don't mind me. This is being talked about all over the country. I get it."

Scott smiled widely. "I like you."

Mano's growl startled Neela and caused Scott to turn red.

Blake cleared his throat. "Any feedback yet on the statement we'd sent out?"

Scott wiped his mouth with a serviette. "Overall, it was received very well. It had the right tone. It was apologetic but also emphasized that your privacy had been invaded. Still, you're going to need to do some work on polishing up your public image."

"Is that what RugNZ wants?" Tim asked.

"Yes and no. Well, not in those exact words. No one doubts you can play, but it would be smart to change how people think of you. It'll keep more sponsorship options open for the future. You don't want to be known as the bloke who had a good time in a hot tub. The hot tub market isn't particularly... uh... hot right now."

Blake groaned at the pun.

"Blake, maybe you should consider doing something with Neela?" Tim said.

"Me?" "Neela?" Blake and Neela exchanged looks.

"Why not? Scott just said the market's ready for more female athletes out there," Tim said.

"I wouldn't say no to doing endorsements, but why would Blake do one with me?" Neela asked.

"To add a fun angle to it," Tim explained. "Liana and Mitch were recently approached to do something together. Liana was keen. Said that years ago, there was a famous coffee commercial that followed the story of two people falling in love. Went on for years and increased coffee sales by hundreds of millions of dollars. But you know Mitch. He wouldn't do anything like that."

"Would Liana do it with someone else??" Scott asked.

The silence that accompanied Tim's, Mano's and Blake's dark looks brought a deeper shade of red to Scott's face.

"Scott, we'll save your ass by not mentioning this to Mitch Molloy," Mano muttered. "Just this time."

"As I was saying," Tim continued, shaking his head at Scott. "Something sweet, not sexy. Something quite different from hot tubs." He looked at Neela. "Didn't I read somewhere that you're one of the most admired athletes in the country?"

Neela scrunched up her face. "I think I made that list as part of the team."

"Good enough. You two should think about it. It'd be good for all female athletes, and people will start seeing Blake in a whole new light."

Scott nodded at Tim in approval. "You think like an agent. If you ever want to drop that animal degree…"

"AgriScience," Tim corrected him.

"Whatever. Let me know."

"I don't think we need to force Neela to be seen with me just to clean up my reputation," Blake interjected.

"Why not?" Tim asked. "I think reuniting two people from one of the most liked sports videos ever seen would be very popular. It could give that coffee ad a real run for its money."

"What video?" Scott asked.

Tim stared at the agent. "You don't know about that video? What kind of agent are you?"

"Do we have to do this?" Blake moaned.

"It's still on YouTube," Mano said quietly.

All eyes now turned to him, but Mano's face remained passive. "It's a good video. It brought a lot of attention to girls in rugby."

Scott pulled out his phone. "What do I search for?"

"Use this phrase: 'Girl tackles Blake Stanton,'" Tim said excitedly, getting up to stand behind Scott.

Neela looked over at Blake, whose face was now resigned. He sat back in his chair, arms folded as if he were preparing for the inevitable.

But he isn't angry. She blinked. *He's not mad that he's about to be embarrassed again. If he were Kyle, he would have grabbed the phone and thrown it out the window.*

She tried to remember Blake's face as a boy. It was only when he was smiling or laughing that she could see the similarities to the young, eager-to-please, highly energetic but smaller boy of her childhood.

There was little of the boy she remembered in the man who was sitting in front of her now. From her own experiences as an athlete, she knew he couldn't have achieved all his success without putting in an extraordinary amount of time and effort.

People tended to forget that before the fancy shirts and the flash car, Blake would have spent hours and hours at the gym and on the field. He might not have been a child prodigy, but once he had a shot at turning pro, he took the opportunities offered and ran with them — literally. One season at the club level had resulted in an invitation to join the National Team. That didn't happen to just anyone.

Scott must have found the right video, as the sounds from his phone were familiar. Neela hadn't seen the video in years, but she could visualize what Scott and Tim were watching on the small screen.

Their class had had a disproportionate number of athletes. At the annual end-of-school picnic, there was always a game of Last Man Standing, with an element of rugby, of course. It was usually just a touch to get a kid out. But as they got older, and once the least athletic among them had been tagged out, touch became optional.

When the video started, they were deep into the "friendly competition," with only a handful of kids left on each team.

Neela heard the shout to start. The giggles and the scream. Then the silence. Then an anonymous voice asked the questions that had made the video go viral: "Did you see the way she took him down? Who is that girl?"

She had kept her attention on Blake as the video played. She watched him remember as she did. He mouthed the words — *Did you see her take him down?* — then a smile rested on his lips.

He looked up suddenly and caught her studying him. She didn't pretend otherwise.

"That was a long time ago," he said softly.

Neela nodded as an unexpected wave of nostalgia hit her. Her dad had been so proud of her that day. "It was."

"That was the first time we played *against* each other."

"They picked you before I could."

"They never did before."

"Because they knew you were good."

Something deep within Neela responded to the gentle brown eyes that were looking at her, and the memories came flooding back. She knew those eyes. They'd once belonged to a boy who had trusted her so completely. Now they watched her from the face of a man she now knew mainly by reputation.

"Was that really you, Blake?" Scott asked. "Shit, you were a tiny little thing."

Blake scowled, and his façade changed. "As an agent, aren't you supposed to be building my self-confidence?"

"No, that's your fan club. I'm just here to help get you as much money as possible during your short professional life. Wow! This would be brilliant in the marketing world. Why hasn't anyone shown me this video before? Do we know who owns the rights to it?"

Blake seemed to know where Scott was going with his question. "No. And it wouldn't matter if we did."

"Are you two together? As adults?" Scott said excitedly. "The possibility of using this would be mind-boggling!"

"We're not 'together,' and whatever you're thinking, Scott, my answer is no," Blake said.

"People would love the idea of the two of you in love," Tim added. No one missed the humor in his voice or that he was enjoying seeing Blake uncomfortable.

"No," Blake repeated.

"Actually, Tim does have a point," Scott said. "If Neela is open to the idea, it can't hurt if you two are seen in public together. One of the heroines from Rio with Blake Stanton? It'll be a feel-good story for the summer."

"No."

"Why not?" Neela asked. "What's wrong with being seen with me?"

Blake stared at her. "Are you serious? He's suggesting we be seen together as if we're going out."

"She's one of the most respected women in our country," Tim repeated. "I don't think you even made the top ten of that list, Blake. Some of that respectability may rub off on your public image, give you back some credibility. When you first became famous, being known as a bit of a dag was all right. But you're a Club captain and one of the National Team's senior members," Tim said, reaching for another pita.

"My credibility is fine," Blake snapped. "If the world wants to condemn me because of a video that I didn't make or upload, so be it. It was supposed to be a private moment between two consenting adults in a relationship."

"It had a million hits as of yesterday," Tim remarked.

Blake didn't bother restraining himself this time. He smacked Tim on the back of his head. Neela bit her bottom lip to stop herself from laughing.

"If you want to be in the running for the captaincy, you need to clean up your image, Blake," Scott said.

Neela raised her eyebrows and returned her gaze to Blake. *The captaincy?* Did the joker of the team have some ambition?

Maybe there was a little more to the adult Blake Stanton than met the eye.

"My strength as a player should be enough," Blake forced out.

Scott continued, "There's a rumor of a new advertising campaign going around that could be perfect for this. If it's what I think it is, maybe that video of you and Neela as kids could be a selling point. Childhood friends become adult lovers."

"No!" Blake said.

"It could pay really well," Scott continued.

"How well?" Neela asked without thinking. She felt Mano's eyes on her immediately.

"Pretty well. It's a well-known name," Scott said.

Blake raised his hands in exasperation. "Am I the only sane one here? Why are we talking about this?"

"Do you want to be captain of the National Team, Blake?" Neela asked.

Mano glanced at Blake, as did Scott. Even Tim stopped chewing. *They don't know either.* Maybe he wasn't as much like an open book as she'd thought he was.

Blake returned her stare. The earlier gentleness she had seen in his eyes was no longer there. Instead, there was indecision. His fingers tapped lightly on the table, and he chewed on the side of his lower lip, now far from the happy-go-lucky persona he usually projected to people. That ten-year-old she had met all those years ago was back. He was still there, underneath the image of the glamour boy from the famous National Team.

* * *

Why does she want to know?

It was something only Scott was privy to until now. Blake looked at his agent, trying to decide if he should be angry at Scott for sharing what had been a personal goal, a secret dream, something he had wanted since he was a teenager.

Blake scanned the table. He had everyone's attention, and usually, he'd revel in it. But this was serious. Admitting it publicly would mean he would be accountable to others for reaching that goal, and he wasn't sure he wanted anyone to share his dream. It would be one thing to deal with one's own disappointments; it was another to see it in other people's eyes.

"Well?" Neela asked again.

Hair held back with a hairband, she was dressed as if she were going to church, wearing a white blouse and a pair of navy trousers. Make-up free, her face was remarkably clear and smooth considering the amount of time she spent sweating and exposing herself out in the sun.

He remembered that voice and those eyes daring him to play when they were in primary school. But when he fell, it was Neela — and only Neela — who would hold out her hand to pull him up. When he wanted to stop because it had gotten too hard, she would watch silently, her expectations of him higher than those he had of himself. She hadn't allowed him to quit. She didn't let any of the kids quit. None of them dared disappoint her back then. Neela Smyth was the one everyone followed. She was their leader.

Now, almost two decades later, he, a grown man who'd played top-level sport with two World Championship teams, was once again being pushed. He didn't have to answer her, except there was no malice in her question. Instead, in her own quiet manner, she was throwing down a gauntlet. Should he pick it up and step into the ring?

Everyone seated at the table continued to wait for his answer: his mentor, his best friend, his agent — and Neela, the girl from his childhood who was actually the first person in his life who'd thought he could be a rugby player.

"Yes," he said. "It's something I'd like to be."

"Okay," Neela said. "Then let me help you change the public's perception of who you are."

Neela's dark eyes were solemn. She was taking him seriously, and to his surprise, Blake realized that her opinion mattered.

"I always give a hundred percent when I play," Blake said. "No one doubts that. If I'm meant to be captain, it will be based on what I do with, for, and when I'm on the team, Neela. Mano earned the captaincy that way. He didn't need to be seen with anyone to change his image."

Neela leaned forward, clasping her hands on the table. "Mano is as squeaky clean as they come. He doesn't even drink soft drinks!"

Everyone turned to look at Mano again.

"Diabetes runs in my family," he said with a casual shrug.

Neela rolled her eyes. "Leading the National Team means representing the best of the best, in both form and character. Think about who the next captain will be succeeding: Molloy, Dane, and Palua. All these men were fantastic players, but they were also role models off the pitch. I agree Mano didn't need to do anything special outside of rugby, but you're just one of those fellas who attract a lot of attention. Heck, I don't read any of the gossip news, and even I know who your last two girlfriends were. The media loves you, and you love them, which gets you in trouble."

"I don't want to discuss this anymore," Blake said impatiently.

"Look, I don't forget it when people help me out," Neela said. "I owe you for getting me out of trouble at the pub."

"I did what any decent human being would do."

"Why can't whatever brain is behind that thick skull of yours process that I want to return the favor?"

"It wasn't a big deal."

"It was a big deal to me," Neela said quietly. "It still is."

Blake lowered his eyes and moved loose shreds of lettuce with his fork. He didn't want to see the sadness he could hear in her voice. That wasn't the Neela Smyth he knew.

She continued, "Let me help out this way. I don't mind being seen with you this summer. We'll just do things together for social media, and people will interpret it as they wish. The girls on the team will be tickled. I think a couple of them will even be jealous."

Blake looked at the four other faces at the table. Only Mano's remained impassive and unreadable. Everyone else was looking at him in expectation as if what was being suggested was logical.

She didn't owe him anything. It also didn't feel particularly good to his ego that a woman would only be interested in spending time with him out of a sense of guilt. "Tim helped you as well," he reminded her. "How are you paying him back?"

"I've already agreed to carry his baby one day," Neela said matter-of-factly.

Mano's granite face turned to Tim, who had begun to cough. "We were in high school! New Zealand had lost the Test that night, and we drank too much. Oh, geez, Neela, come on! You want to pay me back? Don't bring it up again."

Neela grinned at seeing the usually laid-back scientist look flustered. "A promise is a promise."

"Well, I absolve you from that promise," Tim mumbled, then looked nervously at Mano before he took another bite of his pita.

Neela turned to Blake again. "When Tim's in a situation where he needs help, I'll offer it. Right now, I can help you. What's the matter, Stanton? Has your head gotten too big for you to accept help from a woman? I bet I can still take you down on the field."

This time Mano laughed. He crossed his arms; his face thoughtful. "I don't like pretense, but Tim and Neela have a point. If you're seen together a few times, even if all you do is have a cup of coffee, the paparazzi and everyone else with a phone will do the rest. It can't hurt for people to see you are more than the fella who models underwear."

Neela grinned. "See, even my protective older cousin approves."

"And you can take her to her parents' anniversary party since I'll still be on tour," Mano said.

Neela's eyes widened at the suggestion. "Mano—"

"You have to go. Besides, after me, your father says Blake's his favorite player. He'll be chuffed at having the likes of Blake Stanton there."

"Mano—"

"You'd be giving him a present no one else can. And don't worry about him. Blake's good at making friends. You should see him at the meet-and-greets with the team. People love him. And he really likes to eat."

"Mano—"

"He'll take the attention off you, Neela," Mano said. "You have to go. It's important for Rieann."

Blake knew that tone. There was to be no further discussion.

Scott forced a cough, reminding everyone he was still there. "Okay, I don't know what sort of debt Blake owes you, Neela, but if you're also interested, let's see what I can do about getting you two into an ad campaign. I think this video could make a difference. I really do." He stood up and carried his empty plate into the kitchen. "I can see why Liana Murphy recommends a love story as a good marketing angle. I'm feeling happy just thinking about the two of you in an ad campaign."

CHAPTER 6

Blake could hear the low rumbling of voices through the closed bedroom door.

After dinner, Mano had asked if he could have some privacy with Neela, so Blake had followed Tim back to his room for a game of chess. Blake had caught Neela's expression as they left the dining area. She was chewing on her bottom lip, studying her cousin furtively. Under the table, she was wringing her hands repeatedly.

She must have sensed him watching her because she turned to him suddenly. A sense of protectiveness came over him. He knew Mano had the best intentions when it came to Neela, but he found himself wishing he could sit with her while she faced her cousin. He was just about to close the door when he heard Mano say a name he had hoped not to hear again.

Blake looked at Tim, who was setting up the chess board on the bed. "Mano just said 'Kyle.'"

"What?"

"Kyle," Blake repeated. He leaned against the door, resisting the urge to listen in. "That was who Neela had the argument with in the pub last year. Remember?"

Tim made a face. "How could I forget? I had never seen Neela so shaken before." He sat up, took his glasses off to clean them with the bottom of his shirt. "Do you think this Kyle fella is on the South Island?"

Blake shrugged. "I don't know, but Mano's being loud. When was the last time he raised his voice like that?"

"He yells at you all the time at practice."

"You know what I mean."

"It's between them. We shouldn't interfere."

"You're right, but there are only a handful of things that ever get a response like that from Mano. I hope she's okay."

Tim looked up. "Oh? You're worried about *her*, are you?"

Blake looked at Tim irritably. He caught the amusement in his flatmate's face. "Knock it off. I'm just concerned, that's all. Like any decent person would be. Remember, I met Kyle. He's someone no one should meet." He studied the chess board then moved a pawn.

Tim frowned. "Mano wouldn't hurt her."

"You're right, but I can't help but feel something is going on."

"Look, I'm not sure if it means anything, but there was a message from Corrine for Mano on the answering machine today."

"Corrine? Neela's ex-flatmate? I thought she was overseas on a mission or something."

Tim shrugged. "I don't know where she was phoning from. She just said she needed Mano to contact her."

"Did you ask him about it?"

"Why would I? I took the message and left it on the writing pad like I do for all our messages."

"But you think it could have something to do with Neela?"

"Maybe. To be honest, there could be a bunch of reasons for her call."

"Like what?"

Tim looked exasperated. "I don't know. But is it any of our business? Let's play."

Later that night, when Blake heard Mano return after taking Neela back to the art shop, he opened his bedroom door to see the light from the living room still on.

Tim had already gone to bed. Blake looked at the clock on his side table; it was late by Mano's standards. He was disciplined with his bedtime while training, but Blake could hear him continue to move around downstairs.

He found Mano seated on the sofa, head bowed and hands clasped. When Mano looked up, Blake recognized the lines of fatigue and worry etched on his face. It was unusual to see such raw emotions on his friend's face; he rarely showed his feelings.

"Am I interrupting?" Blake asked as he approached the sofa and sat opposite Mano.

"No," Mano said, rubbing his forehead before he wiped his face. "Just needed a moment to ask for strength and guidance."

"Neela?"

Mano paused, his reluctance to confide in Blake obvious.

"Will you indulge me a little? I wouldn't ask what was said between you and Neela, except—could you at least let me know if this has anything to do with what happened last year in Auckland?" Blake asked.

"You know I was and still am grateful you were there for Neela last year. But..."

"I heard you mention his name, Mano. I didn't mean to, but I did. If that Kyle fella is around—you know what I remember about him? He wasn't worried about hitting me. He even saw I had the boys with me, and that only seemed to make him want to prove a point. But he wasn't afraid of hitting me. And he knew who I was and what I do."

Blake waited. He could see Mano struggling with what he should say.

"I'm not going to talk about what happened between Neela and Kyle," Mano said slowly. "You have to ask her about it. I will tell you that I'm worried about her, about her safety."

"Is he on the South Island?"

Mano sighed. "I don't know. I spoke to Corrine today. She's back from her mission and had gone back to their old building to see their neighbor. Some kid the girls would babysit sometimes."

"Leon?"

Mano looked surprised. "Yeah. That's his name. Anyway, Leon's mum said Kyle had come by."

"Neela's not unknown, especially after Rio. If he picked up the papers, he would see which team she plays on. He'd know she wasn't living in Auckland anymore. Why go back to her old place?"

"Neela thinks he's making a point that he knows who the important people are in her life."

Blake raised his eyebrows. "He's playing some sort of mental game with her? Trying to scare her by talking to people she knows? Has he approached anyone else?"

"He's never talked to me, and as far as I know, he hasn't made contact with anyone else from the family."

Blake leaned back in his chair. "It doesn't make sense, and that makes me uncomfortable."

Mano nodded. "Yeah. She won't tell me why Kyle doesn't just disappear. There's more to this, but she doesn't want me involved. Doesn't want her brothers to know, either, and I can't say I blame her. Joe and Sam would go crazy if they found out about him. Nothing good would come out of it. Kyle's a loose cannon as it is."

Blake narrowed his eyes as he remembered Kyle's words at the pub. Did Neela still owe him money? He started to ask Mano but changed his mind. "Is she worried he might be around?"

"She won't say. Just kept going on that I need to mind my own business."

"She told you off?" Blake couldn't keep the smile off his face. "Why am I not surprised?"

"It's bloody irritating," Mano growled, but a smile lingered on his lips.

"I'm around, so let me know if I can help."

Mano leaned forward again. Elbows on his knees, he clenched and unclenched his hands. "I know you're not keen on the idea, but maybe if you're seen with her this summer, Kyle will get the message that she's no longer alone. That there are people here who will protect her."

Blake's eyes widened. *Mano must really be worried to suggest that.* "Would that really help?"

"I don't know. But I'm not going to be around this summer, and I *am* worried. She has to live her life. She's still adjusting to being part of a family again, to having her brothers and sister around. She doesn't talk to her father, and she doesn't want her friends involved. She's always been independent."

"You two are pretty similar, eh? You don't let anyone help you out, either."

"Yeah, but I hadn't realized what a pain it could be until now."

Blake grinned, then leaned back in the armchair and crossed his arms. "I don't know, mate. I want to help, but I don't want her to think she needs to spend time with me, especially not for marketing purposes."

"I know that. But if she feels that she's returning the favor, she won't mind doing it. She may even insist on it."

"You don't mind that your cousin's name may be tied to mine? Even if it isn't true? I don't want to ruin her reputation. Right now, I'm the laughing stock of the country."

"Do you remember when you first started at the Club? Well, here's a confession. I didn't ask you to share the house with me by chance. Connor Dane suggested I take you on as a flatmate."

"What do you mean, he suggested?" Blake eyed Mano suspiciously.

The smile came back briefly. "Well, it was more like Connor telling me I should offer the spare room to you. He was the Club captain at the time, and you don't say no to your captain."

"Why didn't you want me as a flatmate?"

"It wasn't you, mate. I didn't want to live with anyone I could work with. You know our business: we're teammates one day and opponents the next. I wanted to keep my private and professional lives separate. But Connor said you're the kind of fella who, if anything, could be trusted. He wasn't wrong. So, I'm going to trust you with Neela this summer."

"Hang on —"

"Whether you spend time with her or not, that's up to you. I know you're busy. But I'm asking you, as a friend, to just be available. You know, if she needs it."

"Do you honestly think being seen with me will keep Kyle away?"

"I hope so. And if you can make it, go with Neela to her parents' anniversary party. I know it will mean a lot to her sister, but it's not going to be comfortable for Neela. There's still a lot of pain there."

"What do you mean?"

"Her father married Laura six months after my aunty passed away. It took everyone by surprise, but Neela…well, let's just say she moved to Auckland shortly after the engagement. Her father hasn't quite forgiven her for not attending the wedding. It's pretty important for their relationship that she shows up to this anniversary party."

Blake whistled softly. "Under those circumstances, I don't know if I'd go, either."

"She'll go," Mano said confidently. "She won't break her promise to her sister. But I don't think it's going to be fun for her. Uncle Malcolm is a good man, but he doesn't forgive easily. And he never forgets."

* * *

Blake didn't see Neela on his morning run. When he returned home, he discovered that Scott had left a message asking him to call right away.

"I've been tossing out the possibility of you and Neela in a marketing type campaign, and there have been a few bites."

Blake sat on his bed. "That was quick. We just talked about it late last night."

"The internet is a beautiful thing."

"Which companies? What kind of product?"

"I can't tell you yet. But if you can confirm with Neela that she's still interested in doing something like this, she'll need to sign a contract for me to represent her," Scott explained.

"I'll phone her."

"Why don't you give me her phone number?"

"No chance, mate. Mano would kill me."

"Why doesn't he like me, Blake?"

"You flirted with his girlfriend."

"That was harmless."

"He didn't think so. He may be a God-fearing Christian, but he's very protective of people he loves."

"I'm not scared."

Blake grinned. Scott couldn't entirely mask the nervousness in his voice.

"I'll speak to you later."

Blake scrolled through his phone until he found Neela's name, newly entered last night after his talk with Mano. He knew she'd be up and would probably be heading to the gym in a few minutes. It was a schedule he was on. The glamor of his profession was in the big games and especially in the wins, but those wins didn't happen without the daily grind of routine.

He decided on a quick message to her phone:

Blake: **Heard from Scott. Call me when you can.**

. . .

She rang at lunchtime, just as he was changing out of his gym clothes.

"Hey, it's me. Mano gave you my number, did he?"

"Yeah. Is this a good time to talk?"

"Yeah, just finished at the gym. Headed home, but I'm working this afternoon before the evening field session."

"I've just finished my workout. Want to go out for lunch?"

Silence.

"Neela?" Blake asked.

"Is Mano still worried about me? I didn't need a bodyguard a year ago. I don't need one now."

"Mano will always be worried about you, but that's not why I'm asking if you want to have lunch. I'm hungry, and I wanted to talk to you about your offer to… you know, be seen with me in public during the offseason." There. He'd said it. And it had left a bitter taste in his mouth.

"Well, to be honest, I didn't think you'd take me up on the offer."

"Are you saying you're not interested?" He hoped she didn't hear the relief in his voice.

"The offer is there, Blake. I wouldn't have suggested it if I wasn't going to follow through with it. But, yeah, let's talk about it over lunch. Where are you? At the Club's gym? Right—I'll meet you at the sandwich shop on Picton Avenue. I'll send you the address. Can you make it there in thirty minutes?"

When he reached the sandwich shop, Neela was waiting outside. She nodded as he approached. "I have sandwiches. My shout since Mano said you'd paid for the pitas the other night. Chicken or ham. You choose."

"Thanks. We're not eating inside?"

"No maître d' in this one, mate," Neela said. "There's a small reserve not too far from here. You won't be stared at as much there. How's your ankle?"

"Really well. I think I can start doing some full-on skirmishes soon. The boys are ready to give me a good workout. Must say

I'm looking forward to some physical contact. There's only so much gym work one man can do."

Neela led them to a small picnic table that was shaded by long branches of a jacaranda tree. She unpacked the sandwiches and brought out a bowl of cut fruit. Blake added two bottles of water to the table as he climbed over the bench to sit opposite Neela. He reached for the ham sandwich, pleased by the surprisingly large amount of salad and tomatoes included.

"Anyway," Blake began. "Scott said he's heard from a couple of companies, and there's some interest in using the two of us in an advertising campaign."

"That would be quite a coup. They know it's a woman rugby player and not two of you lot from the National Team, right?"

"Scott's not the type to overpromise and underdeliver. He's a good agent. There are a few things you need to look over before he pursues this further. I'll send you his email." Blake took another bite of his sandwich. "This is good. You eat there often?"

Neela nodded. "Yeah. It's all fresh stuff, and it's equidistant from the gym and the field. But back to this ad campaign. This would be good for me, but you have a bunch of things already lined up. Can you commit to another brand?"

"I don't know yet, but any endorsement is good. Extra money can't hurt. I'm one of the lucky ones. People seem to think I'm marketable."

"You are. You come across as honest."

"Honest?"

"Yeah. What did you want me to say? Sexy? You're no Connor Dane, Blake. Sorry to burst your bubble."

Blake grinned. "I thought my underwear campaign was pretty sexy."

She snorted. "Sorry, mate. You've got a good body and all, but you can't pull off sexy. You're the boy next door who mums and daughters think is cute."

He laughed. He should have felt a little insulted; instead,

Neela's frank assessment of his attributes mirrored what his own family thought.

He handed her a serviette to wipe the mayonnaise off her lips. She took it, her head turning as the sounds from the nearby play structure reached them. Two children were screaming and laughing as they swung on the monkey bars.

"Do you remember being that age?" She continued to watch the children.

"No, do you?"

"Yeah, I do actually," Neela said. "I remember my father giving me rides on his back. I used to watch him practice the *taiaha* in our backyard, and he'd tell us kids about his childhood. I miss those times."

"Why?"

Neela's eyes grew distant. She seemed far away, in a different place, at a different time. Her voice was soft. "It was all black and white then, wasn't it? Things either were or weren't. It gets complicated as we get older."

He wanted to reach across the table and hold the hand which rested there. But he wasn't sure how she'd take his offer of empathy. The moment passed when Neela scrunched up the paper that had carried the sandwich. "So, I'll contact Scott. Now, do you want to talk about us being seen together in public?"

"Are you sure you want to do this?"

"I wouldn't have offered if I weren't serious. I owe you."

This time it was Blake who avoided eye contact as he crossed his arms. "Just to be straight, I don't want you to feel like you owe me. You don't."

"I can't help what I feel. I know you won't hold this over me. That's not the point of my offer. Besides, I think you'd make a good captain."

Blake couldn't hide his surprise. "Really?"

"Hey, if there's one thing I know, it's who's a good rugby player. You're good. Besides that, the players like and respect you. But with all the time you boys have in front of the media, everything counts. Opinions about your personal life, despite what everyone says, still count. Character counts."

"Yeah, I'm starting to recognize that more and more. So, how shall we do this? We need a first date."

Neela grinned. "I reckon all we need to do is tweet a photo of us and we'll start the ball rolling."

"What? You want to start now?"

"I know you have an account. I don't. But many of the girls on my team do, so if we tweet a picture, I'm fairly certain they'll see it."

He made a face. This still didn't feel right, even though it was Neela's idea. "I don't know. I usually take my dates out for dinner, especially on a first date. Someplace nice."

"We got to make it believable, right? My friends know I'm not a French restaurant type of date. This is perfect for me: a packed lunch between training sessions."

Makes sense, but... "Okay. But this isn't the first date."

Neela smiled, and Blake was suddenly ten years old again. He was back on the school field during recess. Her face had lit up just for him. He had almost made his first try before being tackled. Seeing her look at him with approval made the pain from being thrown to the ground by the bigger kids disappear. His ten-year-old scrawny self had made the most popular girl in primary school smile. He remembered thinking there couldn't be another girl prettier than Neela Smyth.

Now, years later, that same smile stunned him once again.

"What's wrong? Is there something in my teeth?" Neela picked up a serviette and brought it to her mouth.

He shook his head. "No. Never mind."

He took a deep breath as he pulled out his phone. He'd done crazier things. Being in a pretend relationship just to give himself an edge for the captaincy would be one more thing he'd be able to share with his grandchildren. And Mano had asked. At the end of the day, captaincy or not, he would always be ready to help out a friend.

"Okay, let's do it, then. You ready?"

Blake got up from his side of the bench and sat next to Neela. They were both dressed casually in shorts and t-shirts. When he sat down, he was suddenly aware of how much of their bare skin touched. He cracked his neck and told himself to focus on getting the camera ready. *Relax!*

"Right. Uh… smile?"

She laughed. "Why are you so nervous? You've done this a million times with strangers."

"How would you know? You just said you don't have an account."

"I have foolish friends who follow you."

"Do they now?"

"Don't get big-headed. They follow everyone on the National Team."

Blake held up the phone to catch the selfie. Neela put her head next to Blake's and smiled.

"Really, Blake? Smile! No one is going to believe you like me with a face like that."

"Why don't you do it, then?"

"You have the longer arm. Stop complaining. Smile and shoot. Or do you have too many clothes on?"

He couldn't help it. Laughter erupted, and his shoulders shook. Neela grinned.

"Okay, okay. Got it. I'm smiling. See?" Blake said.

He held up the phone again and leaned closer. He knew she had come straight from the gym, but she smelled fresh. Earthy. Real. He took the picture, then showed it to Neela.

"That's not bad," she said.

Blake re-examined the picture. She was right; it wasn't bad. They actually looked good together on screen, comfortable and relaxed. Who knew? Blake quickly typed a caption before he sent the picture to Twittersphere.

"You know, we don't have to make this complicated," she

said as they started to tidy the picnic table. "Our lives don't have to change too much."

"You're right. I'm just not good at pretending to be something I'm not."

"We're not talking about faking a relationship, maybe faking the dates. We'll just spend some time together, that's all."

"How many times do you think we should…uh…go out?"

Neela shrugged. "How many times did you and Lindsay go out before people took your relationship seriously?"

"I don't know. She'll know. I can ask. The attention was new for her."

Neela paused. "Are you still in touch with her?"

"Who? Lindsay? Yeah. Why not? We're friends. I try to stay on friendly terms with my ex-girlfriends. Even Carla."

"Really?"

"I don't understand why that's odd." Blake looked at his watch. "What time is it in Los Angeles? About four o'clock?" He quickly typed on his phone, then looked up at Neela. "This was nice. Why haven't we had lunch before?"

"Didn't we say we're starting fresh?"

Blake gave her a sideways glance before reaching for his bottle of water. "You're right. We did."

"Why didn't you call me?" she challenged him.

"You're not in the directory. You have no social media presence whatsoever, and I couldn't ask Mano, could I?"

"Why not?"

Blake laughed. "Think about it. I was still dating Lindsay up to a few months ago. Why would your overprotective cousin give me, a man whose dating life he's seen firsthand, your phone number?"

Neela grinned. "Okay, you got me there." She looked at Blake again. "Just because we crossed paths once doesn't mean anything could have come out of it."

"I didn't see you at any of the events after Rio."

"I did my bit. I think you're overestimating how many of those things our team was invited to."

Blake paused. "You scored the winning try in the semis of the Summer Games, Neela. You have a Games medal. How many athletes around the world can say that? You'd have been invited to everything."

She shook her head. "Well, *I* wasn't. Besides, even if we were at the same event, would you have seen me? You're surrounded by a lot of the important, beautiful people. That's just not my scene."

The phone buzzing interrupted Blake's next words. *Lindsay.* He read the message and returned his attention to Neela. "She said the papers started talking about a wedding after our fifth date."

"Five dates? Right, that's not bad. I can handle five dates with you. But I head out to Wellington for training next week."

"Then you start the Sevens season?"

"We'll need to get a few things on the calendar before that, or the summer will fly by without us having a real fake fling."

They began the walk back to where he was parked. "One of our dates can be the party for your parents' anniversary," Blake said.

"You're not invited."

"Mano said I should go."

Neela didn't bother to hide her annoyance. "You're not going."

"Your cousin already told your stepmother I'm taking you."

"What?"

"I was there when he made the phone call. I even said hi to her. She sounds nice."

She stood still. "You spoke to Laura? You're kidding me."

"Mano gave me the phone. What was I supposed to do? Ignore her? Pretend I wasn't there?"

Neela groaned. "Damnit."

"When Mano wants something to happen, it usually does."

"Why didn't you say no?"

"I love parties, and Mano said your brother is going to lay a *hāngi*."

She rolled her eyes. "Oh my God."

He grinned as he threw the rubbish into a nearby bin. "No worries. Since he also approves of us having a fake relationship, I can ask Mano for the date and address. Nothing is keeping me from traditionally cooked meat!"

CHAPTER 7

WHEN THE FIRST NOTES OF HER ALARM SOUNDED, NEELA automatically reached over to silence it, her eyes trained on an imaginary spot on her ceiling. She had been awake for at least half an hour.

The nightmares had begun again. Maybe they had never left, but she remembered them now. Despite putting on a brave face in front of Mano, she had felt physically faint upon learning that Kyle was looking for her and that she probably wasn't imagining seeing him at one of her games.

Mano sensed she was hiding something. He frowned when she argued against his interfering. He argued back, actually raising his voice, something she could hardly remember him doing to her.

At least he didn't press for details, and in the end, continued to respect her wishes not to bring her siblings into the conversation. But when she reached home, all she wanted to do was lie under her covers and forget. Except Kyle's face came back, as did the memory of the slap that had sent her reeling into the wall.

Why is he here?

The only way she was going to find out was to talk to him.

After she'd posted the lastest cheque, she had begun to imagine it could be like when he was gone entirely from her life. Will she eventually forget to look over her shoulder? Even though he had continued to hover in her subconscious, she could — and did— build a life knowing he was far away. But he wasn't anymore.

He was on the South Island.

Somewhere near.

No body of water separated them.

She turned over in her bed and pulled the covers tightly around her. When was the nightmare of this relationship ever going to end?

Neela spied the card that lay next to the clock and picked it up. It was dog-eared and slightly worn. She had held it last night, wondering if it was time to dial the number on it. Dr. Chang, the team doctor, had given it to her at her annual physical. She had inadvertently confessed to not sleeping well. She thought she could see a degree of suspicion in the doctor's eyes and prepared a litany of reasons for her difficulty sleeping. Instead, Dr. Chang had quietly handed her the card and suggested she phone the number when she was ready.

Would she ever be ready?

She sighed and tightened her pinch on the white card, uncertain what the answer was to that question.

A different sound commanded her attention, and she raised her eyebrows when she saw the name flashing on the screen of her phone.

"It's six o'clock in the morning, Blake," she said when she answered.

"I knew if I were up, you'd be up. Listen, I'm meeting the Club trainer this morning, so I won't see you on our run. But what are you doing this afternoon?"

"Working with the girls on some ball-handling skills."

"Where?"

"At the gym on Antigua Street."

"Okay. Should I pick you up from there?"

"Why?"

"Neela, it's Friday."

She drew a blank.

"It's our first date, remember?"

"No, wait. I thought we agreed that we're going to the movies at the weekend."

"I can't over. I've got an event to attend in Auckland. Then you leave for Wellington for training. And tonight's the only night we're both free."

She rubbed her eyes. Trying to organize a schedule that accommodated both their jobs had turned out to be a bigger headache than she had expected. They traded emails and texts for two days. She must have missed one.

"Well, I didn't remember. Sorry. But, yeah, okay. Meet me at the gym. I'll take a bus there instead of my bike. What are we doing?"

"Food trucks at the Esplanade."

"Food trucks? How do you stay in shape when all you think about is food?"

Blake laughed. "And that's why I stay in shape."

Neela smiled when she ended their call.

Her morning run did what it always did. She heard only the rhythmic sound of feet hitting the ground, comforting in its consistency and independence. Even when she was with Kyle, she had this moment when she could quiet the nagging voices that criticized either her decision to stay or her plans to go. Her heart wanted to help fix his anger, to appease his distrust, but her mind said this wasn't healthy, that she wasn't in a good spot.

She had followed her heart, and it had almost ruined her.

Neela quickened her pace, eager to feel the burn in her legs.

Not anymore.

She wouldn't ever let her heart rule her actions again.

* * *

Later that day, Neela pushed open the glass gym door and was immediately greeted by the squeak of shoes coupled with the permanent scent of sweat mixed with plastic. She squinted as her eyes adjusted to the slightly dimmer interior.

The loud clash of weights echoed in the near-empty gym. Neela spotted the lone figure at the end of a row of stationary bikes. She pulled out her notebook before throwing her bag into one of the lockers that lined the wall. She then moved toward the figure that had started to stretch her arms as her feet pedaled at a steady pace.

Leila Harris smiled as Neela climbed onto the machine next to hers.

"Hiya," greeted the brunette with the easy smile and intelligent brown eyes. "Miss me?"

"Not really," Neela replied as she began to pedal. "It was nice to come back home and not have a pile of papers to clear off the dining table. Actually had space for a plate, glass, and cutlery."

"That's what you get when you live with a teacher."

"You came straight here from the airport, did you?"

"After a week of Mum's cooking, I wanted some extra time on this."

Rumor was that Leila was considering a return to the XVs team, a decision that wouldn't surprise Neela. A world championship was up for grabs next year, and Leila would be a welcomed addition. But no decision was made, and she was still committed to the upcoming Sevens season. Neela was privately grateful for that.

Any extra time with a player she had a lot of chemistry with, both off and on the pitch, was not just going to be fun, but beneficial for her own development as a player.

"How was your nan's 70th birthday?" Neela asked.

"Good. Nice to see everyone again. My parents send their regards. Though my sister showed me a very interesting picture last week."

"Oh?"

"She follows Blake Stanton on Twitter."

Neela hunched over the console and started to pedal a little faster. She took a deep breath before she recited the sentences she had been practicing in anticipation of this moment. "We were just catching up. You know he shares a place with my cousin."

"Yeah. But I've never seen you in a picture with him before. I've never seen you anywhere close to him, nor have you ever mentioned knowing him. I met Blake a couple of times when I was playing with the XVs."

Neela shrugged. "We went to primary school together."

"And again, nothing new here. Like all rugby fans, I've seen the video. But that was ages ago. You're dodging the question, Neela Smyth," Leila insisted. "I've lived with you almost a year, and you've not been on a date once. I go away for a week, and there's a picture of you with the National Team's hottest guy."

"We're just being…uh…friendly."

Leila grinned. "He's a good bloke to be friendly with."

"Leila!"

"That picture was retweeted about a thousand times."

Neela stopped pedaling and frowned. She'd refused to set up an account and stayed away from social media as much as possible. But a thousand retweets seemed like an extraordinarily large number. "Seriously?"

"Blake Stanton took a picture of you and him looking happy *together*."

"He takes pictures with lots of people."

"You looked joined at the hip in that picture."

Heat rushed up her body. "We did not."

Leila laughed, grabbed her towel from the handle and got off the bike. She stood askance in front of Neela. "Just saying. Anything he posts gets attention."

Loud voices brought their attention to the gym doors. The rest of the group had arrived. Leila grinned, her ponytail bouncing. "Right. Time to work, but you know I'm not the only one who's going to be asking about this."

"Lovely," Neela muttered as she followed Leila to the corner of the gym where the others had congregated.

"Leila, what the hell is this?" Francine asked. The tall lock who played XVs rugby dangled a printed sheet. "You trying to kill us before the weekend? We only have an hour and a half here, you know. I've got to get to the shops before they close. We're out of milk."

Leila, a PE and math teacher who designed their gym workouts, simply winked. "Then we better start, eh? Grab your bands. We'll warm up the glutes together, then split into pairs. Mel and Jo, you two with the hand weights for Arnold presses. Mona, you and me with the exercise ball. Francine and Neela, supine pulls. We'll rotate after three sets each. Any questions? Let's go, ladies!"

There were six of them today. Sometimes there were as many as ten. Some played Sevens; others were on XVs teams. A couple of the more versatile players, like Leila, switched codes depending on the year. All of them were determined to pursue rugby while juggling families, paying jobs, school, and relationships. They did what they had to do to get the extra edge. Often it meant traveling for an hour to work as a group even though they were each other's competition for spots at the club and national levels.

It didn't matter in the end. Working together only made the sport they loved better.

"So, what's this I hear about you and Blake Stanton?" Francine asked as she began her second set of pull-ups.

"What did you hear?" Neela said, bracing herself mentally.

"Are you two seeing each other?"

"Four...five... We just had lunch. Nothing more."

"Uh-huh."

"We knew each other as kids. Two more. Done." Neela moved under the bar after Francine got up.

"You looked pretty happy in that picture," Francine said, now standing over Neela. "Glowing, almost."

"What does that mean?"

"You know. Glowing like…uh…you know…the moon."

Neela groaned. "The moon? Can we concentrate on this, please? Am I at five or six?"

"They say you start losing your senses when you fall in love."

"I don't think anyone says that, and you're supposed to be keeping track of my pull-ups. Focus, Fran."

"Hey!" Fran shouted over her shoulder. "Neela's not giving me anything about her and Blake Stanton. Anyone else wants to give it a go?"

"Fran!"

"Me! Me!" Mel said. "I love Blake!"

Leila laughed so hard, she collapsed out of a technically perfect pike on the exercise ball.

An hour and a half later, despite the slight distraction of Neela's new "love life," they finished the workout as a group. Sweat dampening her forehead, Neela was preparing for the last round of ball-handling drills when Mel squeaked.

"Is that Blake Stanton by the door? What's he doing here?" The young forward stared openly at the figure that had just entered the gym.

Neela wiped her forehead with the back of her hand and glanced over her shoulder. She met his eyes immediately, and a smile grew on his face, showcasing the perfect white teeth that no rugby player should have.

Mel sighed loudly. "He's so hot, even with his shirt on."

Neela looked down on the mat, biting back a smile. Then she raised her head again and gave him a nod before she faced the circle of women who were all now staring at Blake.

"Leila? We have ten more minutes," Neela said.

Leila looked back at Neela with a cheeky smile that matched the amusement in her eyes. "She's right. Girls? Ten more minutes. Never mind that Blake Stanton is in our gym a week after he posted a picture of Neela and him having lunch. She's got the right attitude. Rugby before love, right, ladies?"

Neela stared at Leila, but before she could say anything, Mel whispered loudly, her already flushed face turning a shade deeper. "He's coming over!"

He walked up to the group casually, careful to make eye contact with everyone.

"Hi! Leila, it's been a while. And I don't think we've met, but I know you," said Blake, extending his hand to Mel. "I'm Blake. You had a good match last weekend. Congratulations."

Mel's face was now completely red, and her mouth fell open. Leila nudged Mel to take Blake's waiting hand, but the latter remained vocally impaired. Blake smiled gently, as if used to such reactions, then turned his attention to the rest of the group.

"Looks like you've been working hard," he said.

"Yeah. We're nearly done. How's your ankle?" Leila asked. She tossed the ball at Blake.

"Fair enough," Blake said, passing the ball back to Leila. "Got the all-clear to start working with the boys soon, but if you could use another set of hands, I'll jump in."

"Now?" Neela asked.

"We use the same ball, don't we? As long as I'm not interrupting."

If Blake saw the looks exchanged by the other five women, he didn't say it. Neela shook her head. He was coming in cold and didn't sound like he had really practiced in several weeks.

"Suit yourself, even though you're not dressed," Neela observed.

Blake looked at his attire and shrugged. "We're just tossing the ball around, aren't we?"

Leila grinned. "Let's go, then."

It was a quick pass, catch and release drill, two balls going in a clockwise circle. They would typically start at a controlled pace, then someone—usually Leila—would quicken the pace with a call. But there was no casual introduction to the drill for Blake.

To his credit, it took a few cycles before he dropped the ball, much to the women's amusement. The next drop came at an unexpected change in direction.

"You're all doing it on purpose, aren't you?" Blake yelled as he ran for the ball again. They laughed unashamedly.

Neela smiled. "Don't be like that, Blake. Admit it, you're terrible at this."

"Not terrible. Just out of practice."

Francine looked at Neela. "I didn't realize you had a thing for sooks. Has he always been like that?"

"I'm right here. Why don't you ask me that?"

"Well, have you?"

Blake took a step toward Francine, their bodies separated by the ball he held between them. He looked at Francine intently, his lips curved into a soft smile, his gaze briefly settling on her lips before meeting her eyes again

Neela blinked at the transformation. He wasn't the cute boy next door, but a man keen on seduction. And judging from Francine's face, the mother of two toddlers was enjoying the attention.

"Only when the occasion calls for it," Blake said, his voice low and sensual. "Sometimes, when I'm desperate, I'm even not afraid to"— he inched his body closer— "beg."

He winked. Mel gasped. Francine's smile grew wider. Neela shook her head, raising her eyes to the ceiling.

"Okay, last round, girls...and boy," Leila announced. "The first one who drops it buys a round after our next practice. Ready?"

This time, it was Blake who took control. He didn't lose the casual air of his throws, but with a release that was a nanosecond quicker every time a ball left his hand, he started to quicken the pace. And suddenly the sense of competition among them heightened. No one wanted to be the player to drop the ball. The synchronous motions among the players were part instinct and part experience. Fast and precise: that was how each of them had grown up playing their rugby. It was how they played now. Always faster, always with precision.

Neela could feel the burn starting in her arms, but they kept the pace up until Leila called for a tighter circle. "One step in. Ready? Three, two, one. Now!"

The ball kept moving as they adjusted their releases to the shorter distances between players. Quick, short throws.

"Time!"

Francine spiked the ball. "And that's how you do it!"

"That was crazy!" Melanie agreed, returning a high-five from Neela.

Leila smiled at Blake. "You've always had good hands, but I think we forget how good they really are."

"The admiration is mutual, Leila," Blake said.

Neela frowned at the familiarity between the two players. She didn't remember ever seeing their names associated with each other, nor had Leila ever mentioned knowing Blake before today.

Blake turned to her suddenly. "Are you taking a shower before we go?"

"Pardon?"

"Shower? Or should we just start our *date*?"

The word hung in the air as Neela felt five pairs of eyes on her.

"A date?" Francine asked.

Neela could hear the smile in her friend's voice. She glared at Blake, who was obviously enjoying the surprise he had given everyone. Then she took a deep breath and turned around to face her teammates. "We're just headed to the Esplanade. For the food trucks. Blake has a friend busking as well."

Mel sighed. "I love food trucks! I've only been to the one at Cathedral Square, but I heard this one was good too. Lots more musicians and more dessert trucks. Can I go too?"

Five pairs of eyes now switched their attention to the blonde.

"They're on a DATE, Melanie," Francine hissed.

Realization swept over her face, and Mel blushed visibly. "Oh, yeah. Right. I forgot. Neela doesn't normally date."

"They do have really good dessert trucks," Blake said. "Maybe we'll see you there? Right, Neela?"

Neela forced a smile onto her face. "Sure. Yeah. That will be fun."

"Well, I'm free, Mel," Leila said, grinning." And I'm always up to doing a bit of research on the best dessert trucks. Would Jack be interested in joining us? Didn't you say he has a friend I should meet? Anyone else?" Leila turned to Blake and Neela. "Maybe we'll see you two there. Don't mind us. Just enjoy your *date*."

Less than an hour later, as Neela and Blake started to join the crowd walking toward the Esplanade, she asked, "Why did you have to use that word in front of the girls?"

"Which word? Date?"

"And why ask them to join us?"

"The whole point of this charade was to get the word out that we're seeing each other."

"It is. I thought they'd see photos of us together. I'd get teased, but I wouldn't lie to their faces."

Blake stopped and turned. "We haven't lied. This is a date."

"You can't even say it with a straight face."

Blake's dimple deepened when he smiled. Why was she even noticing these things?

"You're right," he said. "This isn't my idea of a first date. Getting dinner from food trucks is something I'd do after I've seen someone for a month or so. I'm not a pretty eater. I don't think I've done anything like this for a first date."

"Are you usually so calculating with a first date?"

"That's a strong word. The first date is meant to impress."

Neela scoffed. "You play on the almighty National Team.

You've won the World Championship twice. I don't think you have to worry about impressing anybody."

An unexpected knock by a passing stranger pushed Neela into Blake. His reached up to steady her automatically. "All right?"

"Yeah," she said. Her hand rested on his upper arm. *Such solid biceps.* She ignored the hair rising on the back of her neck.

Blake didn't seem affected by the accidental body contact. He continued. "The rugby may get the girl to say yes, but who I am keeps her interested."

Neela frowned. "Really? You're photographed with a lot of different women."

"I've only had three long-term relationships."

"How long is long-term? A week?"

"At least six months. Though I should count Joy Wong since she gave me my first kiss."

"You went out with Joy Wong?" She remembered the quiet girl only because she had been the smartest student in the whole school, the one who eventually skipped a couple of levels to enter university at sixteen.

"Sort of."

"We walked to school together in fourth year. Joy lived on the same street as us. I'm not sure when we stopped being walking mates and became boyfriend-girlfriend," he replied. "We met in Auckland last year."

"Did you?"

"Yeah. She had actually moved to America to continue her studies. At Stanford."

"Stanford?" Neela whistled. "Wow. What's she doing back here, then?"

"She's opening a bakery in Christchurch, part of the revital-ization movement in downtown."

"A bakery?"

"Yeah. That's why we met. She used to come over to our

house to bake and wondered if I still had the recipe we made up when we were kids."

"You're lying, Blake Stanton."

"Why would I make up these things?"

Neela snorted. "Joy Wong, the smartest girl I've ever met, came back from America to bake cakes?"

"Yes. She's going to name the cupcake after me," Blake announced. "The Stanton."

Neela looked at Blake's face, but he appeared serious. "You are definitely making this up."

"I am not. Check the internet. She started a blog. My brother is an investor."

"Your brother? Which one?"

"Andrew."

"I thought he was the tech genius."

"He is, and that's why he also has the money to help businesses."

"So the Stanton cupcake would be named after your brother and not you."

Blake looked hurt. "It's after me. I'm sure of that."

Neela laughed. "I'm sure Joy is more than happy to let you believe that!"

The crowds started to grow by the time they reached the open space at the far end of the Esplanade. At least half a dozen trucks were parked along the waterfront while smaller booths stood on the green area near the clock tower. Impromptu picnic areas and lawn chairs were scattered throughout. Children's laughter with occasional shouts of caution came from the play-ground. Music merged with the continual buzz of voices.

Neela noticed a few people doing double-takes as Blake passed them, but he wasn't stopped. Wearing an All Whites baseball cap with a plain blue shirt and khaki shorts, he looked unusually sedate. Nothing bright or neon on him. Sunglasses should have kept him anonymous, except no article of clothing known to man could camouflage his well-known physique.

"Ah! There it is. I thought I could smell the barbecue kimchi sauce," Blake said excitedly. He stopped at a busy truck that had a string of miniature Korean and New Zealand flags draped across the front. "That'll be my pick. I tell you what, why don't I queue up for this while you pick something else? Maybe a dessert?"

"Dessert? Some of us are still in training mode," she reminded him.

"Yes, and if I know you, you didn't cheat once this past week. One dessert shared by two adults isn't going to unravel your training."

"I'll find some fruit."

"Oh, come on, Neela. Live dangerously."

"I bet that's what you said to Lindsay in the hot tub," Neela said as she walked away.

"Hey!"

She grinned but didn't turn. She walked through the crowd, inhaling the different smells in the air. Some were traditionally comforting, like fried onions and sausages; others were layered, complicated but also familiar. Neela smiled as she watched an elderly couple grapple with their souvlaki, eventually losing the battle with the creamy sauce.

An excited boy ran past her. "Nan! I think I saw Blake Stanton!"

Seconds later, the same boy dragged a confused-looking woman pass her. *That didn't take long.* But she wasn't surprised. Any time she went out with Mano, the same thing happened. The diehards would know everyone on the National Team, but even to the casual fan, her cousin and Blake were two of the more famous faces. There were few places they could go without being recognized. Fortunately, most people were nice about it.

After wandering around and scouting the offerings, Neela decided on a tray of chocolate-covered strawberries. It *was* fruit.

Her phone sounded.

. . .

Blake: **Meet me near the clock tower.**

"Mel spotted me," Blake said when she found him. "She said we could join her and Leila if you like."

Neela raised her eyebrows. "Would *you* like that?"

Blake shrugged. "I don't mind. I've known Leila for a few years. And only if you're comfortable with doing this in front of them."

"Not a real date, right?"

Blake smiled. "It's as fake a date as I've ever been on."

They found the other rugby players on a blanket close to where a group of musicians was playing acoustic guitars. Besides Leila and Mel, Neela recognized Mel's boyfriend, Jack, who was already digging into his bowl of noodles. There were two other blokes Neela didn't know. One was paying a lot of attention to Leila.

"Hiya!" Mel said as she reached over to embrace Neela. "When I told Jack about the food trucks, he insisted on meeting us. Neil and Harry work with Jack. Boys, this is Neela and Blake."

Leila waved her greetings. Neil nodded quickly at them both but returned his attention to Leila, who looked happy to have it. Harry stood up, wiped his hands on his shorts before offering a handshake. "Good to meet you both. Fan of yours, Blake. Too bad about your ankle."

Neela watched Blake shake Harry's hand, but she didn't expect to feel his arm go around her waist after the handshake. Also unexpected was the gentle but firm pull toward his body, or the jolt of electricity that coursed through her at his touch.

She stiffened at their contact. She knew what his body was like under his clothes; pretty much the whole country did. But feeling his muscles, his hardness… Neela swallowed.

Blake angled his head close to her ear, a gesture that could have been mistaken as something far more intimate than the message he delivered. "Relax, Neela," he whispered. "We're supposed to be going out, remember?"

A part of her wanted to pull away from Blake, to get away from the physical attraction that was building inside her. Another part of her—the competitive side—didn't like how Blake Stanton expected her to comply with his directions.

Those days were over.

Neela turned her body slightly and pressed it closer to Blake's. She felt him tensed up, and a thrill went through her. *He's attracted to me!*

With her free hand, she picked up a strawberry and raised it to Blake's mouth. She pressed it gently to his lips before tracing their outline with the tip of the fruit. But as soon as Blake began to open his mouth, she made a deliberate move to bring the strawberry to her own lips and bit it with calculated slowness. She felt some of the juice trickle out of the corner of her mouth and licked it before it could reach the bottom of her chin.

She couldn't read Blake's eyes, which were still shielded behind his sunglasses. But she could see the vein on the side of his neck pulsing a little faster. She hoped, in return, he wouldn't know how fast her own heart was beating.

For a few seconds, neither of them moved. Neela wasn't sure if she were breathing. The sounds, smells, and sights around them disappeared.

Then Blake smiled his famous smile, the same one he had used with practiced ease on Francine, and Neela was back in the real world.

"Well played, Neela Smyth," he said, his voice low and rough. "I may never see a chocolate strawberry again without thinking of this moment."

"I'm sorry I spoiled the fruit for you," Neela whispered.

Blake rested his sunglasses on his forehead, and his brown eyes met hers. "On the contrary. I think you've only made the fruit more appealing."

When Neela turned to sit on the picnic rug, Mel's eyes were

as big as saucers. She leaned over. "Oh my God, Neela! When did you get to be such a tease? That was so hot! I thought I was watching an X-rated movie!"

Neela's heart was still beating a mile a minute, but she feigned nonchalance. Or at least she hoped she did. "You and Jack need to get out more. Or at least expand your movie tastes beyond *The Little Mermaid*."

"Hey, that's the best movie!" Jack retorted.

The group burst out laughing, and a relaxed round of teasing and banter led to a twenty-minute discussion of everyone's favorite movie villain.

In a crowded field on a busy night with a lot going on, Blake still grabbed a few people's attention. Most people just waved and snap photos from afar, but some were bold enough to step into the group to ask for a selfie or an autograph. There were three other professional athletes among them, including two medalists from the Summer Games. But he was the only one whose fans wanted some time with.

Neela looked at her teammates. No one seemed particularly bothered by the interruption. They continued to eat and talk among themselves. Everyone understood that Blake wasn't asking for any of the attention. It came with being on the National Team. They were the superstars. She and Leila had had their moment of glory when they first came back from Rio. But life had returned to normal quickly. The Summer Games were over. The next match was the only one that mattered.

Everyone stayed into the night, their conversation drifting from movies to rugby to food and back to rugby. It was common ground for them all, both as players and as fans. Once the last of the musicians had finished their set, the group began to pack up. Blake offered his hand to Neela to help her up from the picnic blanket.

She hesitated but immediately sensed Mel's eyes on them. She was supposed to pretend to be on a date, but she had never had a boyfriend who did that, offer his hand to help her. She was a world-class athlete. She wasn't weak. She could get up on her own.

Blake continued to hold out his hand. When she placed her hand in his, he pulled her up effortlessly. She began to pull out of his grasp, but he only tightened his grip.

"Thanks for the good company tonight," Blake said as he looked past Neela to the group. "It was a lot of fun."

"Good meeting you, mate," said Harry. "Good luck with the ankle. The Club will need you back, especially if Mano leaves. Hope to see you back in form in time for the season."

"You and me both, mate," Blake said. "Ladies, fellas? Be seeing you all again, I hope."

Neela and Blake walked hand in hand along the sea wall, the rhythmic sound of crashing waves kept them company. She wondered if she should break their physical contact. It was dark; there was no one to see them now. But it felt nice. Really nice.

CHAPTER 8

Neela threw one more set of trainers into her bag, glad for the distraction. She hated packing and, as always, had left it to the last minute. Leila's bags were already by the door, no doubt meticulously packed according to the list she had tacked to her bedroom wall. She had shaken her head in disapproval when Neela confessed she hadn't even started to get ready for their tour. She did have her uniforms, she assured Leila. Everything else was optional.

"Hello, Scott."

"What do you think about the contract I'd sent?"

Neela walked to her bureau and reached for the thick pile of papers she had printed out a few days ago. "I must say I'm a little surprised. Pastall's is quite a brand. My nephews and nieces spend a fortune on their lollies, even the teenagers."

"You'll get a lot free as one of their spokespersons."

"That would make me a very popular aunty. And this has been cleared by RugNZ?"

"Final approval received today. You're ready to be immortalized in the world of advertising. I just need your signature."

"Blake's also okay with it?"

She hadn't spoken to her fake boyfriend since their date. He had flown to Auckland early the next morning. His presence at a charity event with Mitch Molloy and Connor Dane had made the evening news.

She could lie to herself and say it didn't matter that he hadn't called or sent her a message. There was no reason to. They had already set up their next date. This was all for show, a pretend relationship— except feeling his hand on her back after their fake date had sparked excitement in her body that she had long suppressed.

When he hugged her goodnight, she could feel the strength beneath her palms as they instinctively followed the uneven planes of his well-muscled back. Nor had she imagined his lingering caress on her exposed arm when she stepped past the security door to her building. She had been sorely tempted to ask if he wanted to come up.

"Neela?"

"Sorry. I'm in the middle of packing and got distracted."

"As I was saying, Blake has no problems with the terms. The product is a new one for him. I don't know why, but the lolly people have never seemed interested in Blake Stanton before."

Neela smiled. "Would an electronic signature suffice?"

"I'm a bit old-fashioned and would prefer the real thing. Can I drive by your place and pick up the contract?"

Neela looked at the clock. "I leave for Wellington this evening."

"I forgot. I'm at the Club right now. I have a meeting, but—"

"I can drop it off there if you like. I don't mind getting out of the house for a bit."

"Would you? That would be great."

Neela took one more look at her bag. She would have a little bit of time to throw in any last-minute items afterward. Otherwise, there were shops in Dubai. She was anxious to get out of the house, and a quick ride seemed the perfect solution to her usual pre-travel anxiety.

When she pulled into the Club's carpark, Scott walked out of the Club building. He was dressed casually, but he had a severe expression on his face as he talked on the phone.

She turned off her bike, her actions attracting Scott's attention.

When she took off her helmet, she recognized the surprise that came over his face. This wasn't the first time people had been caught out by the sight of her on a motorbike.

"May I call you back in five minutes? I'll have to pull those numbers for you. Thanks!" Scott said. He smiled widely at Neela as he ended his call. "I didn't know you rode. I do, too. I knew we'd have a lot of things in common."

"That's one thing."

"It's a good start, don't you think?" Scott grinned. He reached for the brown envelope Neela held out for him. "Fantastic. Do you have any other questions?"

"No. Mano went over it with me, and if he's satisfied, then I know it's good," Neela said. "I'm still surprised at the money. I won't lie. It'll be nice to have a little extra."

"You'll earn it. And Blake made sure it was equal."

Neela's head jerked up. "What?"

"It's something he's always insisted on whenever he does a campaign with other people. Everyone gets the same amount. It's part of his contract," Scott said. "Don't tell him I said so, but he's one of the good blokes in the world. Always fair and disgustingly honest."

Scott's phone buzzed. He gave Neela an apologetic look, then frowned when he saw the number. "May I ask another favor? I really need to take this call. I was supposed to meet Blake on the field. Could you ask him if he could meet me at my car? I think this call may take more than a few minutes."

"He's here?"

"Yeah. The players take turns helping out with the after-school camp. Part of the Club's community outreach program."

Neela glanced at the gates leading to the field. "No worries."

"Thanks, Neela. Dinner sometime, eh? To thank you and to celebrate us working together?"

"That would be nice. Nothing fancy, though."

"We'll see. Good luck in Dubai."

She walked towards the pitch, where the gates were open for the afternoon. She could see two, maybe three, different groups of children, with at least two adults overseeing a drill in each group. She walked behind some people she assumed were parents. They were watching the activity in front of them very keenly, some of them commenting among themselves. Cameras and phones were out in abundance. Neela found an empty spot and rested her arm against the metal rail of the chain-link fence.

She spotted Blake quickly, dressed in the Club's off-pitch uniform of a maroon polo shirt and black shorts. Wearing a baseball cap and sunnies, he looked like every other player and coach. But she'd recognize those shoulders anywhere. He shouted out directions to the group he was working with.

Neela studied the players in Blake's group. They must have been about twelve or thirteen years old. They listened intently. Judging by their enthusiastic and energetic attempts, each child was eager to impress the local heroes who were present.

She would have loved the opportunity to learn from a professional when she was that age. But the infrastructure RugNZ had in place now was still in its infancy when she was a child, and girls weren't the target group back then.

A whistle blew at the far end of the field, signaling the end of the day's practice.

The young players began to move toward their respective coaches. Blake checked his clipboard before he gave what would be the final speech for the day. Whatever was said, the participants cheered loudly, and it was another ten minutes of photo-taking and autographs before the pitch began to clear.

As the students began to disperse, Neela walked onto the field, pulling a blade of grass as she did so. A young boy approached her for an autograph.

"Thanks, Neela," he said as she signed. "You're a legend."

"You're most welcome. And keep at it. Have fun with the sport." She gave him a final wave as she watched her new fan run to a waiting parent.

Blake was in discussion with one of the Club coaches when she reached him.

"Hiya! What are you doing here?" he asked and moved to kiss her on the cheek.

Neela prided herself on standing still instead of ducking. She ignored her disappointment that it was nothing more than a cursory peck. She smiled instead, resting her sunglasses on her head so she could meet Blake's eyes. "I just dropped off my contract with Scott. He had to take a call and asked that you meet him in the carpark."

Blake turned his head toward the gates. "That's right. I forgot I was supposed to meet some of his new clients. Glad you and I don't have a date, eh?"

"Would you have canceled on him or on me?"

Blake feigned a wounded look that made Neela smile, "Darl, you first. Always."

She knew he was teasing, but that didn't stop the blush she felt creeping up her neck.

"Did you ride over? I'll walk you to your bike if you have a few minutes," Blake said as he began to pick up the first of a line of fluorescent cones on the field. They walked toward a stocky figure collecting the various equipment that had been used in today's training. "Do you know Jim Wilson? He's in charge of youth development and community outreach at our club," he said as they reached the remaining figure on the field. "Jim, Neela Smyth."

Neela shook Jim's hand. "Hi. Looks like a great program you've got here."

"Thanks. Very good to meet you, Neela," Jim said. "We hope we can get a couple of the ladies from the Sevens to come out for one of our summer camps one of these days."

"I don't think you'll have too much trouble trying to convince us," Neela said. "We've got to get the next generation ready."

She appreciated Jim's questions. It was apparent he loved the sport and had a real passion for sharing it with both boys and girls. As they parted company, she agreed to a follow-up conversation with Jim after her trip.

"What do you have to do until you leave tonight? Sure you don't have time for a quick drink with Scott and me?" Blake asked as he bent to pick up a ball.

"I still have to finish packing, for one."

Blake grinned. "Yeah, I'm a last-minute packer myself. Before I forget, I hope you don't mind, but I just found out today that I have to change our second date. We—my family—are celebrating Mum's birthday a week earlier than usual. Dad suddenly decided he wanted to go on a little holiday with her. Just the two of them."

She swallowed the disappointment that threatened to show on her face. "That's very sweet. No worries. We got plenty of attention with the first date."

"Yeah. Tim was right. As a couple, people find us interesting."

"Let me know when you want to reschedule."

"Actually, I was wondering if you want to keep the date but go with me to the birthday party."

She stopped abruptly. Meet his family? "Are you sure? How does this help get the kind of attention you need?"

Blake tossed the ball in her direction. She caught it with one hand. "Mum's friends are fairly active on the social media scene," he explained. "Trust me, if there's something that needs to be publicized, you won't find a better party to go to. Besides, she's been wanting to meet you again."

"Me?"

"Yeah. Mum's never quite believed we've never spent any time together, especially since I live with Mano.

"Why would that be odd?"

Blake shrugged. "Well, Mum thinks that all rugby players know each other. Like she thinks just because Andrew is in IT that he should know Mark Zuckerberg."

Neela frowned, remembering the cover of a magazine from a few months back. "I thought he did."

"They only just met. Bad example. Anyway, now that there are a few photos of us floating out there in cyberspace, I can't pretend I don't know you anymore."

"Are you going to tell her the truth about what we're doing?"

"I told her we're friends, and I won't say more."

"But you won't tell her the complete truth."

"Do you tell everyone everything, Neela?"

She tossed the ball back at Blake. He caught it and stopped to face her.

"Well?" he insisted.

The wind picked up suddenly, and loose strands of her hair covered part of her face. Before she could push them away, his fingers gently brushed them aside, tucking them behind her ear. It was a barely-there touch, but one that sparked a tingling sensation that swept through her body.

Neela swallowed. He was now close enough that she could see the light flecks of gold in his brown eyes—eyes that were framed by lashes that no man should have but most women would pay for. He had perfected the use of those eyes in count- less photo shoots, but now that they were in front of her, staring at her so intently, she could finally admit to their potent hold on her.

A year ago, she had sensed his ability to get past her defenses, to see beyond the tough image she displayed as a rugby player. Why wasn't she resisting? She knew what could happen if anyone had that much power over her.

Blake raised the ball between their faces, his eyes peering over its top.

"No," she whispered. "Not always."

"Will you always tell *me* the truth?"

She reached for the ball, but he didn't let go. He hadn't blinked. Neither had she. "I'll try."

He wanted a better response to his question. Neela recognized the face in front of her. It was the one he put on when playing. He wasn't going to back down from getting a full answer.

She took a deep breath. "Everyone is allowed some secrets."

He studied her, but his eyes were no longer searching or demanding. He nodded slowly.

"Fair enough. That's an honest answer," he said softly. He released the ball and smiled, easing the tension between them. This was once again the face she could deal with, the casual, relaxed look that was reminiscent of their shared childhood.

They resumed their walk to the gates. "I best give you fair warning," Blake went on. "People tend to dress up at Mum's parties, but don't feel like you need to go out and get something special."

"How fancy will it be?"

"No one will be in their gym shorts, I can promise you that."

"Very helpful."

When they reached the carpark, Neela spotted Scott still on the phone but inside his car, with papers in front of him. His wild gesticulation mirrored the movements of a conductor at the symphony.

Blake followed her line of sight. "He can be a bit aggressive, but he's a good bloke to have in your corner."

"You've known him long?"

He nodded. "Since university. He loves most sport but can't run, throw or catch to save his life. He's even fairly hopeless at fishing."

"Well, we all have our talents."

"Yeah, that's true," he said, his dimple showing. "I guess you'd better be off soon, or you'll arrive in Wellington with nothing more than your uniforms."

Neela laughed. "It wouldn't be the first time."

"That'd be me too. Dressing for work goes against every style choice I'd make personally. There are so many colors to choose from, and we stick to black and white."

"They're our national colors."

"I know. But a little pink or purple never hurt anyone."

Neela giggled, and an odd look passed over Blake's face. "What?" she asked.

He smiled. "Nothing. I'll pick you up the Saturday after you get back? Around four o'clock?"

"That works."

Neela knew she was holding her breath when Blake leaned forward. Her heartbeat doubled the moment she felt his lips make contact with her skin. Her eyes fluttered shut; her nostrils swelled. She inhaled the intoxicating mix of sweat and masculine scent of the man in front of her.

When their gazes met, she saw that he was equally affected by what should have been chaste contact, except her body was demanding more. She squeezed her fists tight, resisting the need to pull him close so she could fully experience what his lips promised.

"I'd normally say 'good luck,' but I know you don't need it," Blake said, his voice low and husky. Would he sound like that in a dark room, his breath on her skin? "You'll be amazing, as always."

"Thanks."

For a second, neither of them said anything. Her eyes strayed to his mouth, and she had to force herself to turn around. But she knew he was watching her as she made her way to her bike.

Get a grip, Neela. This is just Blake. No need to go all weak in the knees.

It was just Blake. He wasn't her type. Never had been; never would be. He flirted, and he smiled too much. He was a ladies' man—except he was showing her that he wasn't. He was still friends with his ex-girlfriends, even shared recipes with them.

What sort of man continued to be liked by his ex-girlfriends?

A good one.

Neela reached for her helmet, then straddled her bike.

She knew that voice. It came from her heart. It was the same one that had told her to trust Kyle, to let him decide things for her.

CHAPTER 9

A FEW DAYS AFTER THE TEAM'S RETURN FROM DUBAI, NEELA STARED at her reflection in the mirror. She leaned in closer and second-guessed her decision to dismiss Leila's offer to help hide the bruise on her cheekbone. She sighed. She'd probably be more conscious about it under makeup than exposed. She wouldn't be sorry for it, though; it was the result of her stopping a try in the finals.

The security door buzzed, and Neela heard Leila call out that she'd get it. She looked at the clock on her side table, which told her that he was right on time. Ignoring the bruise, she resumed tightening the screws of the pearl studs her mother had given her for her sixteenth birthday, then took one more look in the mirror.

This is going to be as good as it gets. It's not a date. It's just a night out with a friend.

But the butterflies in the pit of her stomach were still there. It was one thing to pretend in front of her friends; it was another thing entirely to actually meet her fake boyfriend's family. Too late now. "Nee-lake"— or "the champion rugby couple," as one reporter had titled them — was already featured in various entertainment shows and articles, much to Leila's amusement.

Neela reached for her brown clutch, made sure she had her phone then walked out to the living room to meet Blake.

He smiled when she entered the room. Her heart raced in reaction to his approval at her appearance. That bloody dimple appeared again.

"You look nice," Blake said.

"Best I've seen her look in a year," Leila confirmed. "This must be something special, for her to clean up like that."

Neela shot Leila an irritated glare that only caused her friend to laugh loudly.

"Thanks. You do too," Neela said, hopeful that her voice was carefully moderated.

Blake was dressed in brown khakis and a blue sports coat. His cream-colored button-down shirt was unusually conservative for him. Then she took a closer look at the buttons and grinned.

"Where on earth did you find a shirt that has butterflies as buttons?"

"Butterfly buttons are everywhere."

"Not on men's dress shirts."

"Easy enough to find."

"You had the original buttons replaced, didn't you?"

"So I asked. No harm in that."

"Okay, you two," interrupted Leila." How about a picture?"

Neela groaned.

"Oh, come on. My sister really wants to see this. Blake said it'd be okay to post it to her," Leila said.

Neela bit back a retort on what Leila could really do with the picture. But this was all part of the plan to be seen. "Okay. Just don't make it a silly one."

"Would I do that?'

"Yes!"

Blake laughed and put his arm around Neela's waist. He angled his head close to her ear. "You smell nice. Is that perfume?"

"No. Just your good old-fashioned over-the-counter soap." She risked looking at him, their faces inches from one another.

His gaze stayed on the bruise on her cheek before he met her eyes again. "You make the soap smell really good," he whispered.

The flash from Leila's phone surprised them both, and when the spots disappeared, Neela was greeted by Leila's mischievous grin. "That was perfect! My sister will be so jealous! Don't hurry back. Just let me know if you decided not to come back at all, yeah?"

"Leila!"

As they walked out of the building, Blake asked about her time in Dubai.

"It was pretty perfect. We're always glad for a win, but it was especially nice to get a bit of revenge from the Summer Games," Neela admitted. "As proud as I am of the silver medal, I wanted the gold."

She frowned when he stopped in front of a black sports car and unlocked it. "Where's your ute? The one we drove in to the Esplanade."

"At home. This will be more comfortable on longer drives."

She surveyed the meticulously kept interior, briefly touching the polished wood veneer before she put her seatbelt on. Memories from a year ago surfaced. "Wasn't this what you were driving in Auckland?"

"Yes. It was Andrew's then. He was ready to move on to the next model, so I bought this from him."

"It's pretty flash."

"He bought it because of the technology in it. Trust me, it could look like something from the 1950s on the outside, and he wouldn't care. It's all about what the engineers do inside." Blake pressed a button on the steering wheel. "Can you smell that?"

"I can't smell anything."

"Precisely. It's a custom on-demand air cleaner."

"In a car?"

"You've obviously never had a child get sick in a car before. Andrew had one made after my niece threw up in his last car." Blake pushed another button to reveal the transparent panel of a moonroof. "Mum and Dad are excited to meet you," he said. "When was the last time you saw them?"

"At the same school picnic where I didn't share the Choc Cherry. Your mum's hair was purple that day."

Blake snorted. "It's funny how many people remember Mum's hair color at different occasions."

"How could you forget?"

"Because my brothers and I grew up with her hair color never being the same. I think I was almost ten years old before I found out her natural color was brown."

"She's quite different from your dad."

"They're as opposite as they can get. You remember that Dad was in the Navy, don't you? Even after he left the service, he liked living his life by schedules and discipline. I don't think he knows how he ended up with Mum, but they've been married almost forty years. Somehow, they make it work."

Blake's parents now lived outside of Christchurch, in the seaside suburb of Sumner. The street leading up to their house was already chockful with cars, suggesting to Neela that this was a bigger party than she'd thought. "Didn't you say this was mainly just family and friends?"

"Well, Mum does have a lot of friends."

"Oh, great."

"You can't be shy of crowds, surely? You've played in front of thousands of people."

"On the pitch, I'm a rugby player. I'm focused on the game. I don't pay attention to the people in the stands. This type of event is different. There's no game to distract anyone from who you are."

"Just don't pay attention to the people around you. They'll think you're too cool for them."

Neela shook her head, smiling. He had an answer for everything.

They had reached the house when she realized her hand had been in Blake's as they walked from the car. It was an automatic movement now, as was the feel of his arm around her waist as he steered her through the other guests.

The attention on Blake was different here. He wasn't the famous rugby player in his parents' house but the youngest son of the woman whose birthday everyone had gathered tonight to celebrate.

The "guests" greeted Blake informally, often with nicknames Neela had never heard before. They didn't ask about his ankle; they were more interested in whom he had brought to the party.

"My friend Neela" was how he introduced her to Uncle Jack and Aunty Rose, to Uncle Sanjay and Aunty Priya, to Uncle Mike and Aunty Doris.

"How many uncles and aunties do you have?" she asked when they had a respite between introductions.

He smiled. "Loads. Both my parents were only children, so their mates became family. Most of the people you'll meet here tonight will tell you they knew me while I was still in nappies. Some might even show you a picture of it."

"I have one if you'd like to see it."

She turned to see a near-spitting-image of Blake in front of her, except he was slimmer, had less hair and wore glasses. Bright orange glasses.

"Robbie Stanton, Blake's oldest brother," he said. "You must be Neela, of course. It's an honor to meet you. My daughter is a huge fan of the Sevens team."

"Thank you. Nice to meet you too."

"My daughter's here if there's any chance you'd be interested in meeting her."

"I'd love to," Neela replied.

Robbie grinned, a dimple showing in his cheek. "She's going

to be thrilled. She's holding court with her nan and pop as we speak."

When they entered the rumpus room at the back of the house, Lulu Stanton had a captivated audience of not just her grandparents but at least another dozen guests. Dressed in layers of tulle and chiffon, she was flitting and floating around the small space allotted to her show. When she finally stopped, she bowed dramatically in front of her grandparents, who were seated on their 'thrones.'

Neela smiled as the figure of Clarissa Stanton —with lime-green hair—came rushing toward her granddaughter. With a dramatic flourish, Clarissa swept Lulu into in her arms, tulle, and chiffon fluffing about.

"My word, Lulu-bell! That was simply stunning! The Bolshoi has nothing like you in their company. They'll be falling over themselves when you're ready to dance with them, won't they, everyone?" Clarissa gestured around the room.

Everyone clapped louder and more enthusiastically. Blake whistled his appreciation and attracted Lulu and her nan's attention.

"Uncle Blake! You're here!"

The youngest Stanton wiggled out of her grandmother's arms and launched herself at her uncle, confident he was going to catch up.

"You're a little late," she admonished him, her arms around his neck.

"I am not. I'm right on time. You were early."

"Did you see any of my dancing?"

"I caught some of it."

"I can do it again for you later."

"Would you? I'd be most honored."

Blake gazed adoringly at his niece as they spoke, closing his eyes slightly as he kissed Lulu on her forehead as if he were memorizing the moment. "And I have a friend you might be interested in meeting. Recognize her?"

Lulu screamed. "Neela Smyth! Oh, wow!"

Lulu grabbed her arms, and a flood of indiscernible words came pouring out of the little figure. Neela could only nod, unable to get a word in.

Blake crouched next to Neela, an arm around his niece. "Slow down, Lulu. Breathe, darling, breathe."

Lulu's quick nod was followed by concentrated intakes of air, her eyes widening with each exhale until she burst out again. "We watched the series in Dubai! You were brilliant! Especially when you scored that try against Ireland! Better than any of Uncle Blake's tries, I can tell you that. He always looks like he just makes it across the line, but you just float! You're a legend! Oh, wait. Is that bruise from when you stopped that bigger woman in the finals?"

Neela laughed, catching Blake's smile.

"Lulu, please, let Miss Smyth talk," said a heavily pregnant woman who had just walked up to them. "I'm Sharon, Robbie's wife, and this bundle of energy's mum. God help us all if we have another one like this."

Neela rose from her knees to take the hand being held out.

"Mum! It's Neela Smyth!" Lulu repeated, her eyes not leaving her heroine's face.

"She says my tries are better than yours," Neela teased Blake.

"My niece knows what she's talking about," he responded good-naturedly. "And she's right. You do look like you float when you cross the line."

"Do you have your Games medal with you, Miss Smyth?" Lulu asked.

"I'm afraid I don't," she said. "It's in a small box I keep at home. But maybe I can have your uncle bring it to you one day to see?"

"That's a grand idea, but I have a better one," Blake said. "Maybe, just maybe, we can convince Miss Smyth to show you her medal herself. We can say thank you by taking her on a picnic. What do you think?"

"Oh, yes, please!" Lulu squealed. "Say yes, Miss Smyth! Uncle Blake always bakes the best cookies when we go on a picnic."

"I know. He's already baked some choc chip ones for me," she said.

"Oh, he must really like you, then. He only bakes choc chips for his favorite people," Lulu said, switching her gaze from Neela to Blake. "Is she your girlfriend, Uncle Blake?"

Lulu's voice pierced through the crowd, and a flush crept up Neela's neck, warming her cheeks. She expected to see laughter in her date's eyes. Instead, they stared back, as if studying every detail on her face.

He then bent to meet Lulu's face. "She's just a very good friend."

"That's all right, then. Dad said I don't ever have to have a boyfriend because boyfriends are rubbish anyway, and I should just have lots of friends," Lulu said confidently.

Neela laughed. "Your dad gives good advice."

"And your dad needs to make sure you have your dinner," Robbie said as he reached for his daughter's hand.

"No—"

"Lulu, let's get something to eat."

"Can I—"

"No."

"Please?"

"No."

They watched Robbie firmly march his daughter out of the room, but not before the little girl had turned for one last wave.

"I must warn you, Neela, my daughter was already quite a fan of yours before Rio." Sharon placed her hand over her stomach. "But after Robbie, mean sod that he is, showed her the video of you and Blake at twelve, she's been quite obsessed with you. On behalf of my husband, I apologize in advance for anything she does."

Neela smiled. "I'm flattered. But it seems she also has quite the artistic side."

Sharon sighed. "It's in the Stanton blood. It's not one thing, it's several things. I asked her the other day if she'd like to try ballet or rugby, and she asked why she couldn't do both."

"Good question. Why not?" Blake asked.

"She wants to wear her tutu to rugby practice."

"Again, why not?"

"Remind me to ask you to babysit on those days she has rugby."

"I'm always available to spend time with my niece, Sharon," he said.

Sharon angled her head. "Yeah, but I'm never sure who makes the decisions when you do." She sighed when she caught Robbie waving to her from across the room. "Looks like the doctor needs help with the five-year-old. Honestly, we've been trying to take this family picture for half an hour now, and I'm wondering if it will ever happen. We found you, but Andrew's disappeared."

"What happened to Andrew?" Blake asked, surveying the room.

"Not sure," Sharon replied. "He was here before you arrived."

"Alone?"

Sharon's eyes were troubled. "Yes. Alone."

Blake squeezed his sister-in-law's arm. "He'll be fine. It just means he's going to be involved in everyone else's life a little bit more than usual. But if you'll excuse us, I need to introduce Neela to Mum and Dad."

Neela felt Blake's warm hand on her back. She told herself to move away but didn't. She caught a glimpse of their reflection in one of the windows. They looked like any average couple at a gathering, except they weren't really a couple.

"Happy birthday, Mum!" Blake leaned to kiss his mother

before shaking his father's hand. "And how are you, Dad? You did well to put this together so quickly."

"Darling! So glad you're here," said Clarissa. Voluminous tangerine material covered Blake when his mother embraced him. "Oh, I love those buttons! Did you find that shirt on the website I told you about?"

"Yes. That was a gem of a recommendation. The designer also makes belts. All I need now is a picture of Mano's tattoos."

Neela frowned. Did she just hear that right?

"I'll re-introduce myself to you now, Neela," said the tall man in front of her. "Blake and his mum may go on and on about buttons and forget all about us."

Neela smiled and held out her hand. "Sir, it's good to see you again after all these years."

"Please, call me Walt. And you'll have to forgive them," said Walt. "They've always been like that. Blake was the only one of our children who was excited to go clothes shopping with his mum. Together, they've cost me thousands of dollars in art, crafts, and clothes. When Blake received his first paycheck from the Club, I almost became religious."

She hadn't known Walt Stanton's voice when she was at school. While not unfriendly, he left the socializing to his wife. Back then, he always kept his sunnies on, and his lips were thin and stern. No one could quite match the man to the boy who had made people laugh, whether it was intentional or not. Now retired, the former captain of the Royal Navy still stood with authority, wearing his silver hair in the expected crew cut.

"And congratulations on your success," said Walt. "You've done our country proud,"

"Very kind of you to say so. I'm lucky to be part of a great team," Neela replied. "And thank you for inviting me."

"I understand from my wife that you're keeping our son out of mischief this summer."

"I don't know about that."

"I'm surprised our paths haven't crossed sooner given all that you and Blake have in common."

"Life's sometimes like that, isn't it, Mr. Stanton?"

"Indeed."

Blake returned his arm to Neela's waist. She took a step to face Blake's mother, which he automatically mirrored, drawing her closer. She could smell his cologne again, a scent she realized was becoming familiar and comforting.

"My dear! Look at you, all grown up!" Clarissa exclaimed. Like her granddaughter, Clarissa immediately reached for Neela's hands and studied her face intently. "You were pretty as a little girl, but you're quite simply breathtaking now as a young woman. Those eyes! Fire in them, my dear. I must paint you. I simply must."

Clarissa turned suddenly. The softness of the tangerine fabric brushed against Neela's arm as the cape swirled in a witch-like manner. Clapping her hands, Clarissa commanded the room's attention.

"Everyone, everyone, Neela Smyth, silver medalist from the Summer Games is here. Let's greet her properly. It's her first time with us, so be nice. And don't mind the gossip papers about her and Blake. They're just friends."

Before Neela could blink, Clarissa recaptured her hand and pulled her close. Blue eyes animated and excited, the older woman whispered loudly, "We're so pleased to see you again, darling. I've asked about you for years, but Blake was always coming up with excuses why he didn't know you personally. And now, look at you and him. It's straight out of a romance novel!"

"Mrs. Stanton, like you said, we're just friends."

"The best lovers start as friends, don't you know? Blake has had the loveliest of girlfriends, but out of my three boys, he's never been able to exert an ounce of self-control when it comes to women. But let me introduce you to Shellie. Shellie used to be Stanley Walters. Do you remember him? He directed that dreadful movie about mermaids and pearls years ago. Her work has so vastly improved since the change. Thank goodness. One can only live a lie for so long, don't you think?"

* * *

Blake smiled as he watched his mother commandeered Neela around the room. He suspected she intended to introduce Neela to all twenty of her best friends. Most people were overwhelmed by Clarissa Stanton's enthusiasm and joie de vivre, but when his mum found someone she was particularly interested in, her energy level went up another notch.

His father came up to him and thrust a glass of lemonade into his hand. "How's your ankle, son?"

"Doing better, Dad. Thanks."

"Going to have your brother take a look at it?"

"He's a neurosurgeon, Dad."

"Ankle, shoulder, brains. He had to study everything."

"You might want to think of adding new things to your repertoire, Dad. I've heard this one too often, just with different body parts."

"You're the only one I can say it to since your brothers tend not to get injured."

"Speaking of brothers, I haven't seen Andrew."

"Probably walking by the beach. It relaxes him," said Walt. "He flew down last night."

"How's he doing?"

"As well as he can be. Pat leaving him was unexpected. The last time they visited, Andrew brought up the idea of getting married."

Blake sighed. He'd liked Pat. "They were together a good three or four years, weren't they?"

"Indeed."

"Shall I go look for him?"

"Yeah. Why don't you take Neela with you? If my calculations are correct, Lulu will be done with her dinner. I don't think it's fair for anyone to have to deal with your mother and Lulu simultaneously. We don't want to chase her away after one visit to the Stanton household."

If Neela needed rescuing from his mother, she didn't show it. In fact, she was laughing animatedly at one of his mother's anecdotes. Probably about him, Blake thought. She looked as relaxed as he had ever seen her.

She had done something different with her hair. Maybe it was a little shorter? Hard to tell, since it was usually pulled back into a ponytail or hidden under a cap. Now loose, perhaps styled a little, its vibrant dark mix of brown and black shimmered under the 'mood lights' his mother had in the room.

He watched Neela angle her head slightly as if to hear better. Then she threw her head back, laughing at whatever it was that Aunty Shellie had just said.

Blake smiled in response to the sound of her amusement. He was getting used to Neela's smile. She was the kind of person who laughed from deep within, a genuine and honest reaction when amused.

She should laugh more. It suits her.

She caught him staring at her, her face still flushed from the laughter. Blake moved toward her, unable to stay away. He wanted to be part of whatever it was that had made her happy. When he was close, he held out his hand, and a deep sense of satisfaction went through him when she automatically placed her hand in his. What had once been awkward was now instinctive.

"Everything all right? You're looking quite serious for a Stanton," she said.

"I'm going to look for Andrew. Would you like to come with me?"

She nodded and quickly excused herself from the group.

They were a few meters outside the house when Blake felt a slight shiver go through her. She had a wrap, but the sea breeze, while kind, was cool, so he took off his blazer and draped it over her shoulders.

"Thanks," Neela said as she pulled the blazer closed. "I'll give it back when we go inside. A bit foolish of me to forget how much cooler it is by the water."

"No worries. I rarely get cold. Wear it as long as you like tonight. Mum didn't overwhelm you too much, did she?"

Neela smiled. "I'd forgotten how energetic she is. You get that from her, don't you? She's lovely. Quite unique, isn't she?"

"That's putting it mildly. When we were in England, she didn't fit in with the other navy wives. No one was awful or anything, but she was lonely. Once we got home, she blossomed again. I know Dad turned down some really good postings for them to stay here. Andrew always thought Dad could have done more with his career if he had taken at least one of those assignments. Robbie didn't think Dad wanted more."

"Some people have all they need at home."

"There's truth in that."

"Like you?"

"Are we talking about the offers from Europe I didn't take, now?" Blake remembered their conversation from a year ago.

Neela shrugged. "Mano's taking one."

"He told you that, did he?"

"Yeah. Gave me the inside scoop. Did you know?"

Blake nodded. "He's doing it for Margot. We both know that. He'd never leave her otherwise." He shoved his hands into his pockets and looked towards the water. "We all do what we have to do. He wants to take care of her family, even if it means sacrificing time with her. I don't think I'll ever meet another person who's so clear in his priorities. I respect him more for who he is as a man than as a rugby player and believe me, that's saying a lot."

As they reached the beach, Blake asked. "What you reckon, sand in your toes, or keep those pretty sandals in good shape?"

Neela scoffed. "Sand in toes, of course." She didn't hesitate to take her sandals off as Blake did the same with his shoes.

They walked by the water's edge before Blake led them in the direction he thought Andrew would be. He kept his eyes ahead, searching for movement on the small hill in front of them.

Neela walked ankle-deep in the water, looking lost in thought, her strides creating slight sprays that caught the bottom of his trousers. Her skin was nearly luminous in the light of a bright moon; the bruise on her cheek remained visible.

He'd known it'd be there. He had winced when he saw her tackle the forward who was at least a foot taller—and wider—than she. But like all the good ones, she got up quickly and was ready to move again.

He bet there were a few more dark spots on her body, but she moved unaffected by whatever pain she may have incurred during the competition.

"Two Panadols?"

Neela understood the question. "Every four hours the day after."

"You're moving well."

"RugNZ has some pretty good trainers to keep us loose."

"That they do."

"Why would you want a picture of Mano's tattoos?"

"Don't want to talk about the match, Neela?"

Neela shook her head. "Not really. What's so funny?"

"When people meet me, that's usually all they want to talk about: the footy. Yet here we are, two people who play top-level rugby, and you don't want to have a conversation about how the team played."

"I know how we played," Neela responded. "We break it down after every match. We study the game constantly. I'm all right not talking about it with you. Tattoos?"

Blake grinned. "Okay, okay. No talking about rugby. I want to give Mano something special for his retirement. He doesn't have any belts, and I thought he might appreciate something personalized."

"Like a belt that matches his tattoos? It'd certainly be unique. But have you ever considered *why* Mano doesn't have any belts, Blake?"

"He'll like this one."

Even in the minimal light, Blake saw the flash of amusement in Neela's eyes. "Honestly, Blake, you have more confidence than anyone else I've ever met."

"Oh, I don't know about that. We all have our insecurities."

"What's yours?"

Blake took a deep breath and looked around again. A few meters away, another couple was walking hand in hand. Otherwise, they were alone on the beach.

Blake kept his gaze to the dark path in front of them. "Among the many, I guess the biggest one would be that when rugby is over, there'll be nothing else I'll be good at."

Neela didn't respond immediately. When she did, Blake heard the surprise in her voice. "You have so much going for you."

"I do. But I'm also aware that each year, with each injury, I'm closer to calling it quits. And then what?"

"Didn't you read law at university?"

"How did you know that?"

"Mano mentioned it one day. I guess I remembered because I've never thought of you as…"

"Being able to finish uni?"

"No."

"Being able to get into uni?"

Neela huffed. "Stop interrupting! No, I just never thought of you as a lawyer. You seemed…"

"Not the uni type? Ow! Shit, Neela, that hurt!" Blake rubbed the spot on his upper arm where Neela had pinched him.

She faced him unapologetically. A sudden wind blew her hair wildly across her face, but she ignored it. "I barely touched you, and I just said not to interrupt me! Oh my God, Stanton, shut up, will you? I'm trying to be sympathetic, and you just keep going on. What does a girl have to do to get a word in? How does Mano put up with you?"

Mum was right: she had fire in her eyes, and at the moment he couldn't resist them. He had to know. Could he light the fire inside her with an emotion other than anger?

She wasn't expecting his kiss. Her eyes were still open when their lips touched. Blake recognized the surprise in them when she realized what he was about to do.

But he couldn't keep his eyes open. The intensity that came with the feel of her lips on his eliminated the smell of the sea, the sound of the crashing waves, the grittiness of the sand beneath his feet.

He only sensed her at that moment.

She tasted of wine he didn't know she'd drank, and he wanted more. His body flared when he felt her lips yield to his.

Then a blast of cold air came between them when she pulled away suddenly, her eyes wide and wild.

"What the hell are you doing?" she demanded.

"Uh…"

"Blake! Friends can't kiss like that!"

Blake tried to answer — not that he knew what to say — but the sound of deep laughter caught both Neela's and his attention.

"That's probably the best reaction I've ever seen to one of Blake's kisses!"

Blake continued to breathe hard. He ran a hand through his already wind-blown hair and faced the new person on the scene. "Where have you been, Andrew?"

"In the kitchen having a lovely glass of sparkling white wine with the caterer. Dad said he'd sent you and Neela out to the beach to find me. Why did everyone think I'd be out here in the cold and wind while the real party was inside? Though what I've just witnessed has made the trek out here worth it."

Neela narrowed her eyes at Blake, and he knew they were going to be talking about this later. But when she faced Andrew, it was with a smile that lit up her face. An unfamiliar jolt of jealousy ran through his body, and he shoved his shaking hands his front pockets.

"Hi, Andrew. I'm Neela." She offered her hand. "It's been a few years, but I do remember you from when we were children."

Andrew took Neela's hand and raised it to his lips. He gave Blake a sideways glance before turning on a smile that had most recently graced the cover of an international tech magazine. "I can see why my mother and my niece are obsessed with you. Come, walk with the most civilized of the Stanton boys. Fill me in on your life since we last saw each other."

Andrew carefully folded her hand into the crook of his arm, and Blake was left watching the two of them move toward the house without him.

* * *

"My brother wasn't overstepping his boundaries, was he?" Andrew asked softly as they approached the house.

Neela shook her head. "He did nothing I couldn't handle. I trust Blake. It was just... he took me by surprise. Nothing like that has happened between us before. Nor will it again."

She wasn't going to admit to Andrew Stanton how her lips were still tingling from Blake's kiss, or how close she had been to pulling him closer when sanity prevailed. No, Blake's older brother certainly didn't need to know any of this. "We're just friends," she reaffirmed, as much to herself as to Andrew.

"Oh? The media has you planning your wedding in six months."

Neela shrugged. "Can't control what the media says, eh? Tim's away, and all his other friends are on tour or busy with other things. He's in between girlfriends, so I guess I'm just it for now."

Andrew grinned. "If you say so. Right, well, if you're not really planning a wedding in six months, be careful with Mum, then."

"Blake mentioned that she really wanted me here. I don't understand it. Neither does your brother, apparently."

Andrew studied her intently. He seemed to have made a decision when he spoke again. "He wouldn't understand because Mum will never admit to him that she knew you'd always look out for him at school."

Neela's face went warm. "I didn't. Well, not really."

"I had moved on to high school when she said things got a little rough at school for Blake. He's always tended to stand out, even when he was a little kid. And he was little."

"To be honest, I don't remember doing anything special for him," she said. "He was just someone to play rugby with. We all stood up for our mates. It was a big group of us kids, mucking about with the ball at recess and after school. I remember the girls better because there were fewer of us. It wasn't until he signed with the Club team that I realized he was the same Blake Stanton from school."

"Well, Mum never forgets a face. And she doesn't forget acts of kindness towards her boys," Andrew explained.

They were now standing at one of the many drinks areas set up throughout the house. There was dancing in the room they'd entered, and other guests had made themselves comfortable with plates of food on their laps. Despite the number of people, there was an intimate, friendly feel to the party. Everyone seemed to know each other. No strangers.

Andrew reached for a wine bottle on a nearby table and began to uncork it with practiced hands. "I understand that you and Blake will start shooting the commercial soon. A remake of your Last Man Standing video?"

She spotted Blake entering the house. His hair was now tousled, unkempt by his usual standards, and it only emphasized his masculinity. He searched the room before their eyes met. She knew he was trying to determine if she was still angry. She wasn't, but she didn't want him to know that right now. She still needed to understand her response to his kiss.

She accepted the glass of wine Andrew offered and downed half of it, ignoring his knowing smirk.

"Tell me something, Andrew," Neela said. "How did Blake react when the video of us as kids first came out? It brought me a lot of attention, the good kind. I think it was one reason the coaches started paying attention to me as a junior."

He paused in thought. "Well, we were caught up in the chaos of moving to England at that time. But I remember he said you'd won fair and square, which only made Mum love him more. He wasn't bothered. To be honest, I would have been livid. I think that's what makes him a good rugby player: he knows how to move on. People sometimes think he doesn't care. That's not true. He just doesn't let mistakes weigh him down."

"Yeah, you need that as a professional."

"You need that in life." Andrew placed his now-empty wine glass on the table. "Miss Smyth, would you care to dance?"

Neela was quick to shake her head, but Andrew's natural smile was hard to ignore. Although it was similar to Blake's, it didn't incite any excitement. He had identical eyes, too, but they didn't reach her soul.

"No, thanks, Andrew."

"I know you've got rhythm, Miss Smyth." Andrew's body began to move to the catchy pace of the latest chart-topper. He danced around her. "I've seen you play."

"Rugby is not dancing," she protested as Andrew started to shimmy his shoulders while his head began to shake in odd, jerky movements that were strangely appropriate for him.

"Come on, silver medalist. Show us tech nerds how it's done!" Andrew turned around and... twerked.

Neela burst out laughing. "That's not a good move for you, Andrew!" But she didn't resist when he pulled her gently into his arms and swung her around.

Although she was used to controlling her body in fast-paced, powerful motions, simply swaying and letting her limbs move without intention was strangely relaxing. Laughter came quickly, especially when Andrew started to wiggle his eyebrows to the techno beat that came up next.

Despite the music and a distracting dance partner, Neela felt Blake's eyes follow her. Even when one of the aunties dragged him onto the now-crowded dance floor, she knew he was looking for her.

It was silly, but she made a conscious effort to avoid Blake the rest of the evening. Andrew made it easy. He chose to be her companion for the duration of the party, picking up where Blake had left off and introduced her to various family friends. She sat with Sharon and Robbie while she ate then danced with Lulu for the rest of the evening. She was pretty sure she talked with everyone who came.

All the while, Blake was on the other side of the room. He never lacked companionship and was at ease with people he obviously was fond of. She would admit to looking for him among the strangers, and their eyes would meet at random moments. When she returned his questioning glance with a soft smile, he visibly relaxed. She wasn't angry at him. He deserved to know that at least, Neela thought. *I just didn't expect wanting to kiss you back.*

Blake finally reached her side as guests started to say their goodbyes.

"Are you ready?" he whispered.

Neela nodded. She had kept his blazer on the whole evening, even while dancing. "I'll probably have to dry-clean this for you."

"No worries. Keep it on for now. It'll be cold when we leave the house."

He leaned in, his face centimeters away from hers. She turned, the sound of her heartbeat loud and erratic in her head.

"Are we okay?" he asked.

A shiver went through Neela. She wasn't just hearing his voice but feeling it. She pulled Blake's blazer tighter around her. Swallowing the same nervous energy she usually expected before a match, Neela willed herself to look at Blake. She wasn't a coward. There was nothing to be afraid of.

"Yes, we're okay."

She *should* move. She *should* make her way to Clarissa and Walt, to thank them for inviting her. She shouldn't be staring at Blake's lips or remembering how they'd felt, how they'd tasted.

"Are you leaving already?" Clarissa's loud voice pierced through Neela's confusion.

"Yes, Mum," Blake said. His hand returned to Neela's waist, bringing her closer to him.

She didn't pull away. "Thank you again for inviting me this evening," she said. "I had a wonderful time. Your family knows how to throw a party."

"Well, we've had lots of practice. We celebrate everything. You must come back, even without Blake," Clarissa said, her eyes dancing and her face flushed. "I am quite serious about doing a portrait of you one day."

"I'm not sure why you would, but I'm always willing to try something new."

"That's the spirit!" Clarissa turned to Blake. "And you'll be coming straight back, yes? We expect you to stay overnight as usual, since Andrew is around."

"Yes, Mum. Straight back."

"I mean it, Blake. I may have had a few too many glasses of sparkling wine, but I saw the way you were undressing this girl with your eyes while she was dancing."

"Mum!"

He bent to kiss Clarissa, who whispered something to her youngest son. Blake responded with a shake of his head and an affectionate smile. A sudden image of Neela's last goodbye with her own mother came out of nowhere. It'd been years since she'd thought of that afternoon in the hospital. There had been tears —

lots of them — but Mum had made all her children promise that they would only remember the good times.

"You all right?"

"Yes, why?"

"You were far away, someplace sad."

Neela pursed her lips. "I'm not there now."

Blake looked unconvinced, but he kept his feelings to himself as he led them through the house. After a long string of good-byes, she followed Blake back to his car. He held her hand the whole time. Her mind said to let go, but something else deep within her told to keep it there.

After starting the car, he turned on the radio. She was surprised when the first sounds of the latest pop song came out.

Blake shrugged. "I thought you might want something a little more to your taste. And…well… I'm sorry if kissing you was the wrong thing to do."

In the shadows of the car, his dark eyes held hers. She whispered, "I'm not angry at you. I guess I didn't think we'd… you know."

He sat back in his seat and placed his hands on the steering wheel. He stared ahead, a vein in his neck visibly pulsating. "Could something happen between us?"

Neela's eyes widened, surprise stunning her into momentary silence. She slumped back into the luxurious leather seat. Frowning, she pulled the seatbelt over her. "What do you mean? What does 'something' mean, Blake? A quick one-night stand? I don't do those."

"No, I wouldn't think you did. And that's not what I meant, either. We're attracted to each other, aren't we? We don't have to pretend. We could have the dates we're planning to have be… real. They could mean something."

Neela looked out the window on her side of the car. Clouds had moved in, hiding any light from the moon and stars. Only scattered streetlamps prevented them from being shrouded entirely in darkness.

Oh, Blake. This was supposed to be an easy way to thank you for saving me last year. No more.

"I hope they won't," she said.

He pulled in a sharp breath at her answer. His disappointment weighed heavily between them, but she didn't want to face him yet. Whether she liked it or not, she couldn't ignore that he, out of everyone she had let into her life, could see straight past the walls she'd worked so hard to build. It wouldn't be long before he could see into her soul. She couldn't let that happen. No one needed to know all of her.

But she also wanted to explain. She'd promised him honesty. "Blake..."

He looked at the hand that rested gently on his arm, and her words faltered. Heat emanated from the skin under her touch. She also felt his strength. When she looked up from her hand, there were questions were in his eyes. Mercifully, only questions and no anger.

"I'm damaged goods, Blake," Neela whispered. "You're the prince-in-waiting to lead the greatest team in sports history. We're on different roads."

He shook his head. "I don't believe that."

"Trust me. This could never work between us. We're so different. It's probably why we've never been friends."

"We were friends as kids. We're friends now, and we *do* have a lot in common. You know we do."

"I hope we can stay friends."

"Look, Neela, I'm going to be honest here. I like you. I really do. And I think we could be good together."

"I think it's best that we don't think of ourselves as more than friends. I want to finish what we've started. I owe you. No, you can't tell me what I'm supposed to feel or not feel. I *owe* you," Neela emphasized. "But you must promise me that you won't try to kiss me again. Otherwise, it'll get odd between us, and I don't want to deal with that."

She could tell he didn't like where this was going.

"We're attracted to each other," he argued.

"Yes."

"And that's okay?"

Neela shrugged, pretending that this was the type of conversation she was used to having. "It's what we do with our attraction that changes things. I didn't want to feel something when you kissed me, but I'd be lying if I said you're a bad kisser."

Blake's dimple appeared. "There can be some benefits to being friends."

"No." Neela gripped the clutch on her lap a little tighter. "You kissed me. I stopped it. It's over. We're two adults. This doesn't have to be more than it is. Do I have your promise that you won't try to kiss me again?"

Blake revved the engine. Then he sighed. "Okay. I promise I won't kiss you again. But you can't stop me from thinking about it, Neela. Or wishing that I could taste your lips once more because I really like kissing you."

Breathing became difficult.

Blake Stanton wanted her.

She was grateful for the darkness of the night. She could hide her fears, her desire. *Please stop saying things that make my heart beat faster.* She fiddled with the latch on her clutch, her eyes trained on the polished surface, looking for a distraction.

She glanced sideways just in time to see Blake nodding as if he were making a decision. He checked over his shoulder before easing the car out of the parking spot.

"And, Neela?" he continued, keeping his attention on the road. "My promise doesn't mean that I'll stop *you* from kissing me. And if you ever make that first move, rest assured I will take full advantage of it."

Neither of them spoke on the drive home. Enough had been said. He would glance in her direction ever so often, and she'd do the same. Sometimes, their eyes would meet. He kept the pop music on, occasionally tapping his fingers to the beat, but it was his last words she kept hearing in her head, not the music.

Blake was an easygoing fella. He didn't need to push anyone into a corner. He'd never demand more than what was freely offered, but would he ignore their attraction to each other like she would? Why would he? He trusted his feelings. And that was where they were different. Those were the same feelings she'd vowed she would never indulge in again after the caresses of her last lover turned to blows.

Neela sank deeper into her seat and stared through the moonroof. Still no stars. Only darkness.

CHAPTER 10

Neela groaned when Rieann pushed another dress through the dressing room curtains.

"No more! I'll take the blue. The blue dress is fine. It fits, and it's in my budget."

"You're right, it's fine. I don't want fine. I want fabulous!" Rieann insisted. She pulled open the curtains, ignoring Neela's scrambled movements to cover her naked torso. "Dress for me, sis," she instructed. "I still have about ten kilos to gain before my old clothes fit again."

Neela stopped moving, inhaling deeply as her head dropped.

Before she could say anything, one of Rieann's arms covered her shoulders. "No, none of that. Come on! Don't feel sorry for me. I'm going to beat this thing. Mum dying meant I was checked earlier. That was her gift to us and her granddaughters. We know we're supposed to be diligent about it. We're not going to stop it from happening, but we can fight it earlier."

"Rieann…"

Rieann held her hand up. "Stop. We're changing the subject. I didn't mean to bring it up. Today's not about cancer. Besides, I plan to be extremely envious about this red dress."

Neela blinked at the dress Rieann was now holding against

her body. It wasn't a subtle red, but an 'I-dare-you-not-to-look-at-me' red. Even on the hanger, she could see that this dress would gracefully follow every movement she made; its silhouette reminded her of Marilyn Monroe's famous costume from *The Seven Year Itch*. It was designed to walk the thin line between elegance and sexiness.

Neela narrowed her eyes at her sister, who was still admiring her find. "We're starting the celebration at church. Lunch will be in the church hall. *Church*, Rieann. This is probably not the most appropriate thing to wear to those places."

"You can wear a camisole underneath, and Blake can take it off afterward."

"Rieann!"

Neela was certain Rieann's laughter could be heard at the front of the boutique.

"It's been entertaining to gossip about your love life at work, Neela. Who knew that my little sister dating a celebrity would be so much fun? If it were any other fella, I think the boys would be annoyed. But since it's none other than Blake Stanton, you're not going to find anyone saying they won't approve."

"So if a convicted felon asks me out, as long as he's part of the National Team, no one in the family, including my brothers, would be concerned?"

"Don't be silly," said Rieann. "We have our standards. He needs to have at least one World Championship under his belt to avoid some serious questioning by Joe and Sam. Blake has two, which means he has leave to do pretty much anything he wants."

"That's just fan-tas-tic."

"We've started a pool on when your engagement is going to be announced."

"That's not going to happen, Rieann."

"Oh, hush! Let us have our fantasies!"

Neela groaned as she reached for the red dress. Her fingers touched the hints of gold that were subtly woven into the fabric, adding sheen and shine. When she stepped into the dress and pulled it up, it was as if she had stepped into the arms of a lover, so completely enveloped by its softness. Gentle caresses where fabric met skin caused a tingling sensation up and down her body.

Neela stared at the unknown reflection. Hours on the pitch, years in the gym and a strict diet had all contributed to her muscular physique. She depended on her body for a living, so she worked it hard. She appreciated it, but she'd be the first to admit that she didn't pamper it. She didn't do manicures, and she was uncomfortable doing pedicures.

But in this dress, her pronounced muscles, her well-developed upper arms, her width, and even her thick neck weren't camouflaged, they were celebrated. The simple halter top captured the strong lines of Neela's shoulders, while its deep neckline suggested rather than revealed her cleavage. Neela turned, and a hidden slit teased with modest glimpses of firm thighs whose tan lines remained concealed.

"Oh, my. You're right. Maybe this isn't for church, but you need to get it," Rieann whispered to the reflection. "This was made for you."

Neela suddenly had an image of Blake's hands fingering the material. He'd appreciate the soft texture that contrasted with her hard body, and somehow, she knew he'd take his time peeling off the garment as part of a slow seduction. His words came back: *Rest assured, I will take full advantage…*

"You need to get it," Rieann repeated.

Neela shook her head, willing away the images and voice that would only make things more complicated. When she looked at the price tag, she was slightly relieved. The price made it easier to return the dress to its hanger.

"The blue dress will be perfect for the party," she argued. "It's dressy, and the pastor won't have a heart attack." Neela pulled at the tie, and the dress slipped to the floor. But before she could pick it up, Rieann grabbed it, pulled the curtain aside and walked out.

"Well, this will be from me to you. Merry Christmas!"

Her sister's laugh echoed through the store as Neela returned the stare of the amused salesperson outside the dressing room. With one arm across her breasts, Neela drew the curtains again with the other, then hurriedly pulled on her work clothes. When she reached the cashier, Rieann was ready to leave, the pink paper bag in her hand indicating that it was too late for Neela to do anything about the purchase.

"I'll wrap it up, but you have to pretend to be surprised when you see it," Rieann said.

She sighed as she placed the blue dress on the counter and handed the cashier her credit card. "You shouldn't have. It's quite dear."

"Nonsense. I love it, and you look amazing in it. When's your next date with Blake?"

Neela smiled at the cashier as she paid for the more appropriate and budget-friendly dress. "Are you really interested?"

Rieann looped her arm through Neela's as they left the boutique. "Yes! I'm an old married woman with two teenagers. Your life reads like a bit of a fairy tale right now. 'Medalist Dates World Champion.' You're now part of 'Nee-lake.' How cute is that name? You two look like the perfect couple."

Neela waited to feel some form of guilt, but there wasn't any. "We're just friends."

"If you say so. But let the rest of us pretend there's more, eh?"

"I'm seeing him this afternoon. We're babysitting his niece."

Rieann stopped suddenly and frowned. "What kind of date is that?"

It was Neela's turn to laugh. "Blake offered to watch Lulu a fair bit this summer to give his sister-in-law a break. Sharon's due any minute. And I promised the little one a look at the medal."

"Interesting seduction strategy: bring a child on a date. I thought he'd be more of a fancy restaurant and wine type."

"He may be, but I'm not."

Rieann's eyes twinkled. "You may be but haven't realized it yet. You should let him spoil you a little, Neela. It's the fun part of dating, and if the fella can afford a few luxuries, take advantage of it."

"I cannot believe I'm hearing this from you. Take advantage of Blake's wealth? Did chemo screw up your sense of principles?" Neela immediately slapped her hand over her mouth, horrified. "Sorry! I didn't mean... Quit laughing at me, Rieann! I'm trying to apologize!"

Neela found herself in her sister's arms. The latter's thin body shook with laughter.

"Don't apologize for being you! You've been tiptoeing around this for a year." Rieann stepped back then bent slightly so their eyes could meet. "You, my sister, have always been a bit of a hothead. But you've not been completely yourself with me since you moved back. My instincts tell me it's not just about you tip-toeing about my cancer."

"I don't know what you mean," Neela said. She began to walk but was held back by a sudden grip on her arm.

"We're cut from the same cloth, you and I," Rieann said, her voice surprisingly gentle despite the firmness of her hold. "We're our mother's heirs. We've inherited her people's past. We face our fears. Be you. I know that fierce little girl is still in there. I see her on the pitch. Don't forget that's also who you are when you don't have a rugby ball in your hands."

Neela studied her older sister. Rieann covered her still-bald head with a kerchief. A long-sleeved lime-green poplin dress did little to hide how extraordinarily thin she was.

They were ten years apart. By the time Neela had started high school, Rieann was married to Trey, was a mum to a toddler, and pregnant with her second child. They had never been best friends, but her older sister always made an effort to be on the sidelines or in the stands whenever she played.

"I wasn't sure how much you wanted to talk about being sick," Neela said slowly.

Rieann tilted her head slightly. "I had cancer. You can use the word. And I'm not Margot, if that's what you're wondering. I don't share with the world what I'm going through, but neither will I avoid talking about it. I'm not hiding. It's part of who I am now."

"I've been away for so long. I just thought I'd be the last person you'd be interested in confiding in."

Rieann nodded. "You were away for a long time. We were worried about you. All of us."

"I know. I'm sorry."

"Hey, no more! You don't owe anyone an apology for living your life," Rieann said. "We all knew you had to go. It's okay. And look what you've accomplished by going away. A silver medalist!"

Neela bit on her lower lip, regret lacing her words. "I've missed a lot."

Rieann smiled gently. "Nothing is without sacrifices, and you're here now. I want you to feel comfortable knowing you can ask me anything. Promise me that. Maybe one day I'll ask you about the life you had after you left us. But I'm learning to live in the present right now, and I'm glad you've come home, little sis. Very glad."

Blake bit back the impulse to call out Neela's name. Whatever was being said between Neela and the taller woman seemed personal and private. Besides, he was going to see her in a few hours. With Lulu as a chaperone, no less, but he'd take any time he could get with Neela.

After he'd confessed that he was more than interested in

kissing her, contact between them had remained minimal this past week. She had been right on that point. It could get very odd between them.

Would he dare risk the friendship they were building for a one-off chance that the chemistry between them could be something special? He wasn't much of a gambler, but he decided this was a risk he was willing to take. Neela would be worth it.

He stayed in place as the women exchanged an embrace but didn't continue his walk when he realized the taller woman hadn't moved either. When Neela turned the corner, the woman's gentle, indulgent smile was replaced with a deep frown.

Before he could think twice, Blake jogged to the other side of the road. "Rieann?" he called, taking a guess.

A startled look quickly gave way to a cheeky smile. "Blake Stanton? You just missed Neela."

"I'll be seeing her later today. I was just stopping by to pick up some cupcakes for my niece when I saw you both."

"It's your niece's birthday?"

"No. A bribe."

"Ahh. You're an experienced babysitter, then."

Blake laughed. "I've been properly humbled by Lulu from the day she was born. She has both my brothers and me tied around her little finger. I wouldn't have it any other way, though."

"Children have a way of taking over, even without trying. But they're worth it."

"Yeah. My brother has never looked more tired or happier since he became a dad," Blake said. "If you're not in a hurry, would you like to join me for some tea or coffee? I have a bit of time before I have to fetch Lulu."

"Why not? It's not every day I get picked up by a younger, handsome man. I'll forget the bit that you're dating my sister, though."

They walked the short distance to the cake shop where his

order was ready upon their arrival. He peered into the box, satisfied with the unique designs of tutus and rugby balls. He showed them to Rieann.

"I love it!" she said.

As they waited for their tea and coffee, Rieann plied Blake with questions about Lulu and their plans for the afternoon. He didn't miss the innuendos behind Rieann's line of questioning, and if he were inferring correctly, Neela's sister seemed pleased with the idea of him and Neela dating.

"Promise me you'll take her someplace fancy one day," Rieann said. "So she can dress up."

"Someplace fancy? She barely lets me pay for her lunch."

Rieann smiled. "Yeah, Mum made sure both her girls understood that early on. She told us to always pay our own way so that no fella expects payment in some other form."

Orders in hand, they found seats towards the back of the cake shop. "You're looking well, considering," Blake said.

Rieann brought the white teacup to her lips. "Thank you. I assume Mano mentioned something."

"Not much. He's as private as they come."

"One of our strengths and faults as a family," Rieann said quietly as if to herself. "Did he tell you that Neela will have a hard time at the party?"

Blake stayed silent, unwilling to admit something he knew Mano had said to him in confidence. But Rieann's sharp eyes recognized his reluctance.

"He did say something, then. Good." She surprised Blake by reaching for his hand on the table. "If he said something, then he must trust you. That makes me especially glad you agreed to join us and that you'll be there for her. I love my family, Blake, and I adore my father. He means well, but he can be a mean old codger."

"Neela hasn't mentioned anything about it to me. I know she doesn't want to go, but from what you and Mano are saying, should she even be going?"

Rieann paused, then nodded, her jaw set determinedly. "We're family. We may not always like each other, but we're family. It's the one thing Mum really drilled into us. When Neela left, it was hard on all of us. If my getting sick was what brought her back, then there was a silver lining to having cancer."

Rieann exhaled and leaned back in her chair, her eyes focused on him. "Look, I know Neela doesn't want to go. I know Dad hasn't forgiven her for missing out on his wedding. But they both need to be there. It's the first step in a long journey toward the Smyth family being whole again."

CHAPTER 11

NEELA STARED AT THE CLOTHES LAID OUT ON THE BED AND PULLED A piece of lint from her new blue dress. A light yellow cardigan would give it a pop of color, and simple black flats would finish the outfit.

She turned to her dresser and opened a small wooden jewelry box. Would her pearl studs be okay to wear to the party? Or would their appearance incur her father's displeasure?

She sighed. She didn't know anymore. It was like walking on eggshells whenever they were in the same room. She had only seen her father a handful of times in the last year. Their encounters were always brief, usually at family dinners, surrounded by many people, and Mano was always present. He took the attention off her.

Attending a public celebration of her father and stepmother's anniversary was a big step. She had picked up the phone half a dozen times yesterday with an excuse, but she knew not showing up would be unforgivable. If she wanted any chance for a relationship with her father, she had to go.

But did she really want that chance? Wouldn't it be easier not to have him in her life? Her mum would be disappointed if she answered 'yes.'

Her phone buzzed. "Yes, Blake."

"Well, good morning to you too. I'm sending you a picture of what I thought I'd wear to the party."

"Blake, it doesn't matter."

"I want to make a good impression."

"To be honest, you could be wearing a pair of shorts and a shirt full of holes, and no one would care."

"Just the socks. I want your thoughts about the socks."

"Who pays attention to socks?"

"You'd be surprised."

"I'm not giving you feedback on socks, Blake. I'll see you in an hour."

"Nee—"

"Bye."

She tried to keep a straight face, but the smile remained. She couldn't remember anyone who made her smile as much as Blake. He wasn't Mano, but she knew her family would be more than happy to shower attention on him. Anything to make the day go a little faster would be welcomed.

He was on time, and to the score of *Madame Butterfly*, Neela watched the landscape change from urban to country, the city buildings quickly giving way to wide open land as Blake expertly drove them home.

Home?

Neela guessed it still was. Despite her feelings for her father, it was where she had grown up.

She snuck a look at her driver. He looked content, lost either in his own thoughts or in the music. She had offered to hire a car to take them both, but he insisted on driving. She still couldn't decide whether to be annoyed or impressed that he was interested in joining her for the full day of celebration, which would begin with a church service.

Blake wasn't a churchgoer, but he'd told her he didn't want to show up just for the roast pig. Besides, he argued, when the season started again, he'd have very little time to take the car out for long drives. Roast pig and a long car drive made for an almost perfect day.

"You handle the car well," Neela remarked as they hit the highway.

"Thanks. Took a bit of practice to get used to the power and the sensitivity of the steering, but this is pretty much my dream car. I had to convince Andrew to sell it to me. Stingy bastard wanted more money than I was willing to pay."

"If you really wanted one, why didn't you just buy your own? New, even. Not secondhand." Neela was confused. "You do know you're one of the highest paid athletes in the country, right?"

He glanced at her briefly. "When we were younger, Dad's parents lost their farm. They moved in with us, and my parents did what they had to do to help out. That meant us kids had to do without for a bit. I've never forgotten what that was like. We ate a lot of soup. Maybe that was why I was so puny, eh? But, yeah, as much as I wanted a flash car, I wasn't going to buy it until I was really ready for it financially."

"I never knew."

"We weren't allowed to complain, and to be honest, we learned very quickly that complaining didn't change anything. It motivated all us boys to work hard."

"Your parents must be proud of all of you."

"I think it's more of a relief that none of us ended up in jail," Blake said with a laugh. "Robbie was especially tough as a teenager."

"I don't believe it."

Blake nodded. "Yeah, the neurosurgeon you met had piercings in his ears, nose, and tongue at sixteen."

"We're talking about Lulu's dad, right?"

"Andrew got suspended for hacking into the principal's computer, and we didn't own a computer ourselves. He read a book and just wanted to see if he could do it."

"And to think all three of you have been honored as outstanding citizens of New Zealand at one time or another."

Blake glanced over. "Only two of us. I haven't had the honor."

Neela frowned. "That can't be right."

"It's true. The tech genius got the award first, then the neurosurgeon was honored two years later. The rugby player hasn't been on that list."

Neela heard it then for the first time. It was just a slight nuance in his voice, but she recognized it. It was the same insecurity she often felt when she tried to gain her father's approval, approval he gave freely to her older siblings.

"I'm sorry, Blake. I honestly thought you—"

"No worries. They both earned it."

Neela decided to change the subject. "Do you remember any of my brothers or my sister?"

"Not really." He glanced at her again. "I met Rieann last week."

"She didn't mention anything."

"After you went shopping. She made me promise to take you someplace fancy. Why?"

"Ignore her."

"I don't break my promises, Neela. You know that."

Neela sighed dramatically. "If only you would. We wouldn't be here together if you did."

Blake laughed. "That's a fair point. I do remember your oldest brother, Joe. He was a top rugby player at high school, wasn't he?"

"Yeah, he was. Joe taught me the fundamentals. Played provincial rugby for a bit but hurt his knee after a year."

"He's in the family business, I hear."

"They all are. Joe captains one of the boats. Rieann deals with operations and Sam is in sales."

"Do you see them often?"

Neela looked out the window. "I'm starting to again."

As eager as she had been to leave her father's house, she continued to have fond memories of her childhood in the town that sat in the outskirts of the port town of Timaru. It was a safe environment to grow up in. People looked out for one another without being asked. No strangers. Back then, doors were left open, and kids played freely in each other's backyards. Simpler times.

Neela's heart tightened. She leaned back and stared through the moon roof, watching the clouds pass by quickly.

Blake didn't ask any more questions. He kept the music going, and occasionally he would join the singer in a chorus. Again, there was comfort in their silent companionship. Did he know he was giving her time to prepare for the rest of the day?

When Blake turned into the carpark of the red-brick building, trepidation flowed through her body. Her heart started to beat faster, and she rubbed her palms repeatedly on her dress. She swallowed, wondering whose face she would see first.

They were fifteen minutes early, but already half the parking spaces were filled. The church would be full for today's service in honor of her father and Laura's anniversary. The Smyth family had a long history in the community, and her father was very much respected and admired.

Neela spotted her oldest brother's dark blue sedan immediately. Rieann and Trey's large SUV was parked next to it. Sam's Ranger was also there, as was her father's silver ute.

Familiar faces—part of her past she had yet to revisit—waved in her direction. Were they looking at Blake or at her? No, it was her. They wanted to see her. They seemed glad to see her. Neela swallowed, then forced a smile and waved back. The pounding in her head grew persistent; a rush of adrenaline shot through her body like a tidal wave that demanded that she react. Fight or flight? She knew what she wanted to do. It just wasn't what she had to do.

Suddenly, she felt a large warm hand cover her clenched fist. "It's going to be fine," Blake said softly.

Neela opened her hand and laced her fingers through his. He squeezed it firmly.

Rieann saw them soon after Blake had parked the car. Dressed in a long-sleeved pink sheath with a pearl pendant that matched Neela's earrings, Rieann held her arms out as she approached them.

"You're here!" she cried, pulling Neela into a fierce hug. Neela blinked back tears as her sister whispered, "I know this is going to be hard, but it's important. Thank you. It wouldn't be complete without you. Mum would be so proud you came."

Rieann's continued to smile as she greeted Blake. "Good to see you again, Blake. We're happy you're able to join us today, and no matter what my brothers say, you are not required to throw the ball around with them."

Blake laughed. "I'll do as I'm told by any of the Smyths. It's a role I'm getting used to," he added, winking at Neela.

"The whole town is excited about the commercial being shot at the primary school," Rieann said as they entered the narthex to the church. "The director's already put an ad in the local papers for some extras. I might need to take the day off work."

As her eyes adjusted to the dimmer interior, the first person Neela saw was Malcolm Smyth. Their eyes met for a couple of seconds at most, but it was she who turned away first.

"Fun and games don't pay well, Rieann."

"Oh, Dad," Rieann giggled as their father reached to greet her with an embrace.

Malcolm Smyth commanded a room. Although he wasn't a tall man, he peered at everyone as if he were. White hair contrasted sharply with his deep tan, and his dark, assessing eyes saw everything. He was conservatively dressed in a white shirt and gray trousers, but his broad shoulders and muscled arms rivaled those of his sons'. He often boasted of his ability to still work on the boats and have his sons keep up with his work schedule.

He loved the sea, her dad. For as long as Neela could remember, he'd reminded his four children that both their past and their future were there.

Except she'd gotten seasick when she was ten and had refused to go on another boat ride ever again.

"Dad." Neela hoped she was smiling. "Happy anniversary."

With guarded eyes, he opened his palm to accept her hand as she moved her forehead to his for a *hongi*. She suppressed the desire to break contact, to move away. This was her father. When had it become hard to touch her own family?

When she felt her father move, Neela turned quickly to face her petite stepmother, whose ash-brown hair was pulled tightly back into a bun. Laura moved hesitantly toward Neela, her arms outstretched for a hug. An unexpected but welcome relief tempered Neela's rapidly beating heart. She only saw kindness in her stepmother's face.

"Happy anniversary, Laura. You look lovely." Neela surprised herself with how much she actually meant those words.

"Thank you. We're happy to have you here, Neela."

"And this is my friend, Blake Stanton."

Neela didn't miss the genuine look of delight which crossed her father's face. "Of course! Pleased to finally meet you. I couldn't believe it when Rieann said you'd be coming as well."

"The honor is mine, sir," Blake said, accepting the traditional Maori greeting before shaking the older man's hand. He repeated the action with Laura. "Congratulations on your anniversary."

"Thank you. Hey, let me introduce you to some of the family and our friends," Malcolm said. "We couldn't quite keep it a secret that someone from the National Team was going to join us today."

Neela watched her father guide Blake toward a nearby group of people.

"You're looking well, sis. Smart move, bringing Blake Stanton as your date," teased a loud voice that came from behind her.

She greeted her oldest brother with a soft punch to his upper arm. "Hello, Joe. Not exactly my idea. You have to thank Mano for Blake being here. And don't read too much into it! Rieann told me about the pool you started at work. About an engagement? I'd take my money out if I were you. Blake and I are just friends."

"The way he looked at you when you came out of the car, I think I might just add more money to it," Joe said with a wink. "We're going to have a good time today, eh? Like a family. Like old times."

The Smyths were never ones to mince words. As awkward as the division was between her and her father, her siblings were vocal in reminding her to reach out to them.

"Neela, you look lovely!"

A genuine feeling of warmth came over Neela as a large woman with dark, laughing eyes and a wide smile kissed her on both cheeks before drawing her tight against her ample bosom.

"Hello, Agnes," she said, her voice muffled by her sister-in-law's dress.

"Mum, back off! You're suffocating her!" Neela recognized the voice of her niece, Tanya. "It's my turn!"

Neela glanced over her shoulder to see Blake watching her. She caught his smile before she was overwhelmed by yet another hug. She could hear Joe introducing himself to Blake, and envisioned her brother shaking Blake's hand vigorously. "Shitty refereeing" and "Didn't laugh when you fell on your own ball, honest" indicated Joe's plans to ingratiate himself with the rugby superstar.

She lost Blake as a mass of people entered the church. She nodded, shook hands, exchanged *hongis*, received and gave hugs. Faces and voices flooded her senses.

"Where have you been?"

"We screamed so loud when you made it into the Finals."

"Come over and meet the family, eh?"

Did she say anything offensive? The smiles that danced in front of her suggested she hadn't.

Then a voice from the other side of the narthex called out, prompting family and guests to begin sitting for the church service. Blake suddenly appeared beside her, offering his elbow as they followed the stream of people who entered the church.

"All right?" he asked.

She swallowed and nodded.

Narrow, clear windows allowed the sun to highlight the rich wooden interior while also enlarging what was, in essence, a small building. The floors must have been refinished recently, Neela thought absentmindedly. Intricate designs on wooden wall panels gleamed, their details —carved by an anonymous artist— were lost at first glance.

She looked up toward the rafters. More complex designs of her culture were engraved in the beams above, unique to this church. Subtle but ever-present, they used to keep her occupied during the long sermons whose bold messages she never remembered.

Rieann caught Neela's attention and indicated with a nod that Neela and Blake were to sit in the pew right behind her. Sam and his family were already seated, and her brother's arms were full with her newest niece.

"Everyone is pleased to see you," Blake whispered as they sat down.

"Almost everyone."

The last time she had been here was for her mother's funeral. She didn't remember much from that day, just lots of birds of paradise in the church, Mum's favorite flower. Mum loved color, and her family delivered. No one wore black.

Neela didn't remember the readings, the music, the prayers, or the tears. Try as she could, she didn't see the color, just the darkness of losing the one person who never demanded but only gave.

Blake nudged her gently when the pastor asked the family to stand up for a special prayer.

"You, too, Blake. You're family now," Sam said loud enough for more than a few people to hear.

A warm flush crept up her face. Rieann might not have turned around, but her shaking shoulders indicated she'd heard enough.

This time, it was Neela who slipped her hand into Blake's as he stood up. His squeezed recognized her offer of support.

* * *

Her palms were sweaty.

She'd thought he'd be put out by Sam's loud announcement, that he'd been pushed into an awkward position. It was the farthest thing from the truth, but he was going to relish her concern. He'd ignore the rational part of him that warned him not to read too much into such a simple action. He wanted something—anything—from her that showed a change of heart, that she was beginning to realize they were meant to be together.

He wouldn't tell her he'd turned down a good-paying appearance in Christchurch to be with her today. Nor would he admit that his last thoughts at night were spent wondering what she was thinking. And he definitely wouldn't share how much time he had been spending on coming up with reasons why they should continue to see each other once the summer was over.

When he felt her hand in his as the pastor offered a blessing for the Smyth family, in a holy place he rarely entered, Blake faced the truth of his presence there today. It wasn't for a promise, and it wasn't for the captaincy. It was for the fulfillment of feelings that had started years ago, at a lonelier time when only one person had believed in him.

He loved Neela Smyth.

Even at ten, when his life was full of knocks, scrapes, countless bruises, and endless teasing, he had been able to withstand all of that as long as she was waiting for him at the end of the game. He had loved her then. It was only now, in this house of worship, with words and actions so foreign to him, that he could recognize the truth of his feelings for the woman next to him.

He had never stopped loving Neela Smyth.

But she wasn't ready to know that. He knew that as well. What he didn't know was whether she would ever be ready. Blake bowed his head, his silent prayer joining the pastor's.

Please let her let me love her.

The loud notes of the church organ signaled the end of the service. Malcolm and Laura followed the pastor out of the church, occasionally stopping to greet friends and relatives.

"Sorry about Sam," Neela whispered, her breath bouncing off the side of his neck. "He's the worst out of all of us. It just comes out of his mouth. But if you want to know the secret to the best *hāngi* you'll ever taste, he's your fella."

"I'll make sure to take notes."

Neela must have said something to Sam, as Blake unexpectedly found himself with him immediately after the service. Sam led him outside while Neela stayed inside the church hall. Blake was then introduced to a group of men in charge of the barbecue area. Sam commandeered this part of the celebration. He barked orders, and everyone seemed to know their place in the chain of command. Blake managed to fend off the various offers of beer — "Driving and in training, mate"—but he wasn't able to steer the conversation away from rugby.

Usually, he'd prefer that the talk remain focused on sport; it was a safe subject that made strangers friends. But not today. He just wanted to make sure Neela was all right. *She'll be fine. She's among family. Rieann's with her, and it is Neela. She knows how to take care of herself.* But he wanted to be the one next to her, to have his hand available in case she needed it.

Clear glass sliding doors separated the barbecue area from the hall where the rest of the guests were convening and socializing. Blake spotted Neela among the many bodies.

A casual observer would think she looked relaxed and comfortable. She laughed and smiled, moving effortlessly between groups of people. But he saw how she'd rub her neck, saying enough but never too much. She obliged the requests for photos, but whenever Malcolm Smyth was within arm's length, she moved away.

Similarly, Malcolm didn't seek out his youngest daughter. There was no anger in his actions; he didn't seem to care that Neela was there. His attitude toward her was especially obvious given all the attention Malcolm showered on his other children and grandchildren. He didn't miss the opportunity to squeeze Rieann's shoulder whenever she passed by; he exchanged banter with Joe; he came by the barbecue area to check up on Sam.

Malcolm Smyth was proving himself to be a doting father but only to three of his children.

At lunch, Blake joined Neela at the table with Sam, his family and Joe's children, Aaron and Tanya. Neela looked more relaxed as they ate. She quizzed her nieces and nephews on their summer activities and gave as good as she got whenever Sam teased her.

After their meal, Blake agreed to throw the ball around a bit. To his surprise, Neela excused herself, saying she'd help her sister clear up. He offered to help, but she insisted he go out.

"Give them something to talk about tonight," she said. "There's a little girl in that group who'd love to have you pass the ball to her."

When he came back in, he found her looking through photo albums with Tanya. She caught him staring then gave him a weak smile. She returned her attention to her niece, but her quick glance had been enough to stun him momentarily.

Resignation.

No fire.

That was all he needed to see. He walked toward Malcolm, who was in the middle of a conversation with now-familiar-looking faces. When he got close, Neela's father gave him a huge smile, and for a moment, Blake couldn't reconcile this friendly man with the figure who had barely said a word to his most famous child all day.

"How are you, Blake? Everyone treating you well?" Malcolm asked.

"Very well, sir. The food was delicious."

"Sam is one of the best."

"He lives up to his reputation," Blake said. "I hope you don't mind, but I have to leave now. I'm due in Auckland tomorrow, and I haven't started packing yet."

Malcolm nodded. "Of course. You're quite the busy man. You've done so well for yourself. I'll admit that out of all the kids from Neela's primary school, you weren't on the top of my list to make it onto the National Team."

"You wouldn't be the first to think that, sir."

Malcolm shook Blake's hand. "The missus was tickled you showed up. We hope to see you again soon."

Blake turned to see Neela watching him. He nodded slightly toward the door, and her face lit up when she realized they were making their escape. She said something quietly to Tanya, who responded with a warm hug.

As Blake said his goodbyes, he followed Neela's movement around the room. Rieann embraced her warmly, as did Joe, Sam, and their respective partners.

Then he watched her walk toward her father. With a strained smile, she made a move to hug him. Malcolm returned her action awkwardly, with a quick pat on the back. They both turned away as soon as their embrace was over.

Neela approached Laura, said a few things, and exchanged kisses. Then she turned toward the exit without another glance.

Blake started, surprised to see her leave the room. She wouldn't go without him—or would she?

He sidestepped a few people, telling himself that the sudden sense of urgency was unnecessary. Reason didn't stop him from opening the door with unexpected force.

The sudden glare of the sun blinded him for a moment. He scanned the carpark. His car was still where he had parked it. He turned and spotted Neela jumping over an old wooden fence. She was moving determinedly toward the hill behind the church. There was a sudden gust of wind; Neela rubbed her eyes…from the dirt? Or was she crying?

Shit. Neela never cries.

Blake started after her, the gravel crunching under his hurried strides. "Neela!"

CHAPTER 12

"Neela! Wait!"

The wind had come up suddenly, mimicking the emotional chaos inside of her. She couldn't stop crying, but was it out of rage or despair? Or both?

"Neela!"

She ignored him. She could barely see in front of her; the tears flowed swiftly. She stumbled again. *Bloody shoes*!

She stopped, pulled them off, and for no reason other than that he was her only target, she threw them wildly at Blake.

She turned without checking to see if she'd hit him or not. The shoes didn't have heels. He wouldn't lose an eye.

"Neela!"

"Go away!"

She started to run. Faster, harder. She pushed herself forward. She didn't care about the rough, rocky terrain under her feet or the dirt that covered the bottom of her dress when she stumbled.

"Neela! Wait! Damn it! My shoes are meant for dancing, not running! Stop!"

Instead, she increased her speed, determined to get to the top and drink in the view that had comforted her often in her youth.

"Neela! Stop!"

She had to stop, in the end. There was nowhere to go when she reached the top. It led downhill to an empty field that stretched to Mrs. Lawson's backyard, filled with metal scraps, old tires, discarded furniture, and other things most people would call junk but Mrs. Lawson labeled 'art.'

"Neela!"

She whipped around, roughly wiping her face. She knew it wasn't his fault she was so angry, but the fool insisted on being here. "Why are you following me, Blake? Go back to your fancy car. Turn whatever aria you have on up high. Go home. You can't pretend you're too drunk this time. I can take care of myself."

"Neela—"

She took a step forward and poked Blake's chest.

"Now you know. What does it say about me, eh? I can't be a very nice person if my own father can't stand me! He barely said ten words to me all day! Not that I blame him. I didn't want to say five words to him!"

"Sweet—"

"Don't you dare try to sweet-talk me! I don't need your pity!"

But she didn't try to escape his embrace, which was gentle but firm. The swirling wind masked the sounds of her sobs. So complete was Blake's hold that she didn't feel the cold. She pulled at his shirt, bunches of fabric clenched in her fist, desperate to let out all her anger and disappointment.

When she had no more tears left to shed, she kept her face hidden in Blake's shoulder, and he pulled her closer. In a muffled voice, she repeated her earlier statement. "I don't need your pity."

He held her tighter. "No, you don't. You've never had it. You've only ever had my respect and admiration."

She wasn't sure how long she stayed in his arms. Nothing had ever felt as safe. When she finally moved, she studied Blake's face. "I lost my shoes."

"No, they're right here," he said, nodding toward the ground.

"Your forward throw is pretty bad. It's a good thing you don't play softball."

She smiled despite herself, then saw the creases in his pink shirt, which was now marked with her tears. "I may have to replace this shirt for you."

"Nah. It's going to be out of style soon. You know I like to keep up with the trends."

"You're so vain."

"It's how I express my artistic side." Blake knelt, pulled out the bottom his shirt, reached for one of her feet, and wiped the mud off it. He then gently put one shoe on before repeating the action with her other foot. "Dad does woodwork, Robbie does pottery, Andrew is a photographer, and I—"

"You buy bright-colored shirts," she finished.

"And bake and sing," he said, reaching for her hand again. They began walking down the hill. "Mum always wanted her boys to be well-rounded."

"You're very lucky to have parents who supported you."

Blake stopped to place his hands on Neela's shoulders. "I know your brothers and sister love you. I can see that. I also think your father loves you and your stepmother *wants* to love you. They just don't understand you. And that's okay. You don't have to understand someone to love them."

Her eyes narrowed. "Where do you get these things?"

He smiled and put his arm around Neela's shoulders. Her arm automatically went around his waist as they continued their walk.

"Liana Murphy writes the best books," he said.

"Don't tell me you have all her books."

"Yes, all autographed, in exchange for a lifetime of babysitting Jayne Molloy. I think I have the better deal. I also managed to get her to promise me that I'll get the first edition of anything else she writes. They'll be in places of honor in my library."

"You don't have a library."

"One day I will. A big room with floor-to-ceiling windows, a big red carpet, and a fireplace."

Neela stared at Blake, the corner of her mouth twitching.

"I'm serious. It's on my vision board," he continued.

She burst out laughing, her anger and sadness replaced by amusement and incredulity. "A vision board?"

"Haven't you spent time with the sports psychologist? The mind is a powerful thing."

"No, apparently I haven't spent enough time with the sports psychologist."

"When you're next at the art store, buy a vision board. Fill it up, and we can share."

"Blake..."

"That's what friends do, isn't it? We share our dreams. We already have a history together. Even if I'm never allowed to kiss you ever again, I'd like to think we'll have a future together."

Something caught in her throat.

"I..." She inhaled deeply, trying to clear her mind and calm her emotions. "Sometimes, I just don't know what to say when I'm with you."

The dimple appeared. "Darl, now you know how I feel."

As they began their drive back to Christchurch, he sang along with gusto to the soundtrack of *Les Misérables*.

A future?

Even in the throes of her infatuation with Kyle, she hadn't thought about the future. She'd thought in terms of 'now.' That was how it was with Kyle; he touted a philosophy of complete spontaneity. It had seemed like such an exciting way to live.

Neela frowned as she noticed Blake passing the turnoff that would have taken them to the freeway. "Where are we going?"

"Since we're in the area, I thought we could check out the old school."

"Right now?"

Blake only grinned and continued to sing. He pulled into the school carpark fifteen minutes later. With the engine off, it was eerily quiet. The isolation and silence were a contrast to the busyness and turmoil that had filled much of her day.

"Come on, let's take a look," Blake said.

Neela peered out the window. "And what are we supposed to be looking at?"

"Darl, this is where we first met." His teasing tone accompanied the wink that only a few weeks ago would have annoyed her. Instead, a thrill shot through her, and she fought to dismiss it.

"Blake…"

But he had already left the car. She shook her head but followed him. Hands on his hips, he stood facing the school field, now enclosed by a meter-and-a-half-high wooden fence she didn't remember from her childhood.

He looked at her when she came up next to him. "Want to jump it?"

His eyes challenged hers, and he held out his hand as if offering to help. She frowned at the gesture. The height of the fence wasn't the problem. Her dress flared so it wouldn't restrict her, but it might fly up a little.

She warned him. "If you see my undies, don't say a word."

Neela pushed past his offered hand and ignored the wide grin on his face. She reached for the top plank and pushed off from the bottom, clearing the fence in one motion. She turned to see Blake coming over similarly.

"Leopard print?"

"You promised!"

"I did no such thing!"

"You know if we're both caught, this could spell trouble at RugNZ."

"It's not like we're in a hot tub."

Neela choked back a laugh. "Fair enough."

"We're just former students paying a visit."

"On a Sunday evening with no one about?"

"Come on, I'll race you to the middle of the pitch!"

He took off, and Neela followed. He was running at full speed. When they ran together in the mornings, it was an unhurried, paced exercise to build their endurance. They weren't slow, but neither was there the urgency that came with an explosive sprint.

She was a few seconds behind him when they reached the center of the field.

Hands rested on the back of his head, his chest rising and falling. "Can't believe we'll be back here in a few weeks, after all these years. Are you nervous about the filming?"

"Yes," Neela said. "I don't want to make a fool of myself."

"You'll be fine. Just be yourself. This place hasn't changed much, has it?"

She surveyed the field. It was really like any other sports field found in any neighborhood around their country. There was nothing unique about this one in particular, except maybe that it had produced two players who had gone on to represent their country. How many dreams had been made and dashed here?

"No, not much has changed," she said. "Some things just don't. I'm glad for that."

"Do you have good memories of this place, Neela?"

She picked a blade of grass, flicked it and watched it spiral as it fell to the ground. "Yeah. It was good."

"That's it? 'It was good'? Come on! Ow!"

She grinned. "Why didn't you see that coming?"

"Because most adults don't go around pinching people."

"Didn't I pinch you when we were kids?"

"Actually, no. Then you quit being my protector in our last year of school together."

Neela looked up as the late afternoon sun brought a gold sheen to the blue skies. She never used to appreciate such colors. "You didn't need it by then. You could hold your own. And everyone knew it."

"I sort of missed having you look for me at recess."

She frowned. "Really? Did you look for me?"

He laughed softly, then stretched his arms before resting his palms behind his head again. "Every day. But you'd moved on to take care of someone else. That's when I started baking with Joy."

"Ahh, I see. Wouldn't that make me responsible for a cupcake being named after you?"

He grinned. "Oh, no, you're not. My recipe, my cupcake."

"Bet Molloy didn't have a cupcake named after him."

"You're right." He moved his gaze from her face to the rest of the field that stretched in front of them. "Maybe there *is* something I'll be able to do better than him."

She touched his arm. "Blake," she said softly. "Few players will ever do what he has done. I don't know Mitch Molloy, but I know you. You're a good bloke."

His eyes remain veiled. He was somewhere in the past.

"Why did you tackle me in that video? I mean, we'd always played touch until then."

She shrugged, pulling her hand back to her side. "I honestly can't remember. Something just made me go for it. I saw how determined you were to score, and I forgot we were just playing for fun. I guess I responded to the challenge of stopping you."

Blake sat down on the grass, his arms resting on his knees. "I loved this field. It made sense for me, even when I could barely make it halfway across. The grass feels different in each stadium, you know."

She joined him and threw off her shoes, then dug her toes into the soil. "For me, it's the smell. After the warm-ups, the anthems, I take a deep breath and just remember all the other the times I've played the game, in any field, ever since I started to walk. The same adrenaline that made me tackle you when we were kids kicks in then."

"But something made you walk away from the game. When we moved back from England, I looked for your name on all the rugby teams, in all the clubs. You seemed to have disappeared."

She kept her focus on the grass before raising her eyes to the top of the school buildings, where shadows were forming with the setting sun.

"I stopped playing to hurt my dad."

She caught Blake's raised eyebrows and surprise etched on his face. But he stayed quiet, ready to listen.

Neela lay down on the ground, hands behind her head. "It was really the only thing that we had in common. I disagreed with his politics, with his attitude toward people, how he ran the company, the way I was supposed to worship God... Just about everything. After three perfect children, they had me, the surprise kid. Even as a child, I remember Dad and me not being able to see things eye to eye. The only thing we had in common was rugby. Then it stopped being enough. After one argument too many, I decided I couldn't stay in his house and follow his rules anymore. So I left."

"Rieann thinks it was because of Laura."

She nodded. "Her coming into my life when she did made the decision to go easier. I was the only one living at home when Dad started dating her. He never once asked how I felt about her coming into our house. He basically forced her on me. Then, one night, he insisted she stay for dinner, and she chose to sit in my mother's chair.

"My. Dead. Mother's. Chair, Blake."

Neela took a deep breath. The anger from that evening, so long ago, threatened to return. "Laura didn't know what she was doing—how could she?—but when she sat there, I saw red. I said things that hurt us all. I should be sorry, but I'm not."

"How old were you when you left?" Blake asked.

"Seventeen. I had enough money saved up to leave. I stayed at Mano's place while he was on tour with the National Team, but I knew I couldn't stay there for long. He's really close to Dad. I wanted to get away from the South Island as fast as possible. Then it was odd jobs here and there for a few years. Got by. Joined a bike club and met Kyle."

"So, that's how he became part of your life."

Neela laughed softly. "Yeah. Want to hear something ironic? It was Kyle who encouraged me to try out for the Go for Gold campaign. He knew I had played before and was amused by the opportunity. I wasn't interested at first."

"What changed your mind?"

"This is going to sound weird, but I kept hearing my mother's voice saying I should give it a go. She loved the Games. Always followed them whenever they came on. Then, when I made it past the first round, Kyle was all into it. He helped pay for my training and hired a nutritionist so I'd be ready for the tryouts. I foolishly thought he did it out of love."

"I think that was a fair assumption. Weren't you two together by then?"

"Yes." She paused. *Do I tell him more? Maybe he'll realize there's no need to think of the future.* She forged ahead despite the sinking feeling in her stomach. "He's here. He wants his money back."

Blake angled his body to face Neela, and his dark eyes mirrored his confusion. "He tracked you down to the South Island because of money?"

"It's important to most people. Not everyone earns what you do."

"You don't need to be rich to have a sense of what's right or wrong. In this situation, a person with integrity doesn't ask for their money back. Would you?"

Neela shook her head, and whatever Blake saw in her face softened his countenance. "Do you have the money? I can cover whatever you need," he said.

"It's all right."

"It'll get him off your back. You can file a restraining order and start living your life without looking back. No strings, I promise. This is what friends do. We look out for one another."

Neela reached for Blake's hand and squeezed it. "Thanks. I have enough now. The advance from our ad work has given me some breathing space financially."

He seemed to consider that information. She watched him

clasp and unclasp his hands, marveling at how strong they were. In all the years she had seen him play, she didn't recall him ever dropping the ball in a play.

"Why didn't you leave him? When he began to hurt you?" he asked quietly.

This time, she remained silent.

A few minutes later, she sat up—knees now underneath her — and reached for more grass. She rubbed them aggressively between her fingers then released the shriveled blades to the wind. She raised her fingertips to her nose.

The scent of fresh grass kept her sane. She knew what to do on the pitch. Everything made sense there. Get the ball to the goal line. Stop the other team from doing the same. Simple. Why couldn't the rest of her life mimic the clarity of her sport?

She had kept the details of her relationship with Kyle to herself for so long. It was the biggest mistake of her life to love a man who was so vile. She was ashamed of those feelings now, as genuine as they had been.

Only Mano knew about the abuse, but he wasn't privy to everything. He had never met Kyle, and Neela hoped he never would. Her teammates suspected she had had a boyfriend before she signed with RugNZ, but hers wouldn't have been the only relationship to end because of training commitments. Corrine had never known; Leila had never asked.

"He came into my life when I wanted to be loved again," she began cautiously. "I'd never felt such a need to be with someone before. He made me feel like I was the center of his universe. And I liked that feeling. A lot."

Blake hadn't moved. His silence encouraged her to continue.

"Believe it or not, for a long time, I didn't think what he did to me was wrong. I found excuses for his behavior. When he first slapped me, it was because I had provoked him. When he called me names, it was because he was too drunk. And slowly, before I knew it, I started to believe I deserved how he treated me, that what he thought of me was really who I was."

"Darl…"

Blake reached up to wipe a single tear from her cheek. She turned her head slightly. She didn't want to see Blake's disappointment in her. She took a deep breath and continued.

"I thought that if I really loved Kyle, I had to accept him completely. I wanted to be like Mum: loving all of us despite our faults. She was my example of unconditional love. I wanted to be that person for Kyle.

"When he began to hurt me, I rationalized that it was because he couldn't stop himself and that it was my responsibility to help him control those urges. Because that's what you're supposed to do when you love someone, isn't it? Stick with them through thick and thin?"

Neela closed her eyes as the memories of Kyle's blows came rushing back: the time when she'd come home later than expected; when she'd argued that her rugby training was more important than having his mates over late in the evening; when she'd wanted to visit Mano…

"How long did you live with him?"

"Eight months. And I hadn't planned on leaving him. But one night, Kyle just went crazy. He drank too much, and I was fifteen minutes late coming back from training. This time, after he was done, I couldn't get up on my own. I knew I needed help."

"And you called Mano," Blake said.

"I don't want your pity," she said. "I put myself in that position, and I got myself out of it. It will never happen to me again."

"You're the strongest woman, I know, Neela Smyth. But sometimes, even the strong need to rest, and there's no shame in that," he said roughly. "You don't need to face him alone. I promise I'll be there for you, and you know I don't break my promises."

CHAPTER 13

NEELA KEPT THE RIM OF HER CAP LOW AS SHE HIT THE PAVEMENT. She hadn't slept well the night before, but not for the expected reasons. She was prepared for the mental exhaustion that came with being in the same room as her father. Instead, her tossing and turning had come from wondering what Blake thought of her, given her inability to stop talking. She had said more than she should have.

He had left for Auckland early that morning, but not before waking her up with a phone call.

"What the…"

"Just making sure you don't miss out on your run."

"Blake, I have an alarm clock."

"I know, but I wanted to hear your voice before I left."

Neela covered her eyes with her free hand. "What are you doing, Blake?"

"Being honest. No lies between us, remember?"

She didn't even say goodbye before she hung up on him. She didn't want his honesty. She didn't want his trust. She didn't want him caring for her.

She breathed deeper and increased her pace, not caring that she was using too much energy too quickly. She wanted to feel the burn in her legs. What she didn't want was to feel anything in her heart.

But I wanted to hear your voice before I left.

She shook her head and turned a corner she usually didn't include in her run. The incline would be a physical demand on her that she didn't need.

She tried to rationalize away her angst from hearing his voice this morning, from knowing he now knew more about her than anyone else.

He was going to be in Auckland all week. Besides meetings with RugNZ, he was representing the National Team at a couple of charities. Then there was an endless number of public appearances for sponsors in the build-up to Christmas. Next time she'd see him would be a few days before Christmas, in the same field they had been at last night, to film the commercial. Not for a date.

She was starting to depend on him.

"I only promised five dates," she said out loud. "Five dates. Five *fake* dates."

Even to her own ears, they were hollow affirmations. There was nothing fake about the relationship they were building.

There was a relationship between them. There always had been.

When she reached a clearing, she slowed her run, then stopped altogether. She might not have felt the exertion, but her body had responded accordingly: increased heartbeat, sweat dampening her skin. She inhaled and exhaled deeply as she scanned the park, which was far from empty. Her eyes were drawn to an elderly couple holding hands as they strolled. The woman suddenly laughed at whatever her partner said in her ear. He, in turn, responded by pulling her hand to his lips.

Neela frowned. A deep longing for a future she never thought she wanted surfaced.

"I don't need anyone," she reminded herself. "I'm strong on my own."

She took one last look at the couple before starting her run home.

When she entered her unit, she saw a small wrapped box on the dining table. She pulled out the card that the box was sitting on.

Don't open it until Christmas! I'll call when I arrive home. Merry Christmas! Love, Leila

From the shape, it was either the latest video game or a CD. Neela had slipped her own present to Leila into the latter's handbag last night. They had said it was to be a no-pressie-Christmas. Obviously, neither of them could be trusted.

Leila, too, had left this morning for Auckland. She wanted to spend a few extra days with her family before the team went to training camp in preparation for their next competition in Sydney.

No Blake; no Leila; no team training.

A whole week without commitments.

Alone.

The way Neela preferred things to be, the only way to keep her heart safe. So why did she feel like crying?

* * *

Blake ignored Scott's protest that they should talk on the flight to Auckland. He put on his earphones to let *La Bohéme* flood his senses, but it didn't. All he could see was Neela's eyes from last night.

Absent of fire.

Full of regret and pain.

Whatever anger he felt toward Kyle, it was nothing

compared to the sense of despair when he realized he couldn't erase all the hurt from her past. It was always going to be a part of her.

Blake looked out the window. The rugged coastline of the South Island was now behind them. The sea they were flying over was dark and seemingly calm, its dangers hidden when viewed from up so high. Just like Neela, Blake thought. Calm and controlled on the outside but full of turmoil inside. And all because she had trusted the wrong man.

Whatever it takes, no matter how long, he vowed. He'd be there for her until she was ready to trust again. She deserved better.

Scott nudged him. "You are ready, aren't you? For this meeting?"

"Yes."

"Because this *will* be a talk about the captainship."

"You sound more nervous about this than I am. What's the matter, mate? Don't think I'm up for the job?"

"No. I mean yes. I mean…"

Blake put his earphones back on. "Relax. Enjoy the flight. If I don't get the captaincy, it's back to economy for you, mate."

He *should* be more nervous, but being injured these last couple of months had only reinforced what Mano had drilled into him early in his career: there was a lot that was out of their hands.

Three hours later, he had to once again calm down his agent. "Don't skip, Scott."

"I can't help it. Mate, you're the new captain of the National Team!"

Blake smiled. Scott looked giddy with excitement, taking the news delivered to them a mere half an hour ago with a loud exclamation and a fist pump.

"You got what you wanted!" Scott said. "What you and Neela have been doing this last month has worked!"

"I also happen to be a pretty good rugby player."

"Whatever." Scott smiled wider, his dismissal in good fun.

He thumped Blake's back, stepped in front of him and grabbed his client's upper arms. His voice was suddenly uncharacteristically emotional. "You've wanted this since we were both in uni. I'm proud of you."

"Thanks, Scott. I sometimes think you're a moron, but I've also never questioned that you'd look out for me."

"Why aren't you more excited? Never mind, I'll be excited for the two of us. National Team captain! I wonder if we can get more money out of the next ad campaign."

"Is that all this means to you?"

"I'm kidding! Are you going to tell anyone?"

"No. Nothing's official until the start of the year."

"Not even Neela? There's no real reason to continue being seen together."

"She promised me five dates. There are two more to go," Blake said automatically, not breaking his stride.

Scott stopped walking. His voice echoed down the hallway. "Wait a minute. Are you saying what I think you're saying?" Blake had reached the stairs when Scott caught up with him again. "Hang on, Blake. Is this serious?"

"I don't know what you mean."

"When Lindsay said she was going to break up with you, you shrugged and bought her flowers to wish her well. You never pursue a relationship. I've given you a reason to end a charade that you initially didn't want to take part in, and you tell me you want more?"

Blake stopped at the bottom of the stairs. RugNZ's home office was busy despite the time of the year. It was just a week until Christmas; international rugby season was over while club rugby had yet to begin. But this place never seemed to stop. A constant flow of people coming and going at RugNZ was the norm. Many were familiar faces. Most weren't.

He loved this place. Early in his career, when he was first getting used to being part of the National Team, he would walk the hallways wondering behind which closed door a group of people would meet to decide when his dream to represent his country would be granted…or denied.

Today, that group of people, also behind a closed door, had given him a responsibility he had secretly hope for to since he was a teenager. He should be sharing this news with his family immediately. Instead, he didn't want anyone to know. It might mean Neela would think her role in his life was over, that she could walk away, her 'debt' to him paid.

Blake turned abruptly to face Scott, causing the slighter man to bump into his chest. "No one is to know, Scott, especially Neela. Understand?"

Scott frowned, unused to Blake's tone. "It's worth celebrating. She won't say a word."

"I'm not ready to let her go. I'm going to need my last two dates to convince her that we deserve to be together. Not a word, Scott. I mean it."

* * *

Neela was reading the packaging of her frozen dinner when her phone rang.

"Darl?"

"Blake? You really shouldn't call me that."

"Why aren't you going to Rieann's for Christmas?"

Neela's eyes widened. "How did you know that?"

"Mano sent me a message asking if I knew why."

Neela groaned. "Don't tell me. Rieann asked Mano to ask you."

"You got it."

"Nobody's business, including yours, Blake. Don't you have someone you need to meet for dinner or something? I thought you had a fairly packed schedule."

"Does this mean you're going to be alone at Christmas?"

"I like being alone for Christmas."

"Liar."

Neela's tempered flared. "You don't know me."

"Darl..."

"And stop calling me that!" She turned off the phone. *Damn it.* This was why she didn't tell people anything about herself. They start thinking they knew her, that they could decide what was best for her.

Her mood didn't improve the next morning, but she was determined to concentrate on preparing for the next series in Sydney. With the start of the club rugby season just a couple of months away, she expected Blake to have less time for her. All the pros would be back in the gym, and club workouts would commence. *I should be the last thing on his mind.*

Yes, once Blake Stanton, rugby superstar, was back in full rugby training mode, she could go back to being a figure from his past. Two more dates.

She went straight to the gym, mentally going through the checklist of her morning workout routine. A light cardio on the bike to warm up, then weights. She picked the exercise bike in the far corner, climbed on and quickly put on her earphones. The first notes of her playlist began.

She winced, stopped pedaling then sighed. *Bastard has me listening to arias when I work out now.*

The next unexpected reminder of her fake boyfriend's impact on her life was seeing his car in front of her apartment building. She stared at first, second-guessing her 20/20 vision. It couldn't be his car, but it was. She knew he was in Auckland—he and two players from other clubs had been featured in today's papers— so the last person she expected to see inside was Tim. He had his cap lowered, and he looked asleep.

Neela knocked sharply on the driver's side window. "Oi!"

Tim cursed, his eyes wild. He glared at her as he lowered the window. "I know you could have woken me up in a less shocking manner."

"Why are you here?"

Tim reached over to the passenger seat, picked up a small

brown paper bag and handed it to Neela. She turned her head slightly, suspicious but curious as she pulled open the bag. Eyebrows raised, she picked up part of its contents and stared at the pink and yellow foil wrapper. "You're delivering Choc Cherries? For me?"

Tim shook his head and yawned. "Yes. From Blake. He said he's sorry. He's also worried since you haven't returned his calls."

She leaned on the car window. "You're a Ph.D. candidate at the university. I think I read somewhere that you're supposed to be one of the great minds of our country. Why are you running errands for a rugby player?"

"I'm not. I'm doing a friend a favor."

"That's quite a favor."

"He's not in the habit of asking. The last favor he asked was for a room at the Meriton last year." Tim raised his eyebrows to emphasize his next point. "For you."

Neela sighed. "Okay. You've delivered the lollies. You can go now."

"Why aren't you going to your sister's for Christmas?"

Neela's jaw dropped. "You have got to be kidding me."

"Mano sent me a message."

Neela walked away before she could hear more. She had reached the security door of her building when she paused and looked over her shoulder to see Tim still watching her. She shook her head slightly, annoyed at herself for what she was going to do next.

"You hungry?" she yelled out.

Tim was out of the car before she could blink.

He insisted on making a salad to accompany the sandwiches she offered. After they ate, she held out Blake's bag of apologies.

Tim studied the wrapped chocolate in his hand. "He really likes you, Neela. I've never seen him so confused."

"We're friends. That's it."

"You two look like you're having fun on your dates."

Neela pointed a finger at Tim. "This was all your idea. You were there when we agreed to make it all up. It's all pretend."

Tim shrugged. "He asked me to pick up a bag of your favorite lollies. The scientist in me considers this credible proof that whatever he feels for you is not fake."

"It needs to be," Neela said softly. "I'm not good for him. We're not good for each other. He needs someone who can be there for him, to take care of him. I have to take care of myself."

"He's one of the best people I know, Neela."

There was a tenderness in Tim's tone that made Neela look up. Tim took off his glasses and wiped them with the bottom of his shirt. "He was the first person I came out to. I don't know why, but I knew he'd never judge me."

"Are you in love with him?"

"No." Tim smiled indulgently. "But I do love him. He insisted on coming with me when I decided to tell my family I'm gay. I'll never forget Mitch's face. He automatically looked at Blake as if Blake had had something to do with it. But Blake didn't turn away. He didn't deny anything. He just stared Mitch down, as if he was daring my brother to say something. I'll never forget that moment. Blake confronted his childhood hero, a man he admires and worships, for me. So, if you're at all wondering how to stop him from caring about you, let me just say he's going to, whether or not you want those feelings."

Neela buried her head in her hands. "We're too different."

Tim snorted. "I beg to differ. You two are more alike than you think, but I'm not going to argue with you. Think what you want. I know what I see. But, hey, if you don't have any plans for Christmas…"

"I'm all right. Why does everyone think I need to be with people on Christmas? I'm just fine being alone, thank you very much."

"How about Boxing Day? Mitch throws a barbie every year. Come on. Mano usually goes to that, but since he's away, you can represent the family."

"I don't think so."

"Here's your chance to talk to Mitch Molloy, Connor Dane and Liana Murphy. Consider it research in preparation for the next tournament. Two rugby legends and the woman who brought New Zealand to the top ten of football's world ranking. Sports royalty, Neela." Tim grinned, waggling his eyebrows rapidly.

She smiled reluctantly. "Thank you, but..."

"Blake's bringing Lulu, so she'll distract him from focusing only on you," he added.

Neela shot him a look as she leaned back in her chair. It could be their fourth date. Then only one more to go, and they could go back to things as they had been—connected but not involved. And slowly, she could get used to not having his hand to hold.

As if sensing her hesitation, Tim stood up to leave. "Good. I'll let Mitch and Liana know. But will you please call Blake? His messages are clogging up my phone. I'll see you next week at the shoot."

"What? Are you going to be there?"

Tim nodded as he reached for the door handle. "Oh, yeah. You tackling Blake, and it's going to be documented for all eternity? I wouldn't miss it."

"Maybe you're not quite the best friend Blake thinks you are."

Tim smiled as he headed out the door. "Someone has to keep him grounded. And Neela, this thing between you and Blake—don't think about it too much, eh? Trust your feelings."

After clearing the dishes, Neela brought her laptop to the dining table. She paused, then typed "Blake and Neela" into the search engine.

Within seconds, a list of articles and links to images appeared. She scrolled through them and marveled at how one short month of 'dating' could generate so much attention. Leila had mentioned seeing Neela and Blake featured in various magazines, but Neela hadn't bothered looking. Seeing herself in print was something she avoided, anyway.

But there it was, a history of their relationship going back to the video of when they were twelve: pictures of them at his parents' party, pictures of her visiting him on Club grounds, them at the Esplanade, and with Lulu eating ice cream.

Neela clicked to Blake's public Twitter account. He had half a million followers. Her eyes widened when she saw his latest tweet, posted just fifteen minutes ago.

He was standing at a sports shop with excited fans surrounding him. All of them were holding up the latest line of rugby kits for the Club. He'd tweeted,

@BlakeNZRug: **Would a certain beautiful rugby player like this for Christmas?**

Neela scrolled down through the responses. Most said yes, some said no. Then she caught Leila's reaction:

@LeilaF_Rugby: **Yes, but add something sparkling that comes in a small box!**

Her tweet had garnered a thousand heart emojis. Neela laughed at her flatmate's audacity. Everybody believed this relationship between her and Blake. She scrolled farther, then stopped at the picture Blake had taken which had started this whole thing. She looked relaxed, happy, and content.

She sighed. What was going on with her? This was supposed

to be a simple way to pay back a favor. So why did it feel like she'd been on an emotional rollercoaster with no end in sight?

She reached for her phone and began to type a message. Then she changed her mind and instead pressed the call button for Blake.

"Darl?"

She pursed her lips to stop from smiling, but that didn't stop the warmth that was growing within her. "You really need to stop calling me that."

"Can't help it. It's what I think for you."

"Thanks for the lollies."

"I'm sorry. I shouldn't have assumed anything."

"Are you still at the promo?"

"Stepped away for a bit. How did you know?"

"Saw your Twitter feed. I don't need a new kit, by the way."

Blake laughed. "Okay. No kit."

"Or anything sparkling in a small black box."

"Tin of Milo?"

It was her turn to laugh. "That will do."

"I'll call when I get back."

"I'll just see you at the school field."

"I can pick you up."

"No need. I was going to spend the night at Rieann's. We'll head to the school together."

"Did she manage to get a role as an extra?"

"Yeah. Honestly, the way she was going on about it, you'd think *she* was going to be the star of the ad."

Blake laughed, and this time she didn't stop the smile that settled on her face.

"Are we good?"

Neela sighed. "Yes."

"Then good night, darl."

"Good night, Blake."

CHAPTER 14

A week later, after dinner, Trey shooed her out of the kitchen. "It's nice outside. Why don't you and Rieann take your tea outside? I'll have the kids finish up here. They always behave better when their famous aunty visits."

"They're good kids, Trey," Neela said.

"Yeah, well, like I said, when their aunty visits. David! Jennie! Dishes!"

Rieann wrapped her arms around Trey's waist. "Thanks, darl. Dinner was good. Interesting salad."

Trey kissed Rieann quickly. "Keeping it clean and raw."

"Kids didn't like it."

"Tough."

Neela grabbed a bowl of fruit from the counter and followed her sister, who carried a tray with their tea, to the back of the house. The sky was just turning a deep orange as the sisters sat on the cold concrete steps that led to a large backyard.

Neela held the warmed mug in her hands, her eyes drawn to the changing canvas of color above them. "Remember how Mum would have us do this? Just sit out in the backyard and watch the day disappear?"

Rieann nodded and took a sip from her mug. "Yeah, just her and her girls."

"I don't remember us talking."

"We didn't need to," Rieann said. "Being together was what that was about."

"She sometimes sang."

"Yeah. Always badly."

Neela bowed her head slightly as a chuckle escaped. "You're right there. Mum couldn't quite carry a tune."

"Remember how Dad tried to look like he enjoyed it at Christmas time?"

"Yeah." Neela looked at the dark brew in her hands before she faced Rieann. "He did love her, didn't he?"

Rieann took a deep breath. "He did, very much. In falling in love again, he kept his promise to Mum. She asked him to do what she'd asked you, me, Joe and Sam to do, to keep living after she died."

"It didn't take him long, though."

"I think he knew what he'd lost. And when a chance to be happy appeared again, he didn't think twice. He took it." Rieann sipped her tea. "Dad's always trusted his feelings. It's served him well for most of his life."

Neela exhaled. "What if Dad and I can't ever get along again, Rieann? He hates me."

"He doesn't hate you. You're his child. He'll always love you. Now, the two of you getting on—who knows, eh? But you showing up for the party, that was important. It's what families do. We're there for the important stuff."

"How does he feel about you taking the day off for the filming tomorrow?"

Rieann grinned. "Not happy, but I'm entitled to my shot at fame. Speaking of which, it's best we turn in soon. Are you supposed to check in as early as us extras?"

"Six?"

"Yeah. You sure you don't want to drive up with me?"

"I'm good."

"Not grabbing a lift with Blake?"

Neela knew that wasn't really the question Rieann was asking. "It's complicated."

Her sister squeezed her shoulder as she rose. "Only if you want it to be," Rieann said softly.

The next morning, despite leaving the house and arriving on time, they were far from the first to reach the school.

"Wow! This is bigger than I expected," Rieann said as they walked toward the field. Local police were directing traffic, and pop-up tents were everywhere. The crew was busy setting up and checking expensive looking gear and equipment. Every other person seemed to have a clipboard or wore headphones.

"I guess I go there," said Rieann. She pointed to a tent that had a handwritten sign which said EXTRAS propped on a chair. "I'll see you later? Good luck. You'll do fine."

Neela cracked her neck and rolled her shoulders, scanning the other tents for an idea of where she should go. Her eyes finally settled on Scott, who was standing near the entrance to the field with a phone to his ear.

He smiled when he saw her. "Neela! Right on time!" He kissed her on the cheek. "Let me introduce you to Martin Walker, the director. You've read the script?"

"Yeah. Seems easy enough, especially since I don't have to say anything."

"They just want your face, sweetheart."

"Scott, if we're going to work together after this, you need to know that I don't go by 'sweetheart.' My name will do."

Scott blinked. "Understood. Sorry. It wasn't meant as disrespect."

"None taken, but I'm glad we're clear on it."

"Neela!"

Both of them turned to see Blake walking toward them. Tim was a few steps behind him, a thermos in one hand. He waved at Neela with the other.

"I love it when you're punctual, mate," Scott said.

Blake ignored his agent and leaned in toward Neela. She met him halfway, placing her hands on his shoulders. "You smell good, darl," he whispered before grazing his lips softly against her cheek.

She smiled before glaring at a smirking Tim. "What's your problem? Loads of people are watching us, and we're still supposed to be dating," she hissed.

"Uh-huh. Whatever you say, Neela." Tim chuckled.

Scott ushered Blake and Neela toward a short, bespectacled man wearing a wide-brimmed hat that had seen better days. He looked up from his clipboard when they got close. "Ah, here's the two stars! You're on time. Good. I'm Martin Walker. I take it you've both seen the script? No questions? Good, good. We'll film the scene at the picnic bench first. Should be simple enough. Just smile like you're in love. Yeah? Good. All the extras should be ready in about an hour. But before makeup, Matt over there will go through the choreography for the tackle-scene."

"Pardon?" "Choreography?" Neela and Blake asked in unison.

"That wasn't discussed," Blake said. "What's wrong with her really tackling me?"

"There'll be a tackle, but…"

"It won't be real," Blake finished.

Simultaneously, Neela and Blake folded their arms across their chests. She tilted her head slightly. "You're the director, and this is your commercial. But I don't think we need someone to show us how to tackle without getting hurt."

"Look, we can't really choreograph this," Blake said. "People who have seen us play will know we're holding back."

"Your ankle—," Scott interrupted, his forehead furrowed.

"Is fine. If I can't handle a tackle I know is coming, then I have no business getting back on the pitch." Blake turned to Neela. "You're up to do this for real, aren't you? Like when we were twelve."

"No worries. Like when we were twelve."

"I don't know if that's such a good idea," Scott said. "We should stick to the choreography. The writers…"

"Scott, any rugby fan watching this will know if I gave her the tackle," Blake said. "You need to do better research on your clients, mate." He nodded at her, his dimple appearing. "This isn't your ordinary rugby player. This is Neela Smyth. She doesn't let anyone just pass her."

He said it as a statement of fact. He believed in her capabilities, in her strength, in her determination.

She could no longer deny that here in front of her was someone who truly cared for her. But she didn't want to be important to him. Not Blake, because she could easily fall in love with someone who believed in her so completely.

She couldn't go down that road again, so it was up to her to make sure she could control whatever this was. She needed to be responsible, to keep things simple between them. Like when they were kids.

She shook her head. "Just friends," she whispered to herself.

"Pardon? Did you say something?"

"No."

"What's the matter? The fire's died down in those pretty eyes, Neela." Blake took a step closer to her, ensuring that their conversation would remain private. "You've taken down bigger women than me. You know it's not about the size."

Neela looked up. "It's about the technique and the heart."

His smile widened. "Mano?"

"Who else?" She returned his smile.

"Well, whether it's choreographed or not, it doesn't affect too much of what I do," Martin said. "Let me know what you two think could happen for this shot. I'll decide if it will work with what Pastall's are looking for. Fair enough? Why don't we get you both to makeup, and we'll start with the other scenes?"

What would be less than twenty seconds of screen time took a couple of hours to shoot. There was the shot of them walking off the field together and approaching the picnic tables. Then there was the scene of someone placing the Pastall lollies in front of them, ending with Blake unwrapping one and offering it to her. It was simple enough on paper, but Martin proved to be a stickler for details.

Most of their childhood friends had apparently signed up for roles as extras, and in between filming, Neela and Blake found themselves being reacquainted with faces and names neither of them had seen or heard in over a decade.

During an early lunch, they discussed two simple action sequences to present to Martin, and after a brief conversation with the Pastall's representative, they decided to go for a shot of a straightforward tackle. After a few practices and time to allow Martin to position the lights and cameras, they were ready for the actual shoot.

"Right. Let's do this for real," Blake said to Neela. She nodded, and he smiled, squeezing her upper arm before he turned to Martin. "Get this on the first go, Martin. If you miss it, I promise you, whatever we do afterward will never be as good. I'm coming at her at full speed."

Neela suddenly felt nervous. *On the first go?* "Blake—"

"What's the matter? Is a silver medalist afraid of a world champion?"

The nervous first-time actress disappeared, and the competitor returned. "You wish," Neela murmured, hands on her hips.

Blake grinned. "You know how to play. You know where to go."

"Shut up. Don't tell me how to do my job."

His laughter followed her as she walked to the marker. She could hear Martin in the background yelling last-minute instructions about light and angles. She glanced over her shoulder. Most of the extras from the morning shoot had chosen to stay and watch.

More eyes on her.

"Like when we were twelve!" Blake yelled, now several meters away. He casually tossed the ball in his hand, an easy grin on his face, and nodded encouragingly.

She took a deep breath and closed her eyes. *Stop thinking,* she commanded herself. *Be that scared-of-nothing twelve-year-old who dominated the field over every rugby player at school, both boys and girls. Forget the cameras. It's about technique and heart.*

"Action!"

She reached down to touch the grass and brought the scent back to her nose. She inhaled deeply, then kept her body low and turned her shoulders slightly in. She watched Blake's feet and gauged the speed he'd reach in a matter of seconds. She knew he'd be true to his word, that this would be real. When he was within range, she launched herself at his body automatically, and her arms encircled his waist while she used the full strength of her legs to pull him down.

She heard a gasp from the sidelines as their bodies hit the ground simultaneously.

She automatically rolled around to stand up and reached for the still-lying-down Blake. He took her arm but didn't let go once he was on his feet. Instead, he pulled her close to him, their bodies now in full contact. Her hands were splayed against his chest as he snuck one arm around her waist, holding her as close to him as they'd ever been.

Heat exploded where her body was touching his. Everything and everyone else disappeared. Had the director yelled "Cut!" yet?

It didn't matter. She was lost in his eyes.

"You did that way better than when you were twelve."

She felt goosebumps erupt on her arms as he tucked loose hair behind her ears, a lingering caress behind an earlobe she hadn't known was so sensitive.

She was still breathing hard from the exertion, or so she tried to convince herself. "Thanks. You're heavier than when you were twelve."

Blake threw his head back in a loud laugh, then kissed her on the temple. He covered her shoulders with his arm as they walked toward the enthusiastic group of spectators on the sidelines.

Martin came running toward them. "That was good! Very good! You got some of the PAs sighing with that last look you two gave each other. You were right, Blake. We got the shot we need. I think we're done in record time. Money saved makes everyone happy." Martin turned to Neela. "You're a natural on screen. I wouldn't be surprised if this is the first of many commercials for you, young lady."

"Thanks. Are you sure you don't need us to do this again? Because I'd be happy to give it another go."

"No, I don't think we could recreate that chemistry again. It's really good! The rep from Pastall's loved what we got. We're good! It's all good!"

Blake pulled Neela closer and kissed the top of her head. "You heard the man. Sometimes the real thing only needs to happen once."

Neela turned her head toward Blake's chest. Her arms were somehow already around his waist. "We're still talking about the commercial, aren't we?"

"Yes, but it applies to a lot in life, don't you think?"

"Kiss her, already!"

Neela glared at Tim, who had his phone focused on them.

"And hurry up!" Tim continued. "I want to get the first viral video of the year. Blake beat me last year."

There were a lot of hugs and final requests for autographs and selfies from the crowd when filming was complete. Amidst the happy chaos, something made Neela look toward the far end of the field. Her throat tightened, and a shiver ran down her spine. A lone figure was leaning against the last post of the fence. His face wasn't distinguishable from that distance, but she'd recognize his posture anywhere. He was staring at her. Then, as if he was satisfied that she had seen him, he turned and walked toward a motorbike parked close by.

Kyle.

"What's wrong?" Blake's voice interrupted her thoughts.

"What do you mean?"

"You tensed up." He searched behind her. "He's here, isn't he?"

Neela broke out of Blake's hold. "I don't know what you're talking about."

He caught up with her in half a step, his face a study of controlled emotions. She knew that face. It was the face he had on the field, ready to battle, determined to win.

"The last time you looked like that was after our run last year. You suddenly went stiff and blocked me out," he said.

"Forget about it, Blake."

He pulled on her arm to stop her walking. But he didn't hold on, allowing her the choice to keep moving. She swallowed, crossed her arms but kept her gaze down.

"Neela, you can trust me. Talk to me. Something made you freeze up."

She sighed. "I've got to go. The girls have a catch-up tonight."

He called after her. "Call me when you get home. I just want to know you're safe."

Neela bit down on her lip. She'd heard his concern. She nodded but avoided his eyes.

She started jogging to the trailer where her clothes were. The magic of the afternoon was gone. Her little step back into a time when life had been near-perfect was over. That part of her life was done, never to be reclaimed again.

But that wasn't quite true. A different past had emerged, and she knew he was waiting for her.

Fifteen minutes later, after quick goodbyes to family, she got on her bike. Surrounded by fans, she felt Blake's eyes on her as she rode past him. Judging by the size of the crowd, she expected him to be there for at least another half an hour.

He wasn't the only one who was watching her leave. Tim, leaning against the hood of Blake's car, also studied her movements. She raised a hand, and he returned her acknowledgment with a nod. Then she revved the engine and rode away from the school.

The sound of Kyle's bike coming up behind her wasn't unexpected. He passed her with a quick look. A hand signal indicated he wanted—expected—her to follow him. Her jaw clenched, and adrenaline roared through her body. She heard the faster pace of her breathing, its uneven tempo echoing through her brain.

She revved her engine and rode to his side. This time she met his gaze and shook her head.

No more.

She was never going to follow him. They needed to talk but on her terms.

She went ahead of him but kept her bike at a speed that showed him she wasn't going to outrun him. He wasn't the kind of man who liked following a woman. Even when they rode in a group, he was at the front of the pack. She used to think it was because he was a natural leader. Now she knew better.

He came up next to her, then moved his bike ahead by a couple of meters. She didn't push; she was mentally calculating a place to stop so they could have the conversation he wanted. It had to be in public. A sober Kyle was intimidating, but a drunk Kyle was a trap.

She spotted an exit that led to a convenience store not too far off the main street. It was popular with day-trippers and was seldom empty. She edged her bike up a little and raised her hand to indicated she was going to go off the highway.

As she'd hoped, cars were lined up at the pumping stations. A couple was pulled off to the side, their occupants standing by, drinks in hand. Neela rode to a corner that was private but not isolated. Her screams could be heard if Kyle tried anything.

He was right behind her but chose to park in front of her, blocking any chance of an escape.

She held the cry that came close to spilling out. Her hands shook. She clasped them together, wanting to control that visible sign of her fear. She shoved them into the pockets of her jacket when she couldn't stop the shaking. Helmet still on, she watched Kyle remove his. He smirked as he leaned over the front of his bike, but she expected the eyes hidden behind sunglasses to be cold and assessing.

"Surprised you didn't try to outrun me," Kyle said.

She shrugged. "No point. You were always the better rider than me. You'd catch up."

"Glad you remembered that."

"What do you want, Kyle? My final payment isn't due for another week. You know I'm never late."

"I was on a bit of a holiday. Between jobs. You know how it is. Saw you were filming a commercial. Big bucks in that, isn't it?"

"You're getting most of it, if that's what you're asking."

"I'm not a cheat. I'm only asking for what's mine."

Neela bit back a string of epithets, fear and rage building inside her. "You're getting what's yours. You had no business being at the school today."

"The papers said it was an open set. I wasn't breaking any laws. When did you get so uptight about things, eh, little one?"

"Don't call me that."

Kyle laughed and straightened up. He looked around before putting his helmet back on. Then he turned to her, his voice now low. "I'll call you whatever I want. And I'll do whatever the hell I want. Piss off, Neela. Don't get it into your little head that you decide things for me, understand?"

He made a point of spinning his back wheel enough to leave a blanket of dust in her face.

She remained on her bike after Kyle disappeared from her sight. Fear rooted her to the spot. The taste of blood on her bottom lip started a shaking that transferred from her hands to the rest of her body. Then it was hard to breathe.

She reached up to pull off her helmet and threw it onto the ground as she fell off her bike. The bike toppled from the suddenness of her actions, its loud thud capturing the attention of those around.

The voices that accompanied the concerned faces of strangers seemed so far away. She stared at them blankly, unable to understand the words they were offering.

"You all right?"

"She looks like she's in shock."

"Should we call the ambulance, Mum?"

"No!" Neela cried. "It's all right. I just didn't have enough to drink. Sorry. I'm dehydrated. That was silly of me."

"Matt, get her some water!" instructed the woman.

A bottle was thrust in front of Neela in a matter of seconds. From the corner of her eye, she watched a couple of young guys lift her bike up effortlessly.

"Maybe you should get you inside, darl," said the same woman.

Neela met her eyes. Kind, gentle brown eyes... *like Mum's.* Tears sprung up, but she brushed them away quickly. "No, no, I'm all right." She accepted the arm of one of the younger men. "I'm sorry for the trouble. It just hit me."

The woman nodded. "Yeah, dehydration can do that to you. One minute you're all right..."

"And the next, you've fallen off your bike," said the younger of the two men.

"Well, you make sure you take a breather before you start your ride again. Have you got far to go?" asked the woman.

Neela shook her head. "Only another half an hour."

"Well, that's good, then. But drink up. You gave us quite the scare!" She studied Neela, a small smile forming on her face. "Your color's coming back. Promise me you'll sit for a bit before you get on that bike again."

Neela smiled weakly. "I will. Thank you for your help. You're very kind."

"Of course, darl."

She kept her word, but it wasn't a choice to stay put. She just couldn't move.

CHAPTER 15

IT HAD BEEN A CRAP START TO THE NEW YEAR. ACTUALLY, THAT wasn't entirely true. In a month, he'd be named the new captain of the National Team. The Club team was looking particularly strong with the new signings. Pre-season training would start in a week, and his ankle seemed as good as new.

But he still felt like crap ever since Boxing Day.

Blake thought of the picture Leila had posted on her Twitter account this morning. It was of the Sevens team on their way to a stadium in Sydney for the start of a tournament. Neela was staring into the camera from the back row of the bus, her eyes bright. No fire in them yet; that would come when she got on the pitch.

He shouldn't be annoyed that Neela continued to avoid being on social media. It was probably the saner option in a life that was becoming far too digitalized. But how was he supposed to know what she was up to if she never posted anything? He was left with following her via the team's official account and those of her teammates.

His brothers would have laughing fits if they knew how desperate he was for news of her. Blake smiled as he remembered her face when she'd opened his promised Christmas gift of

Milo tins. If he hadn't realized how much he loved her before, he would have recognized the emotion in that instant.

It hit him so hard that he almost forgot to breathe. She had the widest smile, and her beautiful brown eyes had lit up as a deep laugh erupted. Lulu had caught the infectious sound and joined the giggling. It had been a moment of pure joy that he knew he'd remember all his life.

Neela had him, and he didn't care. He knew he had to give her space. He could wait, but waiting wasn't the concern. What he was worried about was her running away. Unlike the player who was part of a dominating team, Neela off the field was harder to understand. She had built walls around her heart. Should he burst through them or wait for her to open a hidden door that would let him in?

Blake glanced at the GPS on the dashboard. He had taken an alternate route to Mitch Molloy's house today since he had an extra hour to kill. It wouldn't be too long before his schedule became packed again, and aimless long drives would have to wait until the end of the season. When Tim called last night to ask for a lift back from his brother's, Blake had agreed readily. Besides, he still owed Tim a favor for delivering the lollies.

He pulled his car in behind Mitch's SUV and headed to the doorway of a red brick house in a regular middle-class suburban neighborhood. No fancy mansions for Mitch or Liana. Few would suspect that behind such simple walls lived a couple who were each an icon in their respective sport.

Blake heard a familiar scream, a sound that elicited a smile. He rang the doorbell.

Tim swung the door open with force. "You're late!"

"It's barely past nine, mate."

"She's killing me."

"What?"

"Duck!"

But Blake caught the foam ball and threw it back at the little girl with an odd-shaped shooter. "You missed —"

The words were barely out of his mouth when another foam ball hit his forehead.

Tim burst out laughing, falling backward over the sofa in the living room as Jayne Molloy screamed, "Aha! Got you! I've killed all the monsters in the house!"

Blake shook his head but couldn't stop smiling. He looked over at Tim, who was still shaking with laughter. "How long have you been at it?"

"I've been going for cover for an hour."

"She started early."

"It didn't end from last night. Woke up with my two front toes tied."

"Don't you have anything to defend yourself with?"

"She stole it. It's actually my shooter she's using now."

Having had his fair share of babysitting Jayne Molloy, Blake had no doubt that that was precisely what had happened. Blake was convinced that Jayne would either follow in her mother's footsteps and break glass ceilings or end up in jail. The child had no fear.

He was just glad he could observe all this from the sidelines.

"Mitch around?"

"In the back, putting the finishing touches on the ramp."

Blake whistled. "I still can't believe Liana let him build it. Jayne, skateboard, and ramps sound like a dangerous combination."

Tim grinned, getting up from the sofa. "It is. But Mitch used the feminist card on Liana. You know: 'If we had a boy, would you say no?' Liana never has an answer for that. Let me get my things. Fifteen minutes?"

Blake found his former captain in the backyard, on his back, with a screwdriver.

"You're in my sun, Stanton."

"How did you know it was me?"

"Your socks."

Blake looked down at his choice of socks for the day: light

blue with green flowers. "Your daughter gave them to me at Christmas."

"I know. I had to pay for them."

Mitch got up and reached for a leveler, then placed it on the platform. He eyed it and seemed satisfied with the measurement. He looked at Blake. "What you reckon? Will it hold Jayne Molloy on a skateboard?"

Blake jumped onto the ramp and pressed hard with his feet to test the strength. Solid. He jumped again. Nothing moved. "I give it a month," he told Mitch.

Mitch grinned and nodded. "That's what Liana said as well. What's on your mind, mate?"

"I understand that you know."

Mitch looked up briefly, amused. "Yeah. Congratulations."

"Did you have anything to do with it?"

"No. This is all on you. I wasn't involved."

"Your opinion still counts there."

"The only reason I know is because RugNZ wants a photo shoot of past captains together when the announcement is made."

Blake wasn't sure why he was there in the backyard with a man whose career he followed and tried to emulate, except that there would never be another Mitch Molloy. "Thanks. I just wanted to make sure you weren't put in an awkward position. You know, seeing that we're friends."

Mitch stared at Blake suspiciously. "You know that would never happen. What's really going on, mate? Not like you to beat around the bush."

Blake looked past the fence to the Canterbury Mountains. How many times in the last few years had he been in this backyard, admiring the same view, envying the life that Mitch had carefully but diligently built for himself after rugby?

"I'm clear to play," he began. "The ankle is feeling good. But each time I've been injured, it's taking longer to recover and get back to top form. I think I need to start wondering what I should do if—when—I get the type of hit that could end it all."

Mitch nodded. He began to pick up his tools from the ground, wiping them before he placed them into his toolbox. "Plenty of us retire on our own terms."

"Plenty don't."

"Fair enough. Was I wrong in thinking you were someone who puts money aside while you've been playing at the top level?"

"It's not the money. I'm good there." Blake picked up a wrench that had fallen under the ramp and handed it to Mitch. "It's what I'd do next. No one plays forever. I have no idea what I'm going to do when this is over."

"You're a smart bloke, Stanton. I don't believe you didn't have a Plan B if the rugby didn't work out."

"That's the thing. Everything worked out. Better than I had hoped. I had a Plan B at eighteen. Not now."

"You're not even thirty, mate," Mitch said. "Do you still want to play? Still want to win? Good. When you lose that desire, then it's time to think about what's next." Mitch shut his toolbox. "You're still under contract with the Club and RugNZ, so you have time on your side. Just use it to see what's out there. People like you. I think you have more opportunities than you're giving yourself credit for."

They started walking toward the house. "Was it hard for you? To stop having rugby in your life?" Blake asked quietly.

Mitch paused at the step of the veranda that wrapped around the back of his house. "It was. It still is sometimes." He faced Blake again, his expression thoughtful. "Yeah, I do miss the game and being part of the team. That anticipation when we come out of the tunnel? Throwing down the challenge in our country's colors? Nothing like it. I miss those moments. I think I always will. But it helps when there are other things to look forward to. Having Liana come into my life when she did made it easier to move forward. I had my time. I'm one of the lucky ones. I chose to stop."

After returning to the townhouse, Blake went straight to his bedroom. He reached to the back of his closet and pulled out a large black plastic box. Soon after he'd signed his first contract, Robbie and Andrew had practically held him hostage for five hours as they drilled into him the ins and outs of an effective filing system.

They might be flamboyant on the outside, but the Stanton brothers could hold their own in any accountant's office. But it wasn't the finance folder Blake was searching for when he opened the box. He flicked through the folders until he reached the one labeled UNIVERSITY.

It'd been years since he had last seen the contents of it. He shuffled past the various records before settling his gaze on the white paper with the gold lettering and bright red embossed stamp. He smiled. He still wasn't sure how he'd made it through university, but there it was, proof that he did indeed have a law degree. It had taken him a year longer than most people, mainly because he'd had to juggle the demands of his sport with the rigors of academia. He was sure he had just scraped by, but a pass was a pass.

"Blake? I'm just heading out to the shops. Need anything?" Tim appeared at Blake's bedroom door. "Hey, what are you looking at?"

Before Blake could close the folder, Tim flopped onto the bed and reached over to pull the diploma out of his hands. "What made you decide to do an LLB?"

"When my grandparents lost their farm, there was a solicitor who was very helpful. And honest."

Tim's eyebrows rose. "Honest?"

Blake smiled. "Yeah. That's what Dad went on and on about, that finding an honest solicitor was as hard as getting on the National Team. I thought I'd try to do both."

Tim laughed. "And you did. Mate, you're an overachiever."

"That's rich, coming from you."

"No one is impressed with scientists."

"No one likes solicitors."

Tim handed Blake back his diploma. "So, you looking at this means..."

Blake shrugged as he closed the UNIVERSITY folder and put it back in his filing box. "I'm not sure. I just needed to remind myself that there's more to me than playing rugby."

Tim rose from the bed and slapped Blake's back. "Mate, being a rugby player—as good as you are—is definitely not the only thing people associate you with. Hey, are you watching Neela play later in the day?"

"Yeah," Blake said. "What kind of fake boyfriend would I be if I didn't?"

There was no point worrying about when the next injury could happen. It could be next month when the season began or in a couple of years. He had a good run injury-wise until last year, and few athletes could boast that. It was just a matter of time before his body began to succumb to the pressures that came with constant and intense physical activity.

One of the first pieces of advice Mano had given him was to remember that no one played forever.

He reached for the thick white binder he had picked up from the Club last week and immersed himself in the world of scrums, tackles, and formations, taking notes and writing questions until he heard Tim unlock the front door. Then he glanced at his watch and left his room, binder in hand, and headed downstairs to turn on the telly.

"Has it started?" Tim asked.

Blake shook his head. "Not yet. They're just about to take the pitch."

Tim handed him a bottle. "I picked up some light beer. Figured you're back on your diet already. Is that next year's playbook?"

"No. Last year's. Can't hurt to go over what worked well and what didn't."

They moved to the sofa, Tim carrying a plate of vegetable slices and hummus in one hand, beer in the other.

Blake scrunched his nose but reached for a slice of capsicum. "Mate, after all these years of living with you, I still can't decide whether I appreciate or really dislike your thoughtfulness when it comes to my diet and training."

Tim snickered. "Appreciate it. You're ten percent talent and ninety percent raw determination. You need all the help you can get to stay on the team."

Blake grinned. "Between you and Neela, I'm surprised my ego isn't shattered."

"How's it going, then? The dating?" Tim pushed his glasses back up his nose.

Blake narrowed his eyes. "You know something."

"I do not."

Blake raised his eyebrows.

Tim grinned. "She's hot. You must have noticed. If I were into girls, I'd give it a go."

Blake sighed. "Don't make it more complicated than it is, Tim. You saw what she was like on Boxing Day. Every time I tried to get close to her, she went the other way. It was exactly how she acts around her father."

"Oh? That bad, eh?"

"I had a feeling it might be difficult to move our relationship further because of Kyle. She hasn't had the best of experiences with the men in her life."

"I thought she got on with her brothers."

"That's true," Blake conceded.

"You're not her dad or Kyle. She knows that. She just doesn't know what to do with her feelings."

"What do you mean?"

Tim shrugged. "If you were on the pitch, tried a play and failed, would you try it again? Probably. But if it failed a second time, you'd hesitate giving it a go a third time. For Neela, you're the third attempt at the same play."

"A rugby metaphor about my love life? Charming."

Tim grinned and reached for a cucumber. "I think the whole of New Zealand sees something in the two of you that we all want."

"What's that?"

"Two people who were always meant to be together. That's why that video went viral. It wasn't because you were tackled. It was because you two smiled at each other after the tackle. There was something special, even then," Tim said. He bit his cucumber. "Whatever she's running from, she's worth waiting for, you know."

"I know."

Tim smirked, obviously pleased with Blake's answer. "And you two look as cute together now as you did as twelve. I swear Liana kept having this funny look on her face whenever she saw you with Neela. I'm best man material, by the way."

Blake rolled his eyes. That unexpected fourth date was not what he'd planned. It was far from the one-on-one time he craved, but she'd insisted on counting the casual annual barbie at Mitch and Liana's house as a date. She'd even tweeted a selfie —posted on *his* account—of them driving to Mitch's house, just to make it official.

If he didn't know better, he'd think she was trying to create distance between them. Except he'd caught her looking for him at the party, and when their eyes met, he'd felt a mutual understanding, a silent companionship. A connection.

Tim was right. She'd finally recognized that there was something between them.

He just wouldn't walk away this time. He hadn't been brave enough at twelve to ask why she didn't want to spend time with him anymore. This was his second chance with her. He had one more date to convince Neela to give their relationship a go.

"Yeah, come on, girls!"

Tim's enthusiastic cry reclaimed Blake's attention. His roommate might be an academic, but Tim Molloy knew his rugby.

Even though he had only played XVs his whole life, Blake enjoyed the fast pace of the Sevens game. If he were honest, he didn't think he would have been a successful player in the Sevens format. There was no room for mistakes. Everything was do or die. It had to be a flawless display of teamwork. In the shorter time, one mistake could be the difference between a win or a loss.

Neela didn't play with flair or flamboyancy. Her game was efficient and textbook, similar to her cousin's. She played smart. A small shuffle here, a couple of steps there, and the opposition had to change its line. She could recognize potential dangers in an attack, but it was her releases that impressed him most. Quick, precise and sometimes disguised.

"Did you see that?" Tim cried. "She wasn't even looking!"

New Zealand went through their first match with a decisive win over Papua New Guinea.

Tim and Blake kept the telly on for the other matches. Tim surprised Blake with his insight into the other teams participating in the Series.

"When did you become such a Sevens fan?" Blake asked after the next match.

Tim shrugged. "Sometimes, when I need a break, it's a distraction. I get on the internet, and I watch a complete match in fifteen minutes."

New Zealand came on for the second time that day to play against France. It was an aggressive start by both teams, but New Zealand seemed in control. Then the hit on Neela happened.

Blake stood up immediately, already sensing that this wasn't an ordinary tackle.

She wasn't moving.

"Get up, Neela," he murmured.

The cameras panned out, a move toward privacy that, as a

player, Blake could appreciate. But as someone worried about the player, he wished he could at least see if she were awake. Players were told that if something didn't feel right, not to move. They were instructed to always let the medics have a check before they did anything. She could be all right. She was just being safe.

He watched Leila at Neela's side. She seemed to be talking to the injured player. That meant Neela was conscious. Blake breathed again. Leila stood up and indicated to the bench that they'd need to get a sub on.

He didn't miss the look on the captain's face as she glanced back at her teammate. Leila still had a job to do to get the team through to the next round, but the concern for her friend showed.

"They're bringing on a stretcher," Blake said.

"I'm sure she's fine," Tim said.

Blake nodded but left the living room, taking the stairs two at a time. He reached for the phone on his desk and called RugNZ's office.

"This is Blake Stanton. How would I get an update on the injury status of a player on the team in Sydney? I *am* family. She's my girlfriend."

* * *

Neela inhaled deeply, her lungs enjoying the intake of air devoid of scent and dust. Hospital air was always clean.

Eyes still closed, she turned her head slowly, and the low hum of a machine reminded her that she wasn't in a hotel room with the rest of the team.

She opened her mouth slightly, licking lips she knew would be dry.

Pale green curtains surrounded her. She grimaced as she tried to elevate her body farther. A sharp pain sliced up the side of her body at her next move.

Blinking, she looked for a clock and didn't find one, but her instincts told her it was still early in the morning.

Memories of yesterday came back quickly. She'd known she was being stretchered away; she'd heard the doors of an ambulance closing. Lars Goodwin, one of the assistant coaches, had jumped in with her. His presence was reassuring.

A series of specialists had come in to examine her. Then came the bloodwork, x-rays, the MRI. Fortunately, no one saw anything that concerned them, but an overnight stay was deemed a prudent decision.

"Possible concussion, since you did lose consciousness," said the final doctor of the night. "We'll keep you here for observation just to be safe. I suspect you have guidelines on when you're allowed back to practice?"

"Three weeks is standard," Lars said.

Three weeks off the pitch?

She bit back the protest that was ready to erupt from her lips. Then Lars had left, saying he'd update the team and check in on her later.

"Is there anyone at home you'd like me to call?" he asked.

Neela shook her head, ignoring the surprise on Lars' face. "No news is good news, eh?" she said.

Now that she knew there were no real repercussions from yesterday's tackle, she was dreading being in the hospital while the rest of the team was at the stadium. If she couldn't play, she wished she could at least be on the sidelines. But all that was out of her control. She'd just have to be content with the idea of cheering from her hospital bed. The girls would know she was there in spirit.

Neela reached for the remote to elevate herself to a sitting position. Taking another deep breath, then releasing it, she angled herself slightly away from the support of the bed. Concentrating, she went through a mental checklist as to the physical state of her body. She wiggled her toes, bent her knees, flexed and unflexed muscles, rotated her ankles. These were controlled movements she had practiced for years to test the degree of aches and pain after a match.

While she was far from pain-free, nothing was surprising in how she felt. Under normal conditions, pain was welcomed. Numbness would have been a far scarier thing to deal with. The tackle had knocked her out for a few seconds. Silently chastising her carelessness, she reminded herself to study the video of the play as soon as possible.

She would not be caught out like that again.

Sitting up straighter, she could just see out the large window that overlooked a courtyard. The filtering blinds would later prevent direct sunlight from hitting her face, but even at this early hour, she could enjoy the deep blue of the sky, cloudless and vast. Once the blinds were pulled open, she was sure the view would make for a pretty backdrop for the huge display of flowers on the window ledge.

Neela stared. She didn't remember them from last night.

It was a large bouquet of blush-colored roses and princess lilies.

She was just about to get out of bed to pick up the card when a head popped through a small opening in the curtains.

"Good morning," the nurse said in a soft, moderated tone. "We didn't meet last night, but I'm Jo. I'm the overnight nurse. Your coach mentioned that you're an early riser. You also missed dinner, so I wanted to see if you're ready for an early breakfast."

The thought of breakfast was unappealing, but Neela knew she should eat something, just to prove to the doctors that she was fine.

"What would you recommend?" she asked.

Jo smiled as she stepped through the curtains. Blonde with bright blue eyes, Neela detected an English accent. She watched Jo pick up the chart hanging off the base of the bed, flipping through the papers, before she answered Neela's question. "Unfortunately, all hospital food is pretty much the same. Are you on a special diet while you're in training?"

"Sort of. It's more of a recommended list of foods. The truth is, I don't feel particularly hungry."

"That's normal after the night you had. You must have been exhausted, as you didn't move when I came in to check your vitals. A good night's sleep was probably what you needed most, but you're right to think you should eat something anyway. The body needs sustenance to recover. How about we keep this fairly light and simple? Fresh fruit, a cup of yogurt, and toast? If you'd like more, we can check with the kitchen."

Neela's eyebrows rose. "This feels like room service."

"The cook's a rugby fan," Jo said with a wink. "Rumor has it he has a picture of you in his locker. And he's not even from New Zealand. He's English, the traitor."

"Well, I have to thank him personally."

"You may very well make his year by doing that."

Jo started to leave when Neela remembered what she'd been doing when the nurse had appeared. "When did the flowers arrive?"

Jo followed her gaze to the windowsill. "Late last night. I signed for them, actually. It's unusual for us to receive a delivery so late at night. Whoever sent these to you must have a bit of influence." She walked to the display and pulled the card for Neela. "This really is a beautiful arrangement. Oh, yes, I almost forgot. I'm under strict instructions from your captain to make sure you're watching your team play. They're in the semis, I gather?"

"You're not a rugby fan?"

Jo smiled. "No, not really. Maybe I'm the real traitor to England and not the cook. I don't particularly care for sport. I hope you're not offended."

"No, of course not."

After Jo had drawn the curtain for privacy, Neela fingered the heavy linen card. She didn't have much experience receiving flowers. In fact, this was the first time she'd gotten something delivered that she didn't have to pay for.

You should have pinched her. Blake xo

Neela snorted then groaned at the pain.

A soft smile stayed on her lips as she fingered the delicate petals of the nearest rose within her reach. She inched closer and welcomed the whisper-sweet scent that broke the sterile air.

"Oh, Blake," she whispered as tears formed unexpectedly.

She brushed them away quickly and turned on the TV, scrolling to the channel she believed would show the competition. But whenever her eyes rested on the flowers, the smile returned.

Later that afternoon, twenty women with bronze medals around their necks barreled into her hospital room. They were followed by the head coach and his assistants.

"Thought you might want to see what we could do without you," Leila said as she showed Neela the medal. She softened her voice. "You all right?"

Neela nodded. "No worse than usual." She turned to the rest of the squad. "A good result, girls! Always a win to beat Australia! Congratulations!"

Mel sat at the foot of the bed. "Yeah. We managed to pull it off without you. Did you see us look sad for a minute right after the Haka? That was for you."

The team cheered.

"Nice flowers." Leila walked over to the arrangement and read the card. Her smile grew wider, and Neela rolled her eyes, knowing what was going to be unleashed in precisely two seconds.

"Blake Stanton sent these to you?"

Mel reached over to grab the card out of Leila's hands. "He signed it with an X and an O! That's so romantic!"

Neela shot Leila an exasperated look as she watched the card being passed around the team followed by a barrage of questions and suggestions.

The coach stepped out from his corner after ten more minutes of good-natured ribbing. "All right, all right, ladies. Give her a break."

Steve Haughton pulled the card from one of the players and handed it back to Neela. "I hear that the doctor wants to give you one final look-over before they release you." He glanced at the display. "I had a call from RugNZ asking if your boyfriend could get the name of the hospital you were at."

"OOOOOO! Boyfriend," Mel teased as heat flamed Neela's face.

"I'm glad my daughter follows Blake Stanton on Twitter. Otherwise, this would have been news to me," Steve said. He leaned closer to Neela. "You scared me for a minute."

"I'm all right. Just a bit of a harder knock than usual."

Fifteen minutes later, the team prepared to leave. Lars would be back after she was discharged. "You might as well enjoy the peace and quiet while you're here," Steve advised her.

With no other patients in the room, Neela felt the solitude more acutely after the team's departure. She looked at the flowers again. She should message Blake to let him know she had received them and that she was enjoying them.

She hoped this was how he treated all his friends.

She reached for her phone, turned it on and was surprised by the first message that appeared.

Rieann: **Blake called to let us know you were okay. Joe put in another $50 in the pool.**

Neela laughed silently as she leaned back into her pillow.

•   •   •

Neela: **Glad to know I mean so much**.

Rieann responded immediately.

Rieann: **Are you really okay?**

Neela: **Yes. Being discharged later today. Team has a full day in Sydney for PR before flying home. Will need to stay in AUK for a bit. Policy.**

Neela looked back at the flowers. She needed to know.

Neela: **Did Dad say anything?**

Rieann's delayed response was the answer Neela expected.

Rieann: **No.**

Neela put down her phone, ignoring whatever it was that Rieann said next. She suspected it would be the usual excuses for their father's behavior. He was probably out at sea; the game was in the middle of the day; he was working.

She had heard them all before, first from Mum and then from Rieann. At least Joe and Sam never made excuses for Dad. They didn't even try to explain their father's lack of interest in his youngest child.

Her phone buzzed, indicating a call rather than a message.

"Darl?"

"Blake?"

"I haven't disturbed you, have I? Leila said she just saw you."

"You've been in touch with Leila?"

"Yeah. I had to find a way to get an update. I wasn't sure if I would get any news from RugNZ."

"The flowers are beautiful."

"I'm glad you like them. That was quite a hit."

"I'm all right. Really. Lots of fussing for nothing."

"Get some rest. I'll see you when you get home."

"Thanks, Blake."

"You're welcome, darl."

Neela looked back at the flowers, then at the ceiling, trying to squash the warmth that had begun radiating inside her when she'd heard his voice. She pulled a rose from the arrangement. As she inhaled its perfume, the lightness in her heart started to give way to the heaviness of dread.

Damnit, Blake. I can't be someone's disappointment again.

CHAPTER 16

"One more, Blake. Please. That's good. Now, let's turn your face just a little to your right. Perfect. Now, back at the camera. A serious look, please. Yes. That's great."

The photographer stood up and looked at his camera, checking the last few images he had shot. Blake relaxed his pose. He knew the makeup artist from a previous shoot; she moved in quickly during the break to check for any blemishes in her work.

He liked Lucy. She was easygoing, friendly but not overly chatty. "Do I need a touch-up?" he asked.

Lucy held up a mirror to check his hairline. She was the only makeup artist he knew who would do that. He added "perfectionist" to her list of traits.

"No, you're good," Lucy said with a grin. "How's the ankle?"

"All good. But when did you ever care about rugby?"

"Never. I asked because you're one of my favorite models."

Blake smiled. *Model?* He guessed he was, even though it was because of his success on the pitch. "Your favorite?"

"Just one of my favorites. Don't get cheeky," Lucy warned him. "In this industry, my list of favorites rotates quite quickly."

Blake laughed. "That's true in mine as well."

He had flown to Auckland yesterday mainly for today's shoot, but RugNZ wanted to start including him in more management meetings in preparation for his captaincy. It had become a new kind of reality when he entered the conference room yesterday with management, the coaches, and his two teammates who'd be serving as vice-captains. Large windows dominated the room and overlooked the training fields where the National Teams practiced. He had walked towards the view and realized that in all the years he had spent practicing on the pitch, he had never once looked up.

Six years after he was first called up to represent his country, he still felt chills when he walked into the sheds and saw the famous black jersey waiting for him to change into. Not being on the last tour hurt, especially given that it had been Mano's last. It was the first time he had missed one. The invitation to sit at the table today was confirmation that his contributions to the team continued. It also underscored the greater responsibilities that he was about to inherit.

He knew he was ready to move forward, not just professionally but personally. The time away from the game reaffirmed his desire to go on competing, but after spending time with Neela, the sport was no longer the first thing on his mind.

Apparently, his relationship with Neela was also something Andrew thought about.

"Why aren't you meeting her at the airport?" his brother had asked while they were dining out last night.

"I don't know."

"You don't know? I thought you said she'd have to be in Auckland for a few days for a physical."

Blake frowned at the incredulity in Andrew's voice. "Yes. That's standard. Why are you so uptight about this?"

"You just told me you like this girl."

Blake wiped his mouth with his napkin. "I do. A lot. More than like, even."

"Oh?"

"But I can't push it. I don't want to come on strong, Andrew. You saw how she reacted to my kiss at Mum and Dad's. Right now, she just wants us to be friends."

"Okay. Let's go with that, then. Don't friends pick up friends after they've been trampled on the ground?"

"Yeah, but…"

"Do you have anything planned tomorrow?"

"Just the photo shoot in the morning."

"Pick her up. Use my car, if you like. Does she have a place to stay in Auckland?"

"Management usually has something lined up."

"I have the extra room."

Blake frowned and crossed his arms. "Okay, now you're not being you. You don't like to share. What's going on?"

Andrew continued to eat, picking through his salad. "There's something about seeing you with her that appeals to me. When you're with her, you're happy. Not the publicity type of happy, but something quite genuine. And remember, I was sharing a room with you when Neela first came into your life. You were a goner then. What makes you think it's any different now?"

"I was ten then. I'd like to think I've matured since then."

"Who's to say what you felt at ten isn't just as real as it is now?"

"Come on, Andrew."

"Well, I'm just glad we're no longer roommates. It was Neela-this, Neela-that for two whole bloody years. Worst years of my life. When she stopped paying attention to you, you cried for days."

"I did not."

"At least five nights."

"Shut up."

Andrew waved his fork. "Pick her up. You'll figure it out. You always do. That's one thing I've always admired about you: you're a problem solver. You identify the obstacle, find a way to overcome it and move forward. Why are you looking at me like that?"

"Do you mean that? There's something you admire about me?"

Andrew put his fork down and pressed his hands together as if in prayer. He brought the tips of his fingers to his lips, and his face was thoughtful. "There are a lot of things I admire about you. I'm not saying that as a brother, but as a man."

The brothers stared at each other.

"You're messing with me, aren't you?" Blake asked.

"Yeah. Grow up. Go to the airport and show her what it's like to be loved by a Stanton man."

* * *

Neela peered out her window as the clouds parted to reveal her first glimpse of New Zealand. Mel was giggling in the seat behind her, while next to her, Leila continued to work on lesson plans for the new school year.

Neela picked up her phone again, now in-flight mode, and checked the last message she'd received before she boarded the flight.

Blake: **I'll see you at the airport. Lunch?**

She had meant to tell him not to bother, but the truth was, she wanted to see him.

Her screensaver came back on. A new one, courtesy of Leila, who had sent the same picture of Blake's flowers into Twittersphere. By the time they'd boarded the flight to go home, it had five hundred likes.

When the plane's wheels touched ground in Auckland, a sudden charge of excitement flowed through Neela's body. Her heart started beating faster, and she had a sudden desire to giggle.

It had been two weeks since Boxing Day. Two weeks of making excuses not to see Blake. Their fourth "date" at Mitch and Liana's had been harder than she'd expected.

Instead of being less aware of him in a crowd, she'd unconsciously sought him out. It was the most relaxed she had ever seen him. He was at home with the Molloy and Dane families. She'd watched him play tag with Jayne and Lulu, tie Fred Dane's shoelaces and burp six-month-old Eli Dane.

She had been nervous about her Christmas present for him. What did you get someone who could buy anything? Fortunately, Karen had come through when she'd casually mentioned she had found some old Playbills from her time in London, among which were half a dozen musicals whose songs were on Blake's playlist.

His surprised expression on seeing the framed collection was something she would always remember, as would the unexpected caress on her cheek, the softest of touches from the roughest of hands.

He had wanted to kiss her then.

And if he had, she wouldn't have stopped him.

But he didn't.

Because he promised her he wouldn't.

She'd left the Molloys' more confused than ever, trying to regain control of her emotions. She'd stayed away in the weeks that followed: training, extra time at her job, anything to distract her from the feelings that were building inside her. It was safer that way. *Can't trust feelings.*

He didn't try to change her mind. Instead, he'd ring in the morning— "just to say hi"—or send her a funny .gif image in the middle of the day.

Then there were flowers at the hospital.

And now he was waiting for her in the Arrival Hall.

No one had ever welcomed her home before.

The phone buzzed, and she tapped on the screen eagerly. But the name that appeared immediately extinguished her excitement at seeing Blake.

Kyle: **Tonight. 8. At Jack Henry's.**

"Hey, are you all right?" Leila asked as she unbuckled her seatbelt.

Neela blinked. "Er… yeah. Just loads on my mind."

She frowned at her phone one more time. She'd prompted this, but it had taken him a week to reply.

Now or never, Neela. Let's end this.

She took a deep breath and replied.

Neela: **OK.**

"You sure you're all right?" Leila asked. "You looked excited a few seconds ago. Now you look like you're going to throw up. Shall I get Steve? Or Lars?"

Neela edged out of her seat and reached up to the overhead bin. "I'm feeling fine. Honest. I sort of realized how many things I need to deal with now that we're home."

Leila scrunched up her nose. "Don't remind me."

When the team emerged into the Arrival Hall, Neela scanned the large crowd and spotted Blake immediately. His turquoise shirt with the snake motif wrapped around the sleeves would have drawn anyone's attention.

Faces and phones were all directed at him. He ignored the attention, instead engrossed in a conversation with someone she thought was a teammate's latest boyfriend. A young girl interrupted the two men. Blake indulged the request for a photo and signed the back of the young fan's shirt. He stood up as soon as he saw Neela, smiled widely and held up a closed fist. Slowly, uncurling his fist one finger at a time, he revealed a Choc Cherry.

Leila came up to next to her and whispered, "Smile any wider, and all your teeth will fall out, Neela Smyth."

"Shut up." Neela walked toward Blake, aware that eyes and cameras followed her.

"Hiya," she said. "I hope there's more to lunch than a Choc Cherry?"

Blake leaned in to give her a quick kiss on the cheek. Neela was ready for it this time, but expecting the kiss didn't stop her instant response to Blake's body, now pressed against her as he followed the kiss with a hug. She was stunned for a moment but gave in to the warmth and security she felt in his embrace. She hid her head against his neck for a moment before gently pushing back.

"No worries. I've got it covered. As we speak, the famous Stanton marinara sauce awaits," Blake said. Then he studied Neela's face intently. Seemingly satisfied, he nodded. "You look good."

"I have a black eye."

Blake's dimple appeared. "You were working. Part of what we do. Nothing wrong with that." He looked past her but kept his arm around her waist. "Good series, Leila. Welcome back."

Leila smiled. "I'm glad you're here. Are you whisking her off?"

"I hope so. You flying straight home?"

Leila nodded. "After tea with Mum and Dad. You take care of her, Blake. She had a good knock."

"Saw it happen, and I will." He reached for Neela's bag.

"That's all right. I've got it," Neela said as she reached down for the handles.

Blake swiftly switched the bag to the hand farther away from Neela and began to walk. "My pleasure. Besides, what kind of boyfriend lets his injured girlfriend carry her own bags? And before you tell me it's chauvinistic for me to try to carry your bag, I'll have you know I would have done the same for any of the brothers."

"I'm not injured."

Blake stopped suddenly, causing her to bump into him. He held her upper arm as she regained her balance.

"I've got it, Neela." He gave her arm a gentle squeeze that sent tingles down her arm. "Let me help you. Okay?"

She bit the bottom of her lip.

"Neela, I'm just carrying your bag."

She nodded. "Okay."

Blake smiled and took her hand. "So, lunch first before I take you to wherever RugNZ needs you to stay?"

"Is this our last date?"

"Not a chance. Rieann told me about the dress."

"You really need to stop talking to my sister."

"She called me."

Neela smiled. "How did your photo shoot go?"

"Good. The next time you're in Auckland, there'll be a new billboard of me in maroon underwear just in time for Valentine's Day."

"I'll add that to my list of things to do," Neela said dryly.

"If you ask nicely, you could see the real thing."

"Blake!"

"The underwear, of course. Friends don't see friends naked, or do they?" he teased. "Because I suggested it once, and you vetoed it."

As they drove toward Auckland, he peppered her with questions about the tournament and her subsequent hospital stay, thoughtful questions that no one outside their profession would likely have asked. She generally avoided talk about her work with anyone. She'd learned it was easier to keep one part of her life away from other parts. But it seemed natural to let Blake into that world since it was also his.

"That was a tough hit on you. But you didn't do anything technically wrong."

Neela shrugged. "I saw plenty of things I could have done differently. I should have expected her move earlier."

"It was a fast game."

"I need to react and recover faster."

Out of the corner of her eye, Neela saw Blake's dimple appear again.

"So, for our last date, what do you think about going to the opera?" he asked.

Neela stared openly at Blake this time. "The opera? As in, the opera here in Auckland? That's a pretty fancy date. I don't do fancy."

"I have season tickets."

"Not surprised."

"Good. They open with *The Mikado*."

"Gilbert and Sullivan?"

Blake grinned. "Well done, Neela Smyth. Come on, admit it. I'm rubbing off on you."

"I admit nothing. Listen, I thought we agreed to keep it simple."

"We agreed to be who we are. I love the opera. I go every year. I also promised your sister that I'd take you someplace where you can wear that dress she goes on and on about."

"That's a month away. If we go out for dinner tonight, we'll be done."

"You say it like you want this to be over quickly."

Neela turned her head away and studied the approaching city, unsure whether to respond with her head or her heart.

She answered cautiously. "We'll still be friends once this is over."

* * *

It was a whisper, but her words led to a silence in the car that was full of expectation.

"Yes," Blake agreed. "We'll still be friends."

He heard her release her breath. He sensed her fear about the future and silently cursed the two men in her past who'd eroded her sense of self-worth. He was desperate to reach out and offer her a haven from whatever else she was running from. Instead, he tightened his grasp of the steering wheel and feigned nonchalance.

It wasn't time to push for more than she could give; he must be patient. In truth, he had spent most of his life waiting. The difference was that he knew now who he was waiting for. He wanted her, this woman who had fire in her eyes.

He pulled up quickly to the gates that led to an underground carpark, keyed in the security code, and a few minutes later, he opened the door to Andrew's penthouse in the center of Auckland.

The smell of stewed tomatoes and oregano welcomed them in.

"This isn't yours, is it?" Neela walked to the glass sliding doors that led to a large balcony with expansive views of the city and the Auckland Harbor Bridge.

"Too rich even for me," Blake said. "It's Andrew's. He bought it when he sold his first company. He went from Mum and Dad's rumpus room to this overnight. He hasn't looked back."

Blake sometimes forgot how intimidating such a display of wealth could be. He knew he hadn't been able to talk the first time he'd entered the penthouse, which was so different an environment from where he had grown up.

The marble tile floors and high ceilings were impressive, but the view of the city was, nevertheless, the main draw. Andrew had put his personal stamp on the place with wall hangings and fixtures. One of Mum's landscapes hung in the hallway. Blake wasn't a fan of the complicated ball of light bulbs that served as a chandelier over the dining table, something Andrew had labeled as "functional art." Still, if his brother wanted to spend the time and energy replacing so many lightbulbs, who was he to argue?

"Is Andrew joining us for lunch?"

"He's at meetings all day." Blake moved to the kitchen and opened the oven door to check on the homemade marinara sauce he had put together before he headed to the airport. "If you want to freshen up a bit, there's a bathroom just down the hall. You can use the towels there."

Half an hour later, she walked out in a dress, her hair loose and damp but framing her face. She looked relaxed. Even the black eye added to her quiet beauty.

Not yet. Keep it friendly.

"I thought we might eat on the balcony. It's a nice day," he said.

"Can I help bring out anything?"

"It's all done. I just came back in to bring out the drinks."

He thought he knew the way her body moved, but there was a feminine sway to her walk that had escaped him before. She was barefoot and folded her legs underneath her when she sat down.

"Did you make everything?" she asked.

"Yeah." Blake poured some chilled flavored water into Neela's glass. "It's just pasta with a bit of marinara."

She put a forkful into her mouth. Blake tried not to stare at the way her lips lingered on the cutlery. Was it possible to be jealous of a fork? Then she moaned a little, and Blake almost dropped his own fork. He grabbed for his glass of water and drank quickly.

"Oh my God," Neela exclaimed. "This is so good! When you retire, you should think about opening a restaurant."

He tore his eyes from her lips. This was going to be tougher than he'd thought. *Rugby… We can talk about rugby again.*

After the switch to a safer topic, he brought out a plate of brownies for dessert. "I didn't bake these," he confessed and grabbed one after she did. "What are your plans for today? Can I interest you in a walk by the waterfront?"

Neela caught some crumbs and sprinkled them over her plate. "I'm meeting Kyle tonight."

Blake would have sworn his blood froze over the moment Kyle's name was mentioned. Just like that, his "friendly" lunch with Neela had a whisper of evil hovering over it. "Does Mano know?"

"No, and you're not going to tell him either. I'm giving Kyle the last payment. But I want to see him and make sure he understands that this is it. No more. My debt to him is paid."

"I'd like to go with you."

"No."

"Neela, the last time you saw him, he hurt you."

"He won't this time."

"I'll never be able to look at your cousin again if I don't go with you tonight."

"I can handle it."

"You can't tell me you're going to see your ex-boyfriend— this man who used to *beat* you— without me wanting to be there."

"I'm used to taking care of myself, Blake. I need to end this."

"Yes, and I'll drive you there. I'll stay in the car, but I want to be close."

"Blake—"

"Please. Do you honestly believe Kyle won't try to hurt you again? The truth, always, between us, remember?" Blake took a deep breath. "I made your cousin a promise that I would keep an eye out for you. I intend to keep that promise."

"What? Why?"

"Because he was worried about Kyle being around."

"Are you telling me that you hanging out with me this summer was because Mano told you to?"

"Yes. No. You offered to be my girlfriend for the summer, remember? I just took you up on it."

"I can take care of myself, Blake," she repeated.

Blake's phone rang, but he ignored it. Dark, determined eyes stared at him. He wasn't going to back down. Not when she could be in danger. The phone rang again.

"Why don't you answer it? I think we both need a second," Neela said.

He reached for the phone but continued to return her scrutiny. "Hello? Mum? Yeah, I'm at Andrew's. Yeah, how did you know that? When did you start following Leila Farris? Right—let me ask." Blake put his phone against his chest. "Mum would like a word, if you're willing."

Neela took the phone. "Mrs. Stanton? Yes, I'm fine, thank you. No, no expected complications. It's a routine follow-up with our own doctors." She tilted her head slightly as she continued to listen. "Well, yes, I'm sure I'll have some time next month. That will be fine. Thank you. Did you want to talk to Blake again? No worries. 'Bye."

"What did she want?" Blake took the phone back and poured more water into Neela's glass.

"She still wants to do the portrait."

"No surprise there. You'll look beautiful in a painting."

Neela got up abruptly, the soft folds of her dress accentuating her movement. "Please stop with the compliments. You need to stop this." Neela waved her hands around. "I'm not worth trying to impress, right? I'm just a girl from your past. I know we have this thing going on…"

"Thing?"

Neela inhaled deeply, trying to calm down. "That we're attracted to each other. But…"

"This is just lunch." Blake folded his arms. "This is two people trying to have a conversation about keeping you safe. Trust me, if I were trying to impress you, we wouldn't be sitting on my brother's balcony eating pasta."

Neela looked unconvinced. Blake leaned back in his chair and watched a parade of emotions cross her expressive face. He resisted the urge to stand up and pull her into his arms. *Let me love you...*

He cleared his throat. "If I were Leila, would you let her go with you tonight?"

"No."

"Would she insist?"

"Yes."

"I made a promise to your cousin, and I need to honor it. So don't make me do it."

"Do what?"

"Call your sister."

She hadn't expected that ultimatum. Her eyes widened, and her mouth dropped. He picked up her plate, stacked it on top of his and gathered all the cutlery.

"You wouldn't," she said.

"Try me."

"You can't!"

"Whatever I have to do to keep you safe, darl."

He walked back to the kitchen, leaving Neela on the balcony. She came inside a few minutes later with the glasses and the water jug and stood beside him as he filled up the dishwasher.

"I don't mean to sound ungrateful, Blake. This isn't about us. This is about me finishing something. You weren't a part of that life."

Blake shut the dishwasher and leaned against the counter. "I understand that. But I'm part of your life now. How much, we're both still figuring out, and I respect that. And whether you like it or not, Kyle is part of my life as well. I remember every person who's ever hit me, Neela. Every one of them, all the way back to primary school. On and off the pitch. I want to be there, not just because of my promise to Mano, but because I care about you."

Neela fiddled with the washcloth Blake had left on the counter. He was once again tempted to close the distance between them, to reassure her with more than words.

"You'll stay in the car?" she asked.

"As long as I can see you. I don't trust that fella. And Neela, as for compliments? When I think you look beautiful or you do something wonderful, I will tell you. I'm allowed to, and I want to. You're just going to have to get used to hearing people say nice things about you."

CHAPTER 17

THIS FELT LIKE A SCENE OUT OF A MOVIE, EXCEPT SHE DIDN'T KNOW the ending or whether she was guaranteed a full resolution of her problems. She was outside the small pub that she and Kyle used to frequent, and it was unexpectedly quiet. Years ago, it had always been teeming with people. But this was a weeknight, and the crowd she'd expected to help keep Kyle in check wasn't there.

Kyle had wanted to meet inside the pub, but Blake had insisted he'd go in with her if that were the case. Kyle hadn't responded to her last message, but he wasn't inside yet—she'd checked—so she knew she could finish this outside in plain view of any passersby.

It had been in her mind, when she insisted they meet, that this would be a quick exchange. She had two checks: one that would pay off all her debts to him, while the other would be an incentive to stay away, to never get back in touch.

She knew she might be pouring money down the drain. There were no guarantees that he wouldn't try for more. But this was her red line. She would make sure he knew that.

"Why the hell are we meeting out here?"

The voice came from behind her. Neela inhaled deeply then

turned slowly, keeping her hands in her pockets so he couldn't see them shake. "The last time we met somewhere inside, you didn't know how to behave."

Kyle sneered. He threw his cigarette on the ground and crushed it with his boot. Then he looked Neela over, slowly and deliberately. He transferred his attention to over her shoulder. "Your boyfriend's in his brother's car, is he?"

She resisted looking behind her. "What makes you say that?"

Kyle spat and wiped his mouth with his sleeve. He continued to stare past her, his eyes hooded, cold, and dark. How had she ever found him attractive?

"Only one like that in all of New Zealand. I know my engines, and that has a sweet one," he said.

Neela raised her chin and held out the envelope. "Here you are. It's the last of what I owe you. We're done."

"Aww, baby. Why does it have to end like this? Didn't I show you a good time?"

"I don't want to hear from you again."

"You told me you'd love me forever. I remember that moment clearly." Kyle stepped forward, and it took everything inside her for Neela not to step back. "You were naked, on top of me, and those sounds coming out of you…"

"Do not try to contact my family or me again, do you understand?" A fierce grip dug into her shoulder as she turned, causing her to cry out in pain.

A door slammed in the distance.

She looked up frantically. Blake's large body was sprinting toward her, anger palpable in his movements. She knew what Kyle could do. She didn't want Blake hurt because of her. Not again.

She swiftly elbowed Kyle, channeling all her force into the motion, and turned just in time to catch Blake as he reached her side. She pulled his arm, holding him back, with a desperation born out of fear.

"You're dead, Kyle!" Blake bellowed to the figure who was still doubled over.

Kyle cursed loudly. He knelt on all fours as if trying to regain his bearings. Then he suddenly got up and charged. He flung himself at Blake, throwing them all to the ground. Neela fell backward when she lost her grip on Blake, and the force of her body hitting the hard surface caused her to groan.

The sound of punching compelled her to move. Another shot of adrenaline— and something else— kicked in. She knew the force of Kyle's fist, a man who fought with a viciousness honed by life on the streets.

Kyle rolled himself on top of Blake, straddling him. He raised his fist above Blake's head, ready to strike. Neela didn't think twice. She launched herself at him, knocking him off Blake.

She rolled away from Kyle but landed awkwardly. Out of the corner of her eye, she spotted Kyle slowly getting up from the ground, but Blake was already there.

Neela gasped at the sound of Blake's fist hitting Kyle's jaw. Blake pulled the semi-conscious man off the ground and lifted him off his feet by his neck.

A few people had started to come out of the pub. The darkened street might keep them anonymous, but she couldn't risk it.

She scrambled quickly to Blake's side. "We need to go."

"He needs to be taught a lesson."

She held on to Blake's arm. "We're done. This is done."

Blake released Kyle suddenly. Moaning, Kyle curled into a fetal position, breathing hard.

Neela knelt next to him. "Don't contact me again. I've repaid my debt to you. Fair warning: I am going to the police for a restraining order. If you contact my family or me, I will go to the press. You will have nowhere to hide, and nowhere to run."

Then she reached for Blake's hand. "Let's go."

When they got into the car, she could see blood oozing out of the corner of his mouth and nose. "Oh, God, Blake, you're really hurt!"

"I'm fine. No worse than playing South Africa." He wiped his face with the back of his hand then angled the overhead light slightly so he could look at her. Apparently satisfied with what he saw, he quickly sent a message on his phone.

"Who are you messaging?"

"A friend of my brother's."

"Andrew's?"

"No, Robbie's. She's a doctor I've used before. She'll be discreet. Please come back with me so she can check you out. I saw you hit your head on the ground. That's two head injuries in less than a week."

Neela reached for the back of her head. "I don't think I hit it, Blake. I'm sure I'm all right, but you need to get checked out too."

"I'm not hurt. But I'll have her check me out if you will."

"Blackmail?"

"When a man's desperate…"

She paused then nodded. He returned her nod, relief in his face. They drove back to Andrew's penthouse in silence. She should call his bluff, she thought, but he was right. Desperate times called for desperate measures, and he was stubborn enough to ignore his own injuries.

Her heartbeat was finally starting to feel normal again, but she felt far from calm or relaxed. The moment she'd seen Blake being thrown to the ground, she was no longer afraid of what Kyle could do to her. She only wanted Blake to be safe.

When they entered the penthouse, Blake went straight to the fridge. He reached for a beer and showed it to Neela, who shook her head. He then pulled out a couple of ice packs from the freezer and handed one to her. "Put it on your head, just in case."

"This might make the news," Neela said as she took the pack. "A couple of people came out of the pub during the fight."

"Doesn't matter."

"It won't help your chances with the captaincy."

Blake took a drink. "I already have it."

"What?"

"I'm the next captain. RugNZ is going to make the announcement next month."

He got it! Pride swept through her. He was a worthy successor to those who had come before him. He'd be a great captain.

Their plan had worked. Two things had been settled tonight.

She felt his gaze as she studied her hands.

"Darl?"

This was different from the car, where no words had been needed. The silence that followed was pregnant with unasked questions and unknown answers which will eventually define their future.

They could be friends. It was better this way. He would now inherit a responsibility few outsiders would ever understand. She understood it, though; she was part of that world. And she wouldn't be swayed by sentimentality. Letting him move on was the logical thing to do.

She looked up at him. She braved covering his hands with hers, hoping to convey the sincerity behind her intentions. "Congratulations, Blake. You deserve it. I really mean that."

But he knew her too well. "You owe me one more date, Neela. You're not backing out of it."

"There's no reason for it."

He opened his hands to engulf hers, surrounding them with his strength and warmth. "We said five dates."

"We don't need five dates. This was all about giving you the right kind of publicity. It was about me returning a favor. Your promise to Mano has been fulfilled. Kyle is no longer a problem."

"Kyle might show up again."

"He won't. He's like most bullies. Once he's been confronted, he'll stay away. And if he's stupid enough to, I have my brothers.

It's time I trusted them again. You don't need to be a part of this anymore."

"Darl…"

Unwanted tears that had begun to well up. But she'd promised him honesty. "Thank you for helping me face my past, Blake. I wanted to do it alone, but knowing you were there gave me the courage to follow through with seeing Kyle again. I used to run, but I didn't tonight. For the first time in over a year, I know I don't have to anymore. But it's time I walk away from you."

Neela tried to reclaim her hand, but Blake didn't let her. Instead, he kept his grip firm.

"There's something between us that only comes once in a life-time," Blake said. "You're the face I've thought about since I was ten. I've always needed you in my life. I don't like why we started this, but it's been the best two months of my life, knowing you were a part of it. I love —"

She couldn't let him say it. She pulled her hands away from his, desperation made her shout, "Don't! Don't say it, Blake. Once you say it, I'll have to hear it in my head and feel it in my heart forever."

"Would it be so hard to hear it?"

"Only because I can't say it back to you."

"Can't or won't?"

She aggressively wiped away at traitorous tears. "I hope we'll stay friends. But I need to go now."

"Stay, please. At least until the doctor comes."

She heard his pain. To know she was causing it sent her to a place of previously unknown anguish.

"I'm seeing one tomorrow. I'll be fine." She walked toward the door, then paused. "Make sure you get checked out. Please. Do that for me. I need some time by myself. To be independent again. Please, don't call."

He didn't follow her.

She was both grateful and disappointed.

CHAPTER 18

THE EGG DISINTEGRATED BEFORE BLAKE COULD CRACK IT PROPERLY. Much of it was now on his hand; some of it had reached the floor. He cursed and flung the tiny bits of shell into the sink to join the others. It had been six weeks since he'd let Neela walk away, and his anger and frustration had not eased.

Initially, he'd thought he'd give her some time. He'd lasted two days. When he tried to message her, he discovered that her phone number was no longer in use. Part of him was glad that she'd changed it— Kyle wouldn't be able to get hold of her either—but it was one more damn thing that kept him from reaching out to her.

Then the day of what was to be their fifth date came and went. He had planned to pull out all the stops: to romance her with the full force of his love and wealth. Under normal circumstances, he'd have half a dozen people interested in attending the opera with him, but without her by his side, he couldn't go. It made no sense. It was the first opening night at the opera he had missed since he'd become a season ticket holder.

He knew he could get Neela's new number easily. Leila, Mano, even Tim would know. All he'd have to do was show up at one of her team trainings if he really wanted to see her. It was all public information. But he'd heard her plea, and wherever their relationship went next, he was at the mercy of her timing. A less foolish man might walk away, to find someone else to love and who would love him back.

But she did love him. He knew she did. She just needed to admit to herself.

"Blake, mate. Don't take this the wrong way, but we're running out of eggs. I'm sure there's a gym somewhere you can work out all of this frustration. You know, like on a punching bag."

Blake stared at Tim, who had been sitting at the counter watching him try to bake for the last half-hour. "You know I like to bake before a match. Baking calms me down."

Tim peered into the sink. "Yeah, well…"

Blake could feel his jaw lock. He took a deep breath and reached for the silver mixing bowl, but he couldn't stop himself from slamming it on the counter. The bowl rolled and rattled before it settled.

"Ahh. That explains the dents."

"You're not helping!' Blake roared. "Go count some frogs or something!"

"I would, except I'm afraid if I leave, I'll have nothing to eat on tonight," Tim said. "I really don't think you should be in the kitchen."

"I'm fine, okay? I'm fine!"

Tim flinched. Blake turned away. Hands on his hips, he closed his eyes and took more deep breaths. He knew the root of his anger was his fear of losing her. After he'd returned to Christchurch, he'd been caught up in pre-season training and Club meetings. Added to the schedule were more meetings with RugNZ in preparation for his captaincy. But every day, he hoped she'd call, leave a message, something. He was no longer running in the mornings, but he'd wake up anyway and walk to Hagley Park to see if she were there.

She wasn't. She'd disappeared again. How dare she resume her life as if *they* had never existed?

There was a quick knock on the door, and Tim hopped off the barstool to let in Andrew and Walt Stanton.

Andrew looked past Tim after greeting him. "Honestly, Blake. I could hear you yell from down the driveway."

Blake stared at the two figures now standing in front of him. "What are you doing here?" he demanded and yanked at an apron that had the misfortune of being stuck to the hook on the wall. *Damn it!* Blake gave it one last tug, and both the apron and the hook came off, along with some of the plaster.

Four men stared at the spot where the hook used to be.

Blake looked at his witnesses, then at the apron in his hand before he threw it on the floor. Then he pointed at the other men. "You'd think she could at least tell me she's safe, right? I have to read it in the papers! How hard is it to get on the phone? I'll even take an email!"

"Blake…" Walt started.

"Maybe you need to just let her go," Andrew interrupted.

Blake glared at Andrew. "Aren't you the one who said it makes you happy to see her with me?"

"That was before you went a bit crazy…"

"I'm not letting her go!" Blake yelled. "I'm not her father! I'm not Kyle! Why can't she accept that I need her, eh? What's so wrong with letting me love her? I'm the bloody next captain of the National Team of New Zealand, and the one person I want to impress thinks it's the reason she should break up with me! ME!"

"Steady, son, steady." Walt pulled off his sunnies and placed them on his forehead, then scanned the kitchen counter. "Choc chip cookies? Looks like you need a little help. Andrew? Tim?"

"How about I run to the shops and pick up something for all of us to eat for tea?" Tim said. "Blake has to be at the stadium by six. I've tried for an hour, and all I seem to do is increase the destruction of plates and eggs." He reached for his jacket and winked at Blake. "She didn't die, mate. She just needs time."

"Oh, shut up," Blake muttered, his shoulders drooping.

Walt picked up the apron from the floor, casually slipped it over his head, and washed his hands before he opened the refrigerator. He tossed the butter at Tim, then grabbed the last two eggs from the fridge.

"Sit down, Blake," he said firmly. "You need to cool off. Got to get your mind ready for the game. Didn't Nan tell you never to bake when you're angry?"

Blake frowned at his dad. "No. Nan said *to* bake when you're angry. Nothing like beating eggs to let it out. She told me that's how she stayed married to Pop for so long."

"Yeah. We ate a lot of choc chip cookies growing up," Walt admitted.

Blake watched his brother and father move with practiced synchronicity. They had always cooked in pairs: Andrew and Dad, him and Robbie. Mum only burned things.

He couldn't remember when he was last overwhelmed by his feelings. Even in the euphoria of winning championships, nothing came close to the emotional roller-coaster of the last few weeks.

When Neela closed the door behind her, leaving him alone in Andrew's penthouse, the floor seemed to swallow him. He could barely breathe. He couldn't stand. Andrew found him sitting on the kitchen floor, his bottle of beer still full but his heart completely empty.

The sound of the mixer brought his attention back to the kitchen. When the room began to smell of vanilla and chocolate, he tried again. "What are you two doing here?"

"Tim called and said you were being a pain in the arse," Andrew replied. "I told Dad. Dad told Mum. Mum's painting Neela at the moment, so we thought we'd come over here."

"Neela's at the house?"

"She looks great—ow! Dad!" Andrew kneaded the spot on

the back of his head where Walt had smacked him.

"We're supposed to help your brother, not tease him." Walt turned to Blake. "You *are* all right, son, aren't you? Do you need to talk to someone about…uh… what you're feeling?"

Andrew rolled his eyes. "Good lord, Dad. That was terrible." He put the last of the dirty dishes into the dishwasher. "If I understand everything correctly, she still wants to be with you. She just doesn't know if she's ready for more right now. And do you blame her? From what you said, her last boyfriend really did something to her."

Blake crossed his arms. "It's been six weeks. She hasn't tried to get in touch once."

"There's no schedule for this one," Andrew said. "You have a choice: wait or go. Both will have consequences that could last a lifetime."

* * *

"He's heartbroken, you know."

"Mrs. Stanton…" Neela said.

"I've never seen him like this. His dad is even worried, which never happens. He and Andrew are going to watch Blake play tonight."

Tonight? Of course. The start of the Super Rugby season. Those dates were usually ingrained in her head, but she'd tried to avoid all news about Blake these past six weeks.

Clarissa continued. "Blake was always the son who got back up after he fell down and always with a smile on his face. No, Blake wasn't the one we were worried about, even with all the nonsense that came with being on the National Team."

"Mrs. Stanton…"

"Don't move, sweetheart. I'll get the shadows wrong. That's a good girl. 'Ta."

Neela sighed and looked for something to focus on. There were a lot of choices in Clarissa's studio: art, framed family pictures, collectibles, a selection of teacups. She settled on the nodding cat figurine, smiling smugly from its place on the shelf behind Clarissa.

"We knew this was serious when he didn't go to the opera," came the voice from behind the canvas. "He never misses opening night. An opportunity to dress in his best clothes and listen to music he adores? I thought it would take something extraordinary for him to give it up. And I was right."

Neela detected the smug tone in Clarissa's voice. "I'm sure it had nothing to do with me."

"Believe that if you wish." Clarissa stepped back into Neela's line of sight. "Sweetheart, really, you must sit still."

"Sorry, Mrs. Stanton. It's just…" Neela took a deep breath.

Clarissa smiled gently. "He said you told him not to contact you. Why, dear? It's obvious that you miss him too. There's sadness in your eyes where once there was fire."

"I've been busy," Neela whispered. "So has he. He got what he really wanted, the captaincy. You must be proud."

Clarissa laughed. "Well, yes. But he was supposed to be my artist, the singer, the actor. Then one day, when he was ten, he came home and said he wanted to be a rugby player. Just like that." Clarissa shook her head, but the smile stayed.

"Something— or someone— opened a new world for him, and he became great. It's a powerful thing to watch one's children discover their talents. I'm proud of all my boys, Neela. It's not what they do but who they are, and they're all good young men. A little quirky, which surprises me, given that their dad is so predictable. But you're wrong about the captaincy. It's not what he really wants."

Neela stood up, not caring whether she was in the right light. She wrung her hands. "Our relationship was for show, Mrs. Stanton. It wasn't real. I'm sorry to disappoint you, but we've only talked about being friends again. Nothing more."

"He's positively morose at the family dinners. He's starting to depress even Lulu, who's never sad! As for it not being real?

We all saw the way you two look at each other. You can't fake chemistry, dear. But there's nothing wrong with making him wait. I told you, he's always had it too easy with the girls. He'll wait for you. I'll guarantee it. My boys all know quality."

Neela shook her head sadly. "I see where Blake gets his positive attitude from."

Clarissa stilled her paintbrush.

"Actually, I got it from him," she said softly. "I didn't handle the move to England very well. But every weekend, when the boys came back from boarding school, he was the only one who could make me laugh. If you find someone who can do that with you, help you laugh when the world around you is dark, it's a gift." Clarissa turned back to her canvas, brush moving again. "By the way, what do you think of the name 'Corey?' It's such a lovely name. Good for boys and girls."

An hour later, Neela kept her motorbike running, having impulsively decided to keep going after arriving home. Restlessness stretched through her body, especially after she'd sat so still for Clarissa. Fortunately, there'd been no more mention of Blake during the rest of her time there. Not that it mattered, because she had heard enough to resurrect all her feelings for him.

He was never far from her thoughts, and as lonely as it felt without him, she realized she didn't want to lose her memories of his voice, his face, his smile, that bloody dimple— even the ache that came with remembering what it had been like to be in his arms.

She would return to a life without him, she promised herself. She would work hard and keep busy. She would learn how to live without Blake. She'd gotten over Kyle. She could do it again.

The difference was that she still wanted Blake.

And if what she'd heard today was right, he still wanted her.

He loved her.

Neela revved her engine to take a particularly steep hill, and as she turned the corner, she realized she wasn't far from Captains' Field.

A tribute to the men's rugby National Team, the tall cutouts of the more recent captains stood on private grounds which were part of a working farm. Rugby diehards would make a pilgrimage there for selfies. Her dad had brought his children here years ago, long before Neela had had any thoughts of being a professional athlete. He sat all four of them on the fence and recited the stories behind each captain's most famous match. He told them to know the history of the sport, to understand the honor of playing for one's team, whether it was for school or, perhaps, one day, for country.

He had looked at Joe then. No one expected Neela to fulfill the family's secret hopes. But, silver medal or not, her decision to walk away when she did and how she had done so had dampened any joy her father might have felt at seeing her take the field in their country's colors.

She should regret that action, but she couldn't. It was who she had been at that time.

Neela parked the bike on the side of the road. The wooden fence seemed newer now. She climbed it, sat on the top rung, and studied the cutouts, each standing at approximately five meters tall. The team of captains, by its sheer size and numbers, was enough of a reason to stop and stare, especially for fans.

Now, years after she had first seen them and without the impatience of youth, Neela was able to appreciate the artistic impression of each face. The artist had cleverly captured the character associated with each captain. Mitch Molloy looked dangerously impassive. Connor Dane had a regal quality about him. Then there was her beloved cousin: no pretense, no airs. Just strength.

This field was a labor of love.

Blake's image could join this army of captains. He would be a good fit for all the right reasons. He played hard and smart. He was liked not just by the fans, but also by the players. It was a hard position to fill, but Neela knew he was ready for it.

He was a good man, and he was waiting for her to be brave

enough to listen to her heart again.

The clouds were barely moving; their shapes vague and unidentifiable. The sheep in the adjoining paddock had begun to bleat. No one was about. Moments like these were what she used to seek when she wanted a break from her scheduled life. No drama, no worries.

But now she knew a different type of peace. It came from being with someone who never demanded, and who, at that moment, was probably throwing his body against another man for the sake of a small oval ball.

The first match of the season. How was he playing? She had always watched before, both as a fan and as a fellow athlete. She knew her reluctance at turning on the telly was to avoid seeing him again, but it didn't matter. His face, his voice, his smile—they were going to be part of her life forever.

Neela sighed. She had given herself credit for leaving Kyle and finally taking a stand against him. But once again, she doubted herself. From what Clarissa had said, everyone was able to see what she wanted to ignore.

She addressed the captains. "I want to love him, but I'm scared."

The captains stared back, unimpressed. She knew three of them personally and had learned one thing: who they were on the field was because of who they were off the field.

She was one of them. She was a champion, and she played fearlessly. It was the only way she knew how to play. It was time to face the questions she didn't want to ask or answer.

She pulled out her phone and scrolled to the phone number she hadn't wanted to delete. She knew it'd be too late for him to see a message now; he wouldn't check his phone until long after today's match was over.

Neela: **I'm thinking of you today. Good luck!**

. . .

As soon as she pressed "SEND," her heart felt lighter, and she smiled. Having Blake Stanton in her life, even if it was only for a little bit, was worth the risk. Her happiness was worth the risk.

Neela got on her bike and started the engine. There was a local pub nearby with a TV that would probably be showing Blake's match 'live.' She decided she'd watch the rest of it from there, then head out to the townhouse to wait for him.

She didn't know if he'll want to see her, but she could at least be honest with him about her feelings. They both deserved that.

The pub was surprisingly full, and everyone's attention was focused on the large screen taking up most of the far wall. She made her way to the bar, where the last people she'd expected to see were two of the men whose images she had just seen painted on pieces of wood in a field full of sheep.

"Neela? What are you doing here?" Mitch Molloy emerged from the dark end of the bar.

"I was on a ride. Why aren't you at the stadium? I would have expected that they'd have seats with both your and Connor's name engraved on them."

"They do, though they're written with textas," Mitch replied with a grin. "It's a tradition Con and I started after retiring. Just two mates having a drink on the first day of the season. Join us?"

"I don't want to interrupt."

"Rubbish. The second half is about to start. Blake's having a beaut of a game. Playing smart, but also playing…"

"Like a man on a mission," Connor finished. He moved up a seat, nodding to the now-vacant barstool.

Neela sighed. She hadn't been looking for company, but it was hard to say no to either Mitch or Connor, never mind both of them at the same time.

As the players returned to the field, the commentators repeated what Mitch had said. Blake was having a phenomenal match. He looked fit, fast and fierce, and his tight uniform showed off all the hard work he'd put in at the gym during the off-season. This wasn't the easygoing fella she'd seen over the summer; this was the next captain of the current world champions.

The match itself was well-contested, and the ball moved swiftly from end to end. A misstep happened, and the other team took advantage of the gift that had been offered to them. While Blake was playing out-of-his-mind rugby, it was still a team sport. He couldn't make up for some of the new players showing their nerves or a misread play or a bad pass.

With five minutes left, Neela saw a change in the line leaving Blake suddenly vulnerable. She knew the opposition would take advantage of the situation, and she stood up abruptly, willing Blake's teammates to close the hole, to protect their captain. Blake couldn't see the large lock coming at him. She grabbed Mitch's arm as the players collided.

"No!" Her voice joined the other yells of warnings and disbelief.

Then the pub went silent as the camera panned out from the figure lying on the field. Jason Williams, the vice-captain, was waving to the sidelines frantically.

"He's not moving," she whispered.

Mitch threw some money on the counter. "Con, find out what you can. There's only one hospital they'll take him to from the stadium. Message me with any updates. I'll take Neela."

She wasn't going to argue. She needed to be there for Blake, like he had been there for her at the pub, at the airport, at her father's anniversary celebration. And facing Kyle.

"Did you ride here?" Mitch asked. "Con can take your bike back to my place. I'll wait as long as you need and drive you home."

She pulled the keys to the bike out of her jacket pocket. "It's sticky when you shift from…"

Connor took the keys. "Neela, I've been riding since I was seven. Not much out there I *can't* ride. No worries. Go. Take care of your man. He'll need you if it's as serious as it looks."

"I don't think my helmet will fit you."

"Someone here will have a spare. Go!"

She didn't remember much as they drove. She just wanted Blake to be okay. She *needed* him to be okay.

When they reached the hospital, Mitch steered them to the waiting area. Despite being surrounded by a group of rugby and medical professionals, Walt Stanton's eyes met hers as soon she entered the room. He broke away, his hand reaching for hers.

"He's all right. Just banged up," he said, but Neela could hear the concern in his voice.

"It's his shoulder, isn't it? The right one. The way he took the hit..."

Walt's lower lip trembled. "Complete rotator cuff tear."

Neela shook her head. *He just earned the captaincy. This can't be happening.*

"Do you want to see him?" Andrew appeared next to Walt.

"I haven't said a word to him in weeks."

"He's hurt badly, but I think you should see him."

She faced Andrew. "I left him."

"You're here now." Andrew took both of Neela's hands in his. "He loves you, Neela Smyth. He was crazy about you when you were kids, and he's still crazy about you. And I think you being here tonight is because you have equally strong feelings for him."

Everyone seemed to know. "You too?"

Andrew angled his head slightly, a half-smile on his lips. "Mum laid it on you thick, didn't she?"

"She used the word 'heartbroken.'"

"For once, my mother didn't exaggerate." Andrew put his arm around her shoulders. "But he'll wait for you until you're ready. He won't like it, but he will. He's the poor sod who'll hold on to something until he gets it. So, you take your time. He's not going anywhere. But since you're here..."

Neela nodded. "Where is he?"

"Follow me. I'll get you past the scary nurse."

CHAPTER 19

Andrew opened the cream-colored door without knocking and indicated that Neela should walk in. "I'll be right outside if either of you needs me," he said softly.

Neela looked in tentatively. It was a private room, dimly lit and eerily quiet except for occasional beeps and clicks from the machines. Blake was lying in bed, his head turned slightly, his eyes closed. The top half of his body was elevated and bare; his right arm was held in place with bandages.

"Blake?" she asked tentatively.

His eyes opened instantly, and surprise spread across his face. "Neela?" He tried to scoot farther up on his bed, grimacing as he adjusted his body.

"No, don't," Neela pleaded. "I'll come over. That is, if you're okay with me being here."

The dimple appeared.

"Darl," he began "The thought of you entering my room while I'm half-naked and asleep has kept me awake for many nights. If you're not a dream, you better come over."

Neela laughed softly, relieved to hear the humor in his voice. "You must be okay then." She pulled a chair close to the side of his bed, aware that he was watching her every move.

She reached for his hand, and he held on tight. He let out a sigh as he caressed the top of her hand with his thumb. "I've missed you."

"I've missed you too."

His eyes searched hers. "It's not looking good. This one's really serious." She nodded as he continued, trying not to react to how vulnerable he looked. "I'm not going to be captaining anytime soon."

"That's not important. You getting better is."

"I might not be playing at all for a long time. They're talking months at the very least, and that's the best case scenario."

"Oh, Blake."

"You and I both know it was only a matter of 'when.' It's not a game without the hits."

She tightened her grip on his hand. "Whatever happens next, I'm here."

He breathed deeply, looked to the ceiling before he met her eyes again. "I'll keep waiting as long as there's hope, even if it's the smallest of possibilities. But I need to know. Do I— we—have a chance?"

"I hope so, Blake Stanton. Because I haven't been able to stop thinking of you since I left Andrew's apartment."

He stared as if in disbelief before a wide smile spread across his face. "I'm not sure how much drugs are floating inside me right now, but that's the best thing I've heard today. All week. All month. I hope this also means you're here to release me from the promise you asked me to keep."

"Which one? Not to call me or not to kiss me?"

"Both?"

She stood up and sat on the edge of his bed. Gently cupping Blake's cheek in one hand, she lowered her face to his and closed her eyes. When their lips touched, an explosion of awareness engulfed her body. A sigh escaped as she deepened her kiss, focusing on how well her mouth fit with his. She drew one hand down, reaching behind Blake's neck to bring him closer. Her other hand snuck lower, slowly, tracing the finely etched body that was now hers to touch and explore.

She'd started as the initiator, but he met her persistence with demands of his own. And she complied.

When she moved away, she was breathing hard. Blake didn't let her go very far and placed her hand on his chest. "Feel what you do to me? I love you, Neela Smyth. And I hope this means you *are* absolving me from my promise not to kiss you again. Because after that one, I know this is one promise I won't be able to keep."

She recognized the emotions in his eyes. They've been there for a long time.

"Darl, there's no need to cry just because a man says he loves you," he said softly, gently wiping away tears she didn't know were there.

"I just never thought it could be you," Neela said.

Blake raised her hand to his lips. "Ten minutes ago, I started to wonder if I've lost my dream of captaining the National Team. You being here makes me think that if that's the case, maybe I'll have something to replace it with, that there's something to look forward to."

"I'm just so scared to open my heart again. I don't know if I can be the person you need to be with."

"You just be the person you want to be," Blake said. "Whether it's the best rugby player New Zealand has ever seen or the girl who won't share her Choc Cherry with me. I love you. I just do. I always have."

Neela hesitated to speak again. Her relationship with her dad made her question whether she could be loved for who she was while her time with Kyle had conditioned her to second-guess her feelings. There was no rational decision behind being with Blake, except for one.

She loved him.

Could she do it? Could she trust her heart once again? Making decisions with her head had brought her professional success, and it'd kept her emotionally safe. But was a safe life the one she wanted to live?

It wasn't how she played rugby.

Neela reached into her jacket pocket and opened her palm. "I'll share my Choc Cherry with you."

Blake laughed, then groaned. He let go of Neela's hand to find a more comfortable position. "Darl, that's almost as good as a proposal, you know."

"Would you want that?"

Blake's smile grew wider. "A kiss, a Choc Cherry and now we're talking about marriage?"

"Don't you think we should go on a real date first?"

Blake grinned. "I have it on good authority that your brother has a large amount of money riding on us getting engaged."

Neela smiled, but it was replaced with a frown a few seconds later. She wanted him to know first. "I've filed for both protection and restraining orders. I did it on my own, Blake. You helped me get there."

He squeezed her hand. "I'm proud of you, darl. That must have been hard."

"It was once, but after seeing him go for you, I couldn't take a chance that he'd do it again. To me or anyone else I care about."

"When it becomes public knowledge, we'll face it together."

"You've never left my side, even when you didn't know the full story. A lot of others would have."

"I'm now damaged goods, Neela, while you're the princess-in-waiting, poised to be part of a team that will make history," Blake said softly. "I don't know what's in front of me."

"Are you scared?"

He studied her then shook his head. "No. No, I'm not." He smiled gently. "With you next to me, I can face whatever comes with this injury. The idea of losing you scared me more."

"Oh, Blake."

"The last six weeks have been hell, but I'd do it all over again if it means we'd have this moment. It's always been you, Neela. No one else. Always you."

She reached for his face with her free hand and caressed his cheek, finally resting her thumb on his bottom lip. "I love you, Blake Stanton. And I'll take you in whatever shape you're in. If you're willing to stick by a confused and ill-tempered rugby player, how can I not plan for a lifetime together?"

"A lifetime? I'll take that. The answer is yes."

"That's still not a proposal, Blake."

"The answer is still yes." He pulled her close.

She welcomed lips that extinguished the last of her fears. There were none left when she was with him. She was her mother's child, strong and brave. Now that she'd found someone who believed in her, she was stronger and braver than she'd ever been.

"Yes, Neela Smyth. When you're ready to get married, it'll be yes. Always." Blake kissed her lightly on her nose. His dimple appeared again. "Besides being madly in love with you, my mother would kill me if I said no. You know she has the names of our children already picked out. What do you think of the name 'Corey?'"

EPILOGUE

She looked at Andrew. "That's it?"

"Yeah, that's it. You're now in debt for the rest of your life."

Neela was about to smile but bit on her lower lip instead.

"He may be mad for about a minute. He'll get over it," Andrew said.

"I'm not worried about him being mad. I can handle that. It's a lot of money, Andrew. I owe you."

"You'll pay me back. Just get my name off that loan after the honeymoon, eh?."

"It has a library. I had to get it."

"It *is* a pretty impressive wedding present."

"He bought me your car, Andrew. No way was he going to get me the better present."

Andrew laughed. "You two are so competitive. I'm going to enjoy seeing my little brother in this relationship."

Rieann popped her head into the dressing room. "Will you hurry up?"

Neela stuck her tongue out at her sister. "Everyone is supposed to wait for the bride, anyway."

Rieann made a face, then looked to Andrew. "And you need to get out of here. Your mum thinks you haven't shown up. She's pretending to swoon."

Andrew rolled his eyes and held out both hands for Neela.

"Are you sure you want to marry into this family?"

She nodded. "Absolutely."

Andrew leaned over to kiss her on the cheek. "You look beautiful. Blake may faint when he sees you. Now, let me have the paperwork back. I have a pretty envelope that Lulu decorated to put in your suitcase, so it'll look like a proper present."

Neela took one last look at the picture of the house she had just bought and smiled widely.

They had been babysitting Jayne and Lulu at the Molloys' one evening when Neela saw the marketing flier sitting with some other mail on the dining table. Just a street away from Mitch and Liana's house, the house's location was the initial attraction. Then, while Blake was away, she went to one of its open inspections and knew instantly that it was supposed to be theirs.

It needed some work— Blake was going to have a fit when he saw the oven— but one room was perfect. The rumpus room had large windows that showcased the Canterbury Mountains, making the room airy and bright.

The clincher: it had a red carpet.

Scott Warren had worked his magic on her behalf over the last few months, and now that she was signed with three major companies, one of them American, she had enough money for a down payment. She had then called Andrew for advice on getting a loan based on her large but uncertain streams of income. He had surprised her by offering to co-sign until Blake learned about the house. "I don't own anything in the suburbs. It'll add diversity to my portfolio," he had said with a hint of snobbery Neela knew was far from authentic.

Once they understood the severity of Blake's injury and the unlikelihood of a full recovery, it was also Andrew who had suggested that Blake speak to RugNZ about continuing his relationship with them at the corporate level.

Three months after Blake's last match, Chris Hansen, the CEO of RugNZ, offered him a position in the legal department. Blake's role included advising players on their rights and responsibilities when they sign on to play for their country. In addition to any legal advice, he offered the unique perspective of someone who had been through it all himself. One of the perks of the job was that Blake could live anywhere in the country, which meant he often showed up for Neela's matches wearing brightly colored shirts with odd buttons.

When Leila moved back to Auckland, it only made sense for him to move in with Neela. He excitedly took charge of the wedding planning and used his law degree when called on to mediate between his mother, Andrew, and Rieann. Though neither of them was particularly religious, the pastor said he would be pleased to marry them in the church that Neela's parents had been married in.

That appealed to Neela's father almost as much as having Blake Stanton as a future son-in-law. It would seem that Neela and Malcolm's relationship could get past their unspoken problems— until she announced that she wanted to walk down the aisle alone. Had it not been for her stepmother's gentle intervention, Neela wasn't sure her father would be attending today's wedding.

Now, she stood in front of the full-length mirror one more time. The red dress her sister had picked out almost a year ago was finally being worn. A crystal and pearl-encrusted hairband kept her face clear of any loose hair. Her precious pearl studs matched the pearl and diamond necklace Blake had given her for her birthday.

She gently smoothed out the custom-made bolero jacket which allowed the dress to be appropriate for the church part of the day. If the weather stayed warm, she'd be able to take it off at their reception by the beach, which would feature cabanas and a row of barbecues (which Sam insisted he'd be in charge of) to feed the appetites of family and two rugby teams.

A dessert table would offer the newly launched "Stanton cupcakes" along with chocolate covered-strawberries from their favorite food truck.

When she had brought up the idea of wearing a red dress for the wedding, Blake simply said, "It'll match the fire in your eyes, darl."

He didn't faint when she walked up the aisle, alone but far from lonely. As they exchanged vows, his eyes never strayed from hers. She didn't doubt his promise to love, honor and cherish. In truth, that was how he had always treated her, from the time they had first met, on a rugby field, in primary school.

ACKNOWLEDGEMENTS

Always You wouldn't have seen the light of day without so many people cheering me on:

Fantastic critique partners, especially Suja Sukumar and Emile Horne. Your insights and thoughtful comments were valuable and spot on.

The many participants from The Writing Gals FB group – my 24-hr Emergency Help Line!

Beta readers, proofreaders, and the wonderful readers from "Always There" whose feedback and enthusiasm encouraged me to keep going, especially on those long days when a single word seemed impossible to write.

My parents, sisters, cousins, and friends who enthusiastically bought AND spread the word of my books, even when they "don't usually read romance!" I'm truly humbled by your support.

And finally, my family, who didn't mind when their mom/wife shut the door on them to spent time with those characters in her head.

www.ingramcontent.com/pod-product-compliance
Lightning Source LLC
Chambersburg PA
CBHW050337190726
48284CB00007BB/2047

* 9 7 8 1 9 4 9 8 2 3 0 5 9 *